TEARS OF REQUIEM

TEARS OF REQUIEM

SONG OF DRAGONS, BOOK TWO

DANIEL ARENSON

Copyright © 2011 by Daniel Arenson

ISBN: 978-0-9866028-9-4

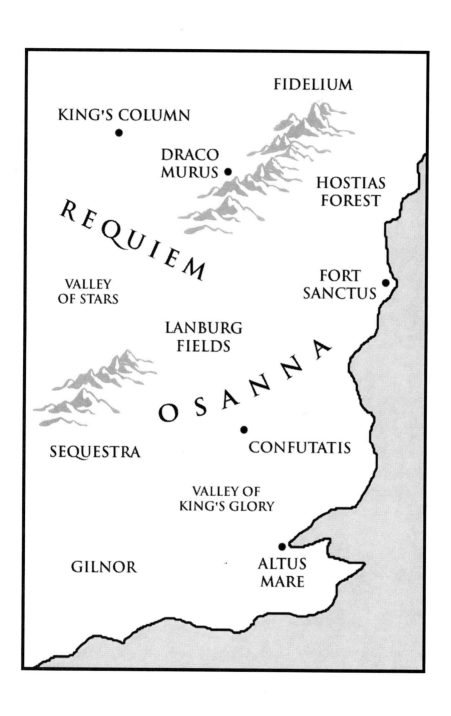

FIDELIUM

KING'S COLUMN

DRACO
MURUS

HOSTIAS
FOREST

REQUIEM

VALLEY
OF STARS

FORT
SANCTUS

LANBURG
FIELDS

OSANNA

SEQUESTRA

CONFUTATIS

VALLEY OF
KING'S GLORY

GILNOR

ALTUS
MARE

FOREWORD

Tears of Requiem is the second volume of *Song of Dragons*, a series of fantasy novels inspired by Mozart's Requiem.

The first volume, *Blood of Requiem*, introduced us to the Vir Requis, an ancient race of men who can turn into dragons. *Tears of Requiem*, this second novel, continues their story.

This novel assumes you've already read *Blood of Requiem*. If you haven't, I think you'll still get the gist of things here... though I do recommend reading *Blood* first.

With this introduction out of the way, I welcome you back into a world of blood, steel, and dragonfire.

KYRIE ELEISON

Kyrie was collecting firewood when he heard thunder, shivered, and saw the smoke creature.

The smoke was distant, a league away, but Kyrie could see there was something wrong about it. It coiled through the sunset, serpentine, moving toward him. A wisp of some campfire? A cloud? No. Whatever this was, it moved like a living creature. Kyrie's fingers went numb, and he dropped the branches he'd collected.

"Agnus Dei!" he whispered through clenched teeth. "Where are you?

She didn't answer. Kyrie tore his eyes away from the smoke and scanned the woods for her. In the twilight, he saw rustling oaks, birches, and elms. He saw fleeing animals: birds, squirrels, and a deer. But he could not see his companion.

"Agnus Dei, where are you?" he whispered again. He dared not speak louder. "There's something coming over, and it doesn't look friendly."

Still she did not appear, and Kyrie cursed and returned his eyes to the smoke. It was so close now, Kyrie could see that it was indeed alive. Arms and legs grew from it, and its eyes glinted like diamonds. Teeth filled its maw. Whatever this creature was, it was no wisp of smoke. It seemed to see Kyrie and approached him, soon five hundred feet away, then only a hundred, then a dozen.

Kyrie considered shifting into dragon form. Like all Vir Requis--or at least, the five that remained after the war--he could become a dragon. He could blow fire, slash with claws, bite with fangs. But as the creature approached, Kyrie remained human.

Turning into a dragon was dangerous; men hated dragons and hunted them. And besides, Kyrie doubted even dragonfire and fangs could kill this smoky being.

Instead, he addressed the creature. "What are you? Turn back!"

The creature seemed to laugh. Its laughter was like thunder, shaking the trees. It floated above Kyrie, thirty feet long and undulating. It wasn't made of smoke, Kyrie realized. It seemed woven of darkness, but even that was inaccurate. Darkness was merely the lack of light. This creature was the opposite of light, deeper and blacker than mere darkness.

"Leave this place!" Kyrie demanded. He glanced around the forest. Where was Agnus Dei? He would not let this creature harm her. He had to protect her. He loved Agnus Dei more than anything; he would beat this creature to death with his fists, if he had to.

"You...," the creature whispered. Its voice made trees wilt, turn gray, and fall to the forest floor. "...are... Vir Requis...."

Kyrie wanted to attack. He wanted to flee. He wanted to find Agnus Dei. He wanted to do anything but just stand there, hearing that voice--no, not a voice, but merely an echo--a sound that made his insides shrivel up.

"I...," he began. With fumbling fingers, he managed to draw his dagger. "You will...."

He could say no more. All he saw was that creature of blackness, its diamond eyes, its teeth like wisps of white smoke. He felt as if he too became smoke. His soul seemed to leave his body, flowing from his nostrils and mouth. He could see his body below, wobbling on the forest floor--just a kid, seventeen years old with a shock of yellow hair and too many battle scars.

And then he could see too much.

He screamed. He saw the universe. Not only the three dimensions of his world, but endless others. His spirit was no longer confined to his skull. It spread through the forest, through the empire of Osanna, through the multitudes of dimensions beyond. So much space! So much pain. So much fear. Kyrie whimpered. He wanted to hide, to weep, but had no eyes for tears.

"Please," he whispered. "Please, it's so... open. So much space. So much pain."

The creature laughed, and Kyrie knew he would soon join it, become smoke and blackness and flow through the endless, empty spaces.

"Agnus Dei," he managed to whisper. "I love you...."

A voice, worlds distant, answered him.

"This is no time for romance, pup. Get out of here, run!"

Hands clutched his shoulders. Shoulders! Yes, he had shoulders, and a body, and a physical form. He had tears, he had a voice, had--

"Pup, snap out of it!" said the voice. He felt a hand slap his face. He could feel! He could feel his body again. His soul coalesced, and his body sucked it back in. It felt like water flowing back into a jug. His spirit slammed into his skull, and he convulsed, and jumped to his feet. He hadn't realized he had fallen.

"Agnus Dei!" he said. Tears filled his eyes. His beloved knelt above him, her tanned face so beautiful to him, her curls of black hair tickling his cheeks. "What, where--"

She hoisted him to his feet. "Run, pup. Run!"

She pulled him up, and they ran through the forest. When Kyrie glanced over his shoulder, he saw the black creature. It was chasing them, flowing between the trees. Every tree it passed wilted and fell.

"What is that thing?" Agnus Dei cried as they ran.

"I don't know," Kyrie said, boots kicking up leaves and dirt. He almost fell over a root, steadied himself, and kept running.

"Don't look into its eyes, Agnus Dei. It did something to me. I'm not sure what. But don't look at it. Just run."

"I am running, pup. And I'm a lot faster than you."

"Agnus Dei, this is not the time for another race." He panted. "Everything is a competition with you, even who can flee faster from a flying smoke demon."

The creature shrieked behind them. It was a sound like fingernails on glass. Kyrie and Agnus Dei covered their ears and grimaced while running. Birds fell dead from the sky. Bugs burst open on the ground, spraying blood. The creature shrieked again, and Kyrie screamed in pain; his eardrums felt close to tearing.

It was dark now. The sun disappeared behind the horizon, leaving only red and orange wisps across the forest. The creature grew in darkness. When Kyrie looked at it again, it was twice the size.

"I think it likes darkness," Kyrie shouted. It was rumbling and cackling behind him, and trees kept wilting. The boles crashed around them, maggoty and gray and crumbling.

"Then we'll roast the bastard with dragonfire," Agnus Dei said. She leaped over a fallen tree, spun around, and shifted.

Leathern wings grew from her back. Red scales flowed across her. Fangs and claws sprouted from her. Within seconds, she was a dragon. With a howl, she blew white-hot fire at the smoky creature.

Kyrie ducked and rolled, the fire flowing over his head. He shifted too. Blue scales covered him, he ballooned in size, and soon he too was a dragon. He blew the hottest, whitest fire he could, hitting the creature head on.

It screamed. Trees cracked. Boulders shattered. Kyrie too screamed, his ears thudding, but kept breathing fire. Agnus Dei blew fire too. And yet the creature lived, swirling and crying. Kyrie felt its tug, felt his soul being sucked out, drawn into those empty spaces. He shook his head and gritted his teeth, clinging onto himself.

"We need light!" Kyrie shouted. "The light bothers it, not the heat. Let's light this forest."

Agnus Dei nodded, and they began blowing fire in all directions. The trees, moments before lush and green, had wilted around the creature. They were now dry and caught fire easily. They crackled, blazing, and the creature howled. A crack ran along the earth, and sparks rained from the sky. The creature seemed to suck in the light. Wisps of light flowed into it, and it howled.

"Leave this place!" Kyrie shouted to it. "There is light here, light that will burn you. Fly away into darkness."

It howled, surrounded by firelight, and gave Kyrie a last glare. Its eyes were so mean, small, and glittering, that Kyrie shuddered.

Finally it coiled, spun around, and fled into the night.

Kyrie watched it flee, then turned to Agnus Dei, who still stood in dragon form. "Let's contain this fire," he said.

She nodded, and they shoved the burning trees into a great pyre. With dragon claws, they dug ruts around it, so it would not spread, and tossed the dirt onto the burning boles. They worked silently until the fire died to embers.

Their work done, they shifted back into human forms and collapsed into the ash and dirt. Kyrie was bone tired. Blowing so much fire had taken a lot out of him, and he shivered to remember what the creature had done. Out of his body, his soul had glimpsed something... something Kyrie shuddered to remember. He pushed it out of his mind. He had seen a horror beyond the world he did not want to ponder.

"You all right?" he asked Agnus Dei.

She lay beside him, chest rising and falling as she panted. Ash smeared her cheeks and filled her mane of curls. He reached out, touched those curls, and kissed her cheek.

She shoved him back. "Am *I* all right?" she said. "Oh, thank you for asking, brave hero, defender of distressed damsels. But if I recall correctly, you're the one who almost died. I had to show up to save your backside. So the question is, pup: Are *you* all right?"

He grumbled and rose to his feet. "I'm fine, and I've told you a million times. You might be a couple years older than me, but don't call me pup."

She stood up, brushed ash off her leggings, and smirked. "Okay, puppy pup." When he scowled, she walked up to him, mussed his hair, and kissed his cheek. "For what it's worth, I'm glad you're all right. But you're still a pup."

Kyrie looked to the night sky. The creature was gone, but he could still imagine it, and his belly knotted. "Have you ever seen anything like that? What was it?"

Agnus Dei scrunched her lips and tapped her cheek. "I think it was a nightshade."

Kyrie raised an eyebrow. "A nightshade? I've never heard of them."

"I don't know much about them," Agnus Dei said. She too looked to the sky, as if scanning for its return. "But my mother used to tell me stories of them. She said they were made of unlight."

"Unlight?"

Agnus Dei nodded. "The opposite of light. Did you see how our firelight disappeared into it, as if the creature and light cancelled each other out? That's unlight."

"Scary stuff." Kyrie hugged himself. He remembered the firelight flowing into the nightshade, like wisps of cloud. Had his soul looked the same when the creature pulled it? "Do you reckon Lacrimosa knows more about them?"

"Maybe. Mother knows a lot. You and I never read much growing up, but Mother was raised in Requiem before it was destroyed. She spent her childhood in libraries. Let's find her. I hope Mother and Father didn't meet that nightshade too."

They walked through the forest, heading south toward their camp. The Draco constellation shone above between the boughs, the stars of Requiem, guiding them. Crickets chirped, and Kyrie held Agnus Dei's hand. Her hand was slender and warm. It was hard to believe that, only a week ago, they'd been fighting Dies Irae. It seemed a lifetime ago that they'd stolen the tyrant's amulet, freed his griffins, and found sanctuary in this forest. A chapter in Kyrie's life had ended when he'd sent Dies Irae fleeing, wounded, back to Confutatis. A new chapter had begun now, it seemed, and Kyrie didn't like how it started. Not one bit.

They were still far from camp when they heard boots trudging toward them. At first, Kyrie wanted to flee. He was used to footfalls heralding pursuit--Dies Irae's soldiers with swords and crossbows. But then he heard Lacrimosa's voice calling, "Agnus Dei! Daughter, do you hear me?"

Agnus Dei cried, "Mother! I'm here."

Soon Lacrimosa emerged from between the trees, carrying a tin lantern. Kyrie couldn't help himself. Whenever he saw Agnus Dei's mother, the queen of fallen Requiem, he paused and stared. Lacrimosa, pale and dainty, seemed woven of moonlight. Her hair was a gold so fair, it was almost white. Her eyes were pools of lavender, and she wore a pendant shaped as a bluebell.

"Agnus Dei, are you all right?" Lacrimosa said. "We heard fire and howls, and I heard you scream."

Agnus Dei hugged her mother. The two looked nothing alike, Kyrie reflected. Agnus Dei had tanned skin, curly black hair, and blazing brown eyes. Lacrimosa was starlight; Agnus Dei was fire.

"We saw a nightshade," Kyrie said to the two women. "Well, we did more than see it. The bloody thing nearly killed us before we blinded it. Do you know much about nightshades, Lacrimosa?"

Lacrimosa grew even paler than usual.

"Nightshades," she whispered.

A voice spoke ahead between the trees, deep and gruff. "Impossible."

With snapping twigs and ragged breathing, Benedictus-- King of Requiem and father to Agnus Dei--emerged from the trees. He held a torch and walked up to them. His chest rose and fell. Sweat soaked his leathery face and matted his graying black hair. He glared at Kyrie, fists clenched.

"I'm telling you, we saw a nightshade," Kyrie said to his king. At least, Benedictus had once been his king, back when Requiem still stood and a million Vir Requis still flew. "Tell him, Agnus Dei."

Agnus Dei spent a moment describing their ordeal to her parents. When she was done, even Benedictus looked pale. The king closed his eyes and seemed lost in old, painful memories. For a long time, the others stood in silence, waiting for Benedictus to speak.

Finally Benedictus opened his eyes and said, "We leave this forest. It's no longer safe."

He began trudging through the woods. The others hurried to keep up.

"Why?" Kyrie demanded. "What do you know of these creatures? Speak, Benedictus!"

The older man, a good four decades Kyrie's senior, scowled. "You don't want to know, kid."

They continued walking through the night. Their boots rustled fallen leaves and damp twigs, and the wind moaned. Kyrie tightened his cloak around him, but found no warmth. He tried to speak a few times, but Benedictus scowled and silenced him, saying these woods were full of ears. And so Kyrie walked silently, thoughts rattling in his skull. He remembered floating over his body. The nightshade had tugged his soul, and was taking it... where? To a place colder and darker than this night, than any night. Kyrie shivered. He didn't know how long they walked through the forest. It seemed like hours, but time felt lost to Kyrie. Finally he could bear it no longer.

He grabbed Benedictus's shoulder. "That thing did something to me, Benedictus. I don't know what, but it scared me."

Benedictus grumbled. "The night is no time to speak of these things."

"I don't care. It seemed to... pull me, Benedictus. Not my body, but whatever's inside my body. My soul, if you'd believe it. And I saw things. Well, I didn't see them, but I felt them. Dimensions, and space, and other worlds. My soul seemed to balloon to fill them, like smoke in a jar, and...." His stomach knotted. He took a deep breath. "I think I've earned the right to learn more. Tell us what you know."

Benedictus growled, still stomping through the dark woods. "You want to know about nightshades, kid?" He pointed his torch to his left. "Look."

Kyrie looked, and saw that they had chanced upon a road that ran downhill, cut through a farm, and ended at a village. The village burned. Kyrie saw bodies between the buildings. A dozen nightshades swarmed above them, coiling, their eyes glittering. The creatures laughed, their voices like thunder.

"Stars," Agnus Dei whispered. She placed a hand on Kyrie's shoulder. "Are those people all dead?"

Benedictus shook his head, staring at the village below. "Not dead. Something worse. Their souls are with the nightshades now, lost in the worlds beyond this world, in lands of darkness and fear. They will remain there forever. They are already praying for death, but no death will release them."

For a long moment, the companions--the last surviving Vir Requis--stared down at the village. Finally Kyrie nodded.

"Great!" he said. "Just great. We finally defeat the griffins, and now these guys show up. As much as I'd love to fight them too, and start a whole new war, I think I'll pass. Not our problem. Osanna is infested with nightshades? Let Dies Irae handle them. Come on, Benedictus. Let's return to Requiem, or at least, what's left of it. This is not our war."

"But it is our war," Lacrimosa answered for her husband, voice haunted. "I remember tales of these nightshades. They were sealed centuries ago. Only the one who sits upon Osanna's throne could release them. That means these creatures work for Dies Irae now. And that means...."

Kyrie clutched his head and finished the sentence for her. "They're hunting us."

The nightshades below shrieked as one. Though they were a league away, and the companions were hidden in the trees, the nightshades saw them. Their eyes blazed, and they abandoned the village. They came flowing up the declivity, heading to the Vir Requis.

"Fly!" Benedictus shouted. He shifted into a black dragon, flapped his wings, and flew into the night. "Only light can stop them. Fly after me, we seek sunrise!"

The others shifted too, and the four Vir Requis flew in dragon form.

Dozens of nightshades howled behind them, chasing in the night.

GLORIAE

Gloriae the Gilded, Steel Maiden of Osanna, stood upon the walls of her palace and watched the city crumble.

Confutatis was known by many names. The Marble City. The Jewel of Osanna. The Cradle of Light. It was a sprawling city of a million souls. A city of forts, snaking walls, and gilded statues of Dies Irae. A city known for a military might that cowed the world. Today, as Gloriae stood upon the battlements of Confutatis, she did not recognize it. She saw no military might, no Sun God light, no glory for the poets to sing of.

She saw death, darkness, and cracking stone.

"Nightshades!" she cried, standing atop the tallest steeple of her palace, overlooking the city. "I have summoned you. I am your mistress. I sit upon Osanna's throne as my father lies dying, and you will obey me."

They swirled across the city, like wisps of black smoke with diamond eyes. Their teeth appeared as but mist, but they toppled towers, statues, and temples of the Sun God. Thousands of people ran through the streets. The nightshades dipped into every road, square, and alley, shrieking. People fell before them, and even from here upon her palace, Gloriae knew that nightshades were sucking up their souls. Bodies littered the streets, not dead but mindless, soulless.

"Nightshades!" Gloriae cried again. "I am the one who freed you. I sit on the throne. You will cease this destruction and obey me."

They laughed at her. A dozen flew toward her, eyes mocking, and swirled around her. They lifted her into the air, flapping her hair like storm winds, seeping under her armor to caress her skin.

"Gloriae the Gilded," they whispered in her mind. "Our mistress."

They laughed, a sound like thunder. She felt them tugging her soul, side to side, toying with her, like dogs fighting over a steak. They pulled wisps of her left and right, snapping her out and into her body.

"Stop this!" she screamed, burning with fury. "You will obey me. You will hunt the Vir Requis."

They hissed like water on a frying pan. "Oh, yes, great mistress. We will destroy the Vir Requis, yes. We will destroy all souls who live entombed in flesh. We will free them. We will free you."

They bore her into her palace, past halls and chambers, knocking down pictures and candlesticks and suits of armor. Servants fled before them. Guards attacked them with swords, only to fall soulless. The nightshades carried Gloriae into her court, and placed her upon her father's throne. They swirled around her, draped around her neck, and wrapped around her legs.

"Sit upon your throne, mistress," their voices mocked. "Rule us from here, oh mighty empress."

Gloriae's belly ached with fear. She had made a mistake, she knew. A horrible, shattering, tragic mistake for her and her empire. Father had warned her. Why hadn't she listened? Why had she freed these creatures?

She clenched her fists and snarled. "Release me, beasts. I gave you one task, and one task only. Hunt the Vir Requis."

They laughed. "Should we hunt you too then, Gloriae of Requiem?"

"I am not from Requiem," she said, but heard the doubt in her voice. Tears stung her eyes. She remembered what

Lacrimosa said. *I am your mother.* She remembered shifting into a golden dragon in her chamber, of swearing to hide her shame. "Lacrimosa lied to me. She gave me her illness, the lizard's curse. I hate the Vir Requis. I will kill them all."

"Then will you kill yourself?" the nightshades asked.

They swirled around her like a hurricane, tugging her soul. She screamed. She felt herself split into a hundred pieces, then a thousand, then a million. The tiles of her court cracked. A column fell. And then Gloriae was inside the nightshades, not just the dozens around her, but the thousands that filled the world. Her soul had scattered and flew within them.

She saw Confutatis from their eyes. She saw temples fall, buildings collapse, streets rise and crash, raining cobblestones. She saw the multitudes dying, the rivers boiling, children crushed with stones. Other parts of Gloriae flew in the east. She saw nightshades attack the griffins, those griffins Dies Irae had once ruled, but now lost. She saw the griffins shriek, bite and claw, try to attack, but fall lifeless in the night. Their souls too had been claimed and tossed into darkness. Gloriae flew in the west, countless pieces of her soul within each nightshade. She saw them attack the salvanae, the true dragons of legend, and fell so many of those ancient, proud creatures.

And she saw herself.

In the shards of her soul, she saw a broken woman. She saw a woman broken in childhood, stolen. A woman raised in lies, in light that blinded her. She saw the old courts of Requiem, before her father had destroyed them. She walked there with Lacrimosa, her mother, in the halls of the Vir Requis. She heard their harps, and saw their birches, and--

No! Lies, all of it. These were the images Lacrimosa had planted within her, false memories.

"Where are the Vir Requis?" Gloriae said, speaking from every shattered part of her, into the mind of every nightshade.

They laughed and hissed, and her soul dispersed and collected within them. She found the nightshades who chased the Vir Requis, and she gazed upon them from countless eyes.

They fled through the night, four dragons. Benedictus, their king, black and cruel. Lacrimosa, his wife of silver scales, beautiful and deceiving. Agnus Dei, the red dragon who'd attacked her in the ruins of Requiem. Kyrie Eleison, the cub, the boy who'd gored her leg with his horn.

"I will kill them," Gloriae vowed, urging the nightshades onward. "Destroy the world if you must. But destroy them with it. I command you."

As they hissed and howled, Gloriae sensed that she commanded nothing of their actions. They were humoring her. *So be it*, she managed to think even with her soul splintered across countless of these beings. *So be it.*

"So long as the Vir Requis die, I've done my job."

Slumped in the throne back at Confutatis, the body of Gloriae twitched, clenched its fists, and smiled.

DIES IRAE

Dies Irae awoke to pain.

He tried to open his eyes, but only one would open. His left eye blazed in agony, and when Dies Irae brought his fingers to it, they touched bandages. More bandages covered his arm, which hurt too--the pain of fire.

What had happened? He could not remember. He could barely remember his name. Grunting, he moved his head, though it shot stabs of pain through him, and looked around. He lay in a Sun God temple. Candles covered the floors and walls, a golden disk shimmered behind an altar, and priests in white masks moved about, chanting.

"Lord Irae," spoke one priest, kneeling above him. The man wore all white--white robes, a white hood, and a white mask. "The Sun God has woken you."

Dies Irae struggled to push himself up on his elbows. The priests had placed him upon white marble tiles. Dies Irae grunted. Couldn't they have given him a bed? But Sun clerics had always been an odd lot; powerful, yes, but strange of ways.

"How long was I unconscious?" Dies Irae asked. It felt like a long time. His memories were still fuzzy. He remembered riding out on Volucris, the prince of griffins, but little else.

The priest bowed his head. "Seven days of glory, your lordship, and seven nights of tribulation."

"Seven days!" Dies Irae said, feeling the blood leave his face. He struggled to his feet. The cleric watched silently. When he was standing, Dies Irae found that his knees shook. He had to lean against a column. A servant brought him a bowl of soup, and Dies Irae wanted to wave it aside, then changed his mind and took the bowl. He drank deeply. Hot beef broth.

"Seven days," he repeated softly. What in the Sun God's name had knocked him out so soundly? He frowned, and the movement made his left eye scream in pain. He felt blood trickle down his cheek, and he tasted it on his lips.

The taste brought the memories back. They hit him like a blow, so hard he dropped the bowl. It cracked, spreading broth across the floor like blood.

Benedictus.

His brother.

"Yes, you did this to me, brother," Dies Irae whispered. "You thrust jagged metal into my eye. You burned me. You--"

Dies Irae froze.

He reached for the amulet that would always hang around his neck. The Griffin Heart. The tamer of griffins.

It was gone.

The weredragons had taken it.

Rage blazed in Dies Irae, stronger than the pain. Dies Irae swung his left arm, the iron mace arm. He knocked down a candlestick. When a servant ran to lift the candle, Dies Irae swung the mace at him too. The mace hit the boy's head. Dies Irae heard the crack of the skull, a beautiful sound. He had missed that sound. The boy fell to the floor, head caved in and bleeding.

"They took the Griffin Heart," Dies Irae said, turning to stare at the priest.

The priest nodded.

Dies Irae stared silently, trembling. Then he marched to the doorways and burst outside. He was barefoot and clad in temple robes, but he didn't care. He had to see Gloriae. He had to see his daughter.

Outside the temple, more pain awaited.

The city lay crumbled and burning around him. In the twilight, Dies Irae saw nightshades flowing across the skies, toppling forts and towers. Three nightshades flew toward a towering, gilded statue of himself, of a young Dies Irae with two arms and both eyes. As he watched, the nightshades toppled the statue. It fell and crushed a house beneath it.

Dies Irae laughed.

He wanted to rage, to scream, to kill. But he only laughed.

The priest stood behind him, silent. Dies Irae addressed the man. "I'm wounded in battle. One week later, my griffins are gone, the weredragons have escaped, and the nightshades have fled the Well of Night to destroy my city. Am I missing anything?"

The priest lowered his head and said nothing.

Ice flowed down Dies Irae's spine. He grabbed the priest's shoulders. "What else? Tell me. By the Sun God, speak."

The priest raised his eyes. Behind his mask, they were black, deep set, aching. "Your daughter, my lord. The lady Gloriae the Gilded. You... you must see her."

Dies Irae began marching through the city, leaving the priest behind. Nightshades howled around him, toppling buildings. The streets were deserted. Only stray cats and dogs, a few beggars, and some soldiers remained; they were fleeing the nightshades, scuttling from ruin to ruin. A nightshade swooped toward him, mouth of smoke opening, revealing white teeth. It shrieked, then seemed to recognize Dies Irae. It spun around and fled. Dies Irae allowed himself a small smile and kept walking.

He hadn't seen such ruin since Requiem's fall. Confutatis, the Marble City, was utterly destroyed. A few buildings remained standing, but nightshades swarmed over them. Bodies littered the roads, both of soldiers and civilians. They were not dead, but neither were they alive. Their hearts pulsed, and their lungs pumped air, but no souls filled the shells. Those souls, Dies Irae knew, now screamed in the realms of night.

Finally Dies Irae reached the palace grounds. The Palace Flammis still stood, though one of its towers and its western wall had collapsed. Bricks and dust covered the courtyards and gardens. Dies Irae stepped around the ruins, entered the main hall, and found bodies inside. Servants, lords, ladies, and soldiers all huddled on the floor, lips mumbling, eyes blinking, but no other life filled them.

Dies Irae walked through this devastation until he reached the throne room. His daughter would be there, he knew. She would have sat upon the throne while he lay wounded. Only one who sat upon Osanna's Ivory Throne could free the nightshades.

Dies Irae pushed open the oak doors and stepped into his throne room.

He was a strong man. He prided himself on his strength. But now, a cry fled his lips.

A hundred nightshades filled the throne room. They swirled above the Ivory Throne, a cocoon of blackness and smoke. Gloriae hovered within them, her eyes closed, a butterfly inside that cocoon of night. She was nude, her body white. Her golden hair flowed around her, as if she floated underwater.

Dies Irae snarled and marched forward. He reached into the cocoon of nightshades, grabbed Gloriae's foot, and pulled her down. The nightshades resisted, tugging her, but Dies Irae kept pulling until she fell into his arms.

"Mother," the girl whispered. She was nineteen, but she seemed so young now, a child. "Mother, may our wings find the sky."

The nightshades howled, eyes blazing. The room shook. Cracks ran along the walls. One nightshade lunged at him, and Dies Irae felt his soul being tugged from his body. Ignoring the feeling, he placed Gloriae on the floor, walked to his throne, and sat upon it.

The nightshades shrieked. Chunks of rock fell from the ceiling, one narrowly missing Gloriae. Dies Irae shut his eyes, clenched his good fist, and tightened his lips. He could feel the nightshades now. The throne gave him power to tame them, the way the Griffin Heart had allowed him to tame the griffins.

Dies Irae had never tried to tame nightshades. Nobody had in two thousand years. They were more powerful than griffins; he felt that at once. Their minds were like furnaces, their hatred exploding stars.

Dies Irae growled. "I am the true ruler of Osanna!" he called out. The throne rattled. "You have claimed my daughter. You will obey me."

They fought him.

They fought him well.

Thousands of them shrieked across the empire, coiled in the night sky, and sent their fire and hatred into him. They tugged at his soul, threatening to rip it into a million pieces.

Dies Irae refused them.

They lifted his throne. They flowed around him. They hurt him. They lifted Gloriae and tossed her against the floor, again and again.

Dies Irae refused to release them. "The old kings bound you to this throne. You still owe it your fealty, beasts of unlight. *You will obey me.*"

With a shriek that shook the city, the throne room shattered. A wall came down. Through the nightshades' eyes, Dies Irae saw the north tower of his palace falling.

Still he clung to them.

He wrestled them into darkness, until they bowed before him, a sea of smoke and shadows.

Dies Irae rose to his feet. His eye no longer hurt, and when he raised his arm, it was no longer burned. Black light flowed in his wounds, powerful, intoxicating. Through the eyes of the nightshades, he could see his face. His bandage had fallen off, revealing a gaping hole where his eye had been. His hair had gone white, and his good eye blazed a bright blue.

Dies Irae laughed. "You are mine now."

Across the empire, the nightshades hissed and bowed to him.

Dies Irae walked across the cracked floor toward his daughter. Gloriae lay there, nude and battered, her hair covering her face. She looked up at him, eyes huge, deep green, haunted.

"Father," she whispered.

Dies Irae removed his robe, leaving himself in a tunic and leggings, and tossed it at her. She draped it around her nakedness and stared at him, cheeks flushed. Her lips trembled.

"Father, I-- I thought that--"

Dies Irae had never hit his daughter. When she'd been a child, and misbehaved, he would beat her handmaiden, forcing Gloriae to watch. For years, he had spared her pain. For years, he had coddled her.

Today he hit her. His fist knocked her to the floor, spattering blood.

"Gloriae, daughter of Osanna," Dies Irae said, staring down upon her. Nightshades flowed above him. One draped across his shoulders. "I banish you from this city, and from Osanna. You have a day and night to run. Then I hunt you. If I catch you, your life is forfeit."

Her eyes widened. Rage bloomed across her cheeks.

"Father," she said and took a step toward him. Blood filled her mouth.

Dies Irae raised his fist again, and Gloriae froze.

"I will hear no excuses," Dies Irae said. The nightshades shrieked above him, and he pointed at the door. "Leave this place. You are banished from this kingdom. You are disowned. You are cast out in shame. Leave, Gloriae the Gilded, and never return. Today I have no daughter."

She stared at him, bared her teeth, and clenched her fists. She seemed ready to speak, and Dies Irae kept staring at her, driving his stare into her green eyes.

Finally Gloriae spun around, tightened the robes around her, and marched out of the shattered court.

LACRIMOSA

They flew east, wings churning clouds, breath hot in their lungs. Moonlight glinted on their scales. When Lacrimosa looked over her shoulder, she saw the nightshades. They were darker than the night sky, and their eyes burned, red stars.

"They're getting closer!" she cried, and heard the pain and fear in her voice. She blew fire back at the nightshades, as bright as she could make it. The other Vir Requis--her husband, daughter, and Kyrie--roared flames too.

The nightshades shrieked. The light hurt them. But they kept flying.

"I don't get it," Agnus Dei said. The young red dragon flew by Lacrimosa. "When a nightshade attacked Kyrie and me, firelight sent it fleeing. We had to nearly burn down the forest, but eventually it fled. Why don't these ones flee?"

Benedictus, a great black shadow in the night, grumbled. "You and Kyrie saw one nightshade, a scout, when twilight still filled the world. Nightshades are stronger in the night, and stronger in numbers. Firelight will no longer stop them. Sunrise burns behind the horizon. Fly! Faster!"

The nightshades shrieked again, and Lacrimosa could feel them. They tugged at her soul, as if trying to pull stuffing out of upholstery. She gritted her teeth, flapped her wings harder, and fought them. *You will not claim me. You cannot.*

She scanned the eastern horizon. Where was the sun? They flew so fast, faster than she'd ever flown. Lacrimosa felt ready to collapse, and the nightshades gave her soul a tug so powerful, she cried in pain. She left her body and floated a foot behind it. Benedictus grabbed her shoulder, and the pain jolted her soul back in.

"Fly, my love," Benedictus said to her. "We're almost there."

Tears streamed down her cheeks. Her wings burned. Her lungs felt ready to collapse. "I fly for you."

Hadn't she always flown seeking sunrise? For nearly two decades--since Dies Irae had raped her, toppled the courts of Requiem, and stole her daughter Gloriae--she had flown seeking light. Darkness had chased her for years.

Screeches rose around her, cutting off her thoughts. They were so loud she had to cover her ears. Ten more nightshades took flight, left and right, and flew at them. The nightshades behind shrieked too, welcoming their companions. The world shook. Lacrimosa screamed.

"Fly!" Benedictus shouted. "Fly fast, the sun shines behind the mountains."

Lacrimosa flew hard. Tears streamed down her cheeks, her wings screamed, but she flew. The nightshades tugged at her. One flew only a foot away, grinning, showing its smoky teeth.

"Lacrimosa...," it hissed, and she couldn't help but stare into its eyes. They were two stars, glittering. Beckoning. There were worlds beyond those stars, dimensions that swirled and spun, a space so much wider for her soul to travel. She would be free there. In darkness. In pain.

She could see her body flying below her. A silvery dragon, so delicate, so small. The worlds in those eyes were endless. Her dragon wings stilled. She began to fall. She saw Benedictus fly toward her, grab her, dig his claws into her shoulders.

"Lacrimosa!" he cried, shaking her in midair. Kyrie and Agnus Dei flew by him, nightshades wreathing them.

"You should not struggle," Lacrimosa tried to say, but she had no voice. "Join the unlight. Join the worlds. There is loneliness here. There is pain. There is darkness to fill. Join."

"Lacrimosa!" Benedictus shouted, and he slapped her face.

Pain. She felt pain. She felt her body. *No!* It sucked her back in. It pulled her. She slammed back into her body, and that pain filled her, and she saw the world through her eyes again.

She wept.

"I'm here, Benedictus. I'm here. I'm back. Fly!"

She could see hints of dawn now. It was only a pink wisp ahead, but it filled her with hope. Benedictus saw it too, and he howled and blew fire, and flew with more vigor. The nightshades swarmed around them, hissing and laughing.

"Mother!" came Agnus Dei's voice, frightened, almost childlike.

Lacrimosa saw that a dozen nightshades swarmed around her daughter, forming a shell of smoke and shadow. She struggled between them, as if floundering in water, and screamed.

"Agnus Dei!" Lacrimosa called and flew toward her daughter. She blew fire at the nightshades. They shrieked. Benedictus and Kyrie shot flames at others. Agnus Dei screamed, the horrible sound of a wounded animal.

"Mother!" she cried, tears falling.

Lacrimosa blew more fire, but the nightshades would not leave her daughter. *No. No! I already lost one daughter. I will not lose the other.*

"Take me!" she said to the nightshades. "Leave her and take me."

They laughed their hissing laughter. Their voices were only an echo. "We will take both, Lacrimosa. We will torture you both in the worlds beyond."

Lacrimosa saw them inhale around Agnus Dei. Silvery wisps rose from the girl's body, entering the nightshades' nostrils and mouths.

"No!" Lacrimosa screamed and blew fire.

Agnus Dei went limp. She began to tumble from the sky.

As Kyrie blew fire at the nightshades, Lacrimosa and Benedictus swooped and caught Agnus Dei. Her eyes stared blankly. In their grasp, she returned to human form. She seemed so small. A youth, that was all, only nineteen. A girl with a mane of black curls and scraped knees. She lay limply in Lacrimosa's grip, eyes unblinking.

"The sun!" Kyrie called. Tears flowed down his cheeks. "Let's get her into light."

They flew eastward, blowing fire at the nightshades that mobbed them. With a great flap of their wings, they cleared a river, and sunrise broke over a cover of mountain. Light drenched them.

The nightshades howled. Their screams made the river below boil. Trees wilted and fell, and a chunk of mountain collapsed. A barn burst into flame.

"Agnus Dei!" Kyrie cried, flying toward Lacrimosa. "Is she dead?"

Lacrimosa was weeping. "No." *She is something worse.*

The nightshades tried to swipe at them, to bite and claw, but they sizzled in the light. Howling, they turned and fled back into darkness.

"Yeah, you better run!" Kyrie called after them and shot flames in their direction. Then he looked at Agnus Dei, eyes haunted. "Let's get her on the ground."

Lacrimosa nodded and descended to a valley. She landed by a willow and placed Agnus Dei on the ground. The girl lay on her back, eyes staring, not blinking, mouth moving silently. They all shifted into human form.

"Agnus Dei," Kyrie said, kneeling by her. He clutched her hand. "Are you here? It's me, Kyrie."

She said nothing. Her eyes seemed not to see him. Her hand hung limply in his grasp.

Tears ran down Kyrie's face, drawing white lines down his ashy cheeks. He kissed Agnus Dei's forehead, and shook her, but she wouldn't recover.

"Agnus Dei, you wake up right now," Kyrie demanded. "Do it, or I'm going to kick your butt so hard, it'll fall off."

Normally, Lacrimosa knew, the taunt would rile Agnus Dei into a fury, and she would be wrestling Kyrie to the ground and calling him a worthless pup. Today she only stared blankly over his shoulder. Lacrimosa also wept. She knew that Agnus Dei was not here, not in this body. Her soul was shattered and lost in the night worlds.

She and Benedictus both held Agnus Dei's other hand. The sunlight fell upon them, but would not find their daughter. She seemed cloaked in shadows. They tried shaking her, slapping her face, pinching her, singing to her, pleading with her. Nothing helped.

Kyrie looked up, eyes huge and haunted. "What do we do?" he whispered.

He looked so young to Lacrimosa. Sometimes she forgot he was only seventeen, still a youth despite all the battles and fire he'd been through.

"I don't know," she said and hugged Agnus Dei.

Her daughter was cold and limp in her arms.

GLORIAE

She rode across the countryside, eyes narrowed. She had taken little from Confutatis: Her horse, a white courser named Celeritas; her sword, crossbow, and dagger; her gilded armor, the breastplate curved to the shape of her body, the helmet a golden mask shaped as her face. Celeritas's hooves tore up grass and dirt, and Gloriae spurred the beast and lashed it with her crop.

"Faster, damn you," she said. Once she had ridden griffins, could cross a hundred leagues in a flight. Horses were slow and stupid, needed more rest than griffins, and frayed her nerves.

"Move your hooves, you mindless beast," Gloriae said and lashed her crop. Celeritas whinnied, and her eyes rolled, but she kept galloping.

Mindless beast. That was what she herself had been only yesterday, was it not? Yes. She had floated, naked and mindless, among the nightshades. Her soul had been broken, had filled thousands of nightshades across Osanna. She'd seen through their eyes, travelled through their planes. She had seen the weredragons fleeing into the east. She had seen Lacrimosa, the silver dragon who had infested her with the reptilian curse. She had seen Kyrie and Agnus Dei, the youths she had fought. And she had seen Benedictus, the Lord of Lizards, the man who claimed to be her true father, the man she had sworn to kill.

"I know where you are," Gloriae hissed through clenched teeth, the wind claiming her words. "I will find you, weredragons. I will slay you with my crossbow, and sever your heads with my sword. I will drag your heads back to Dies Irae, to my real father, and he will forgive me."

Gloriae nodded and tasted tears on her lips. Shame burned within her. Dies Irae, her real father, had trained her from birth to hate and hunt Vir Requis. She had killed many for him, but failed him now. She had failed to set the nightshades on them, had allowed the creatures to destroy the empire.

"But I will make amends," Gloriae vowed into the wind. "I do not need the nightshades. I will kill the weredragons with crossbow and blade."

Dies Irae's men hunted them too, Gloriae knew. Those who'd survived the nightshades would be patrolling every corner of the empire, armed with blades and ilbane. Whoever killed them would become a hero, a favorite son of Osanna, a lieutenant to Dies Irae. But they did not know where the weredragons cowered. She, Gloriae, had seen them through the nightshades' eyes. She had felt the nightshades tug Agnus Dei's soul, bite it, and rip it apart. Dies Irae might control the nightshades now, but Gloriae had seen enough.

As she rode, spurring Celeritas, she gazed upon the ruin of Osanna. It was daytime now, and no nightshades crawled the empire, but she saw signs of them everywhere. Forts lay toppled upon hill and mountain, blackened with nightshade smoke. Cattle lay dead and stinking in the fields. Farmhouses smoldered and bodies lay outside roadside inns.

I did this. The thought came unbidden to Gloriae's mind. She forced it down, refusing to acknowledge it.

"No," she whispered. "I will feel no guilt. The weredragons made me do it. I will redeem myself when I kill them."

She drove Celeritas out of the fields and down a forest road. The leaves were red and gold. Autumn was here, and cold winds blew, biting Gloriae's cheeks. Other than her armor--a breastplate, helmet, greaves, and vambraces--she wore little. White riding pants. A thin woolen shirt. She had brought no cloak in her haste, and she regretted that now. It was cold, colder than autumn should be. She saw frost on grass and leaf, and even Celeritas's hot body could not warm her. She shivered.

"The light and heat of the Sun God are leaving the world," she whispered. "Nightshades and weredragons have filled it, but my heart still blazes with the Sun God's fire. I will light the world with it, even if I must burn it down."

She let Celeritas rest, eat grass, and drink from a stream. Gloriae dismounted and stretched, ate dried meat and crackers from her pack, and drank ale from her skin. She dipped her head into the stream, scrubbed her face, and looked at her reflection. She was thinner than she'd ever been. Her eyes looked huge in her pale face, too large and green. Her hair was long, cascading gold, like a lion's mane. She was still beautiful, Gloriae thought, but sadder now. Haunted.

She thought back to that day in her chamber. The day she had met Lacrimosa, contracted the disease, and shifted into a dragon. With a shiver, Gloriae pushed that memory aside. She might be cursed now, but she would hide it. She would never become a dragon again. She would remain Gloriae the Gilded, human and healthy, a slayer of weredragons and never one of their number.

She was riding Celeritas again, and heading around a bend in the road, when the outlaws emerged.

They stepped out from behind trees, dressed in brown leather and patches of armor. There were three--tall and thin men, a hungry look to them. One bore a chipped sword. A second outlaw hefted an axe. The third pointed a bow and arrow at her.

Gloriae halted her horse. She raised her shield, raised an eyebrow, and stared at the outlaws from behind her visor.

"So," she said. "A swordsman, an axeman, and an archer. You must be mad. I'm on horseback and wearing armor. You don't stand a chance, so scurry along and find easier prey. You might find children you could steal sweets from."

The archer laughed, an ugly sound. "Aye, but there's three of us, and we're hungry."

He loosed his arrow.

Celeritas whinnied and bucked. The arrow hit her neck, spurting blood. Gloriae fell from the saddle and hit the ground hard. The outlaws rushed at her.

Gloriae could barely breathe, and pain filled her, but she wasted no time. She rolled, dodging the axe; it slammed down by her head. She kicked, and her steel-tipped boot hit the axeman's shin. A sword came down, and she rolled again and raised her shield. The blade hit the shield, chipping the wood and driving pain down Gloriae's arm.

She leaped to her feet, swinging Per Ignem, her sword of northern steel. It clanged against the swordsman's blade. She heard the axe swing behind her, and she ducked. The axehead grazed the top of her helmet. An arrow flew and hit her breastplate; it dented the steel, drove pain into Gloriae's side, but did not cut her.

"Who's mad now?" the swordsman said, grinning to reveal yellow teeth.

Gloriae feigned an attack, but jumped back and over Celeritas. The horse was dead. Gloriae crouched behind the body, as if hiding there, and grabbed her crossbow from the saddle. She rose to her feet to see the outlaws bounding toward her. She shot her crossbow, hitting the archer in the face. He stumbled back, screaming a gurgling scream, and hit the axeman.

Gloriae leaped over the horse, swung Per Ignem, and met the swordsman's blade. She thrust, parried, and riposted. The axeman attacked at her left; she blocked him with her shield, thrust her sword, and slew the swordsman.

The archer had fallen and was screaming, clutching the quarrel in his face. Gloriae faced the axeman. He paled and turned to flee.

Gloriae would not let him escape.

She placed a foot on her crossbow, pulled back, and loaded a new quarrel. She aimed, one eye closed, and shot. Her quarrel hit the fleeing axeman in the back, and he fell.

Gloriae walked between the trees, Per Ignem in hand, its blade dripping blood. She had fallen hard off her horse, and her side hurt, but she was otherwise unharmed. When she reached the axeman, she stood above him. He writhed at her feet, blood spreading down his shirt, and rolled onto his back.

"Please," he said, trembling. "Mercy."

Gloriae stabbed him through the chest. Blood filled his mouth and dripped from his wound. Gloriae twisted the blade, then pulled it out and walked away.

She returned to the road. The swordsman was already dead, but the archer was alive. He sat against a tree. He had managed to pull the quarrel from his face, revealing a gushing wound. When he saw Gloriae, he struggled to his feet and threw a rock at her.

The stone hit Gloriae's breastplate, doing no harm. She walked toward the man, her sword raised. He rose to flee. She chased him down and slew him between the trees. His blood soaked the bluebells that carpeted the forest floor.

Bluebells. The flower brought memories to her. She remembered seeing Lacrimosa wear a bluebell pendant, even as the creature had cowered in the dungeons of Confutatis. Gloriae had been shocked at Lacrimosa's beauty, fragility, the moonlight of her hair. How could a creature so evil seem so beautiful?

"I am your mother," Lacrimosa had said. "You have our magic, you can shift too, become a dragon."

Yes, Gloriae had shifted that night, become a golden dragon of scales, fangs, and claws. But she knew this was no gift, as the weredragons claimed, no lofty magic passed down from kings. It was a curse. Dies Irae was her father, and Lacrimosa had infested her with disease.

Jaw clenched, Gloriae again stabbed the body at her feet, as if stabbing the memory of that day.

She took what supplies she could carry from her slain horse: a rolled up blanket, a cast iron pot, three skins of ale, and a pack of battle rations. In the outlaws' pockets, she found a few coins and took those too. She slung her shield and sword over her back, and continued down the path with her crossbow in hand. She kept a quarrel loaded. Should more outlaws attack, she would shoot them. She left her horse behind, bloodied on the road; the wolves would dispose of it.

The road was long, overgrown with weeds and burrs, and rocky. Soon Gloriae's feet ached. A thistle snagged at her leggings, tearing them at the knee. Blood and mud stained her leather boots. Gloriae was bone-tired, and evening began to fall, but she refused to rest. She had to find the weredragons. She had to kill them. Had to.

"I will regain your trust, Father," she whispered through shivering lips. A cold wind blew, sneaking under her armor like the icy hands of a ghost.

When darkness fell, Gloriae wished she had brought her tin lamp and tinderbox. She had forgotten it upon her horse's body, and she cursed herself. How would she light a fire? Her horse was too far behind now, so Gloriae trudged on. Owls hooted around her, and jackals howled, but Gloriae did not fear them. Worse creatures emerged in the night.

The trees soon parted, and Gloriae found herself walking in open country. Clouds cloaked the sky, but once when they parted, revealing the moon, Gloriae saw hills and a stream. She recognized this place. The weredragons had flown here before Dies Irae had taken the nightshades from her, stealing their eyes.

"Where are you, weredragons?" Gloriae whispered, clutching her crossbow. The quarrel was coated with ilbane-- weredragon poison.

A screech above answered her.

A nightshade.

Gloriae ran. Her shield and sword clanked over her back, and her boots squelched through mud. The nightshade saw her. It dived toward her, eyes blazing. She loosed her quarrel, but it passed through the creature, barely dispersing its smoky body. Gloriae cursed and kept running. The nightshade chased.

"Father!" she shouted. "Call it off!"

The nightshade only shrieked. Was Father controlling it? Was he watching through its eyes and could stop it? If so, he did not. The nightshade swooped and flowed across her. She shivered; the nightshade was so icy, it made the night winds seem warm. She swung Per Ignem at it, dispersing some of its smoke, but it only laughed.

Light. I need light! Why had she forgotten her lamp? Gloriae ran. She felt the nightshade tugging her soul, felt her spirit being torn, tugged from her body. She screamed and swung Per Ignem, but the nightshade only laughed and kept tugging. She no longer sat upon the Ivory Throne; a nightshade would show her no quarter now.

Then she saw light ahead.

It was still distant, but burned bright. A ring of fire in the valley. Gloriae ran toward it, swinging her sword and shouting. She had never run faster. With a great tug, the nightshade pulled her soul clear from her body. For a second, she saw herself from above. But the jolt of her body tripping on a root pulled her back in, and she kept running.

She reached the fire. She leaped over the flames, ignoring the pain, and spun around, panting. The nightshade hovered outside the ring of fire, ten feet above the ground. It glared at her, drooling wisps of smoke.

Gloriae grabbed a burning branch and held it before her. She stared at the nightshade, daring not remove her eyes from it.

That was when she noticed, from the corner of her eyes, that others stood in the ring of fire.

The weredragons.

Gloriae gasped, spun to face them, then spun back to the nightshade. She didn't know who posed a greater threat, but she knew that she would die. She could not defeat both these enemies.

All four weredragons were there--Benedictus, their king, a gruff man with a tangle of black curls; Lacrimosa, his wife, a dainty and pale woman; Kyrie Eleison, the boy who had wounded Gloriae's leg. Agnus Dei was there too, but she lay on the ground, eyes open but unseeing, and Gloriae knew what that meant. The nightshades had gotten her.

In a flash, Gloriae realized that she herself had claimed Agnus Dei's soul--or at least, lived in the nightshade that had done so. A shard of that soul still pulsed within Gloriae, weak but crying inside her. Now that she gazed upon Agnus Dei, she could feel it inside her, weeping, crying for release.

She had no time to ponder it further. The three standing weredragons looked at her, then shifted. Soon three dragons blew fire beside her. Gloriae ducked and hid behind her shield, but the dragons were not burning her. They were shooting fire at the nightshade. It screeched, and Gloriae watched, mouth hanging open. The creature seemed to suck in the light, to cancel it out. The dragons kept blowing fire at it, white hot fire that drenched Gloriae with sweat.

I can shift too, she thought. *I can help them. I can also blow fire. I shifted once.*

But no. She dared not, would not. She had vowed never again to shift. She would not allow the curse to claim her.

The fire kept burning, and finally the nightshade shrieked and flew away. Gloriae watched it disappear into the night, fleeing into the forest.

The weredragons shifted back into human forms. For a moment, they all stared at one another.

Then Gloriae raised Per Ignem. She would have shot them, but had no quarrel in her crossbow, nor time to load one. She pointed her blade at Benedictus.

"You will not touch me," she hissed. The ring of fire crackled around them. "Take one step forward, lizard, and your head will be my trophy."

Benedictus scowled, Lacrimosa shed a tear, and Kyrie rolled his eyes.

"Oh, give it a rest!" said the boy. He pointed his dagger at her. "Gloriae, you are denser than a mule's backside, and just about as pleasant. Even I figured out Benedictus and Lacrimosa are your parents by now, and I'm not even related. Can you really be so dumb?" He spoke slowly, as if spelling out a truth to a child. "Benedictus is your father, not Dies Irae. Lacrimosa is your mother. Dies Irae lied to you. You are a Vir Requis. Get it? Good. Now sheathe your sword, before I clobber some sense into your pretty head."

Gloriae gasped. Nobody had ever insulted her like that. If anyone ever had, they'd be broken, slung through a wagon wheel, and left to die atop her city. She took a step toward Kyrie, sword raised.

"I will cut your lying tongue from your mouth."

He gave her a crooked smile. "I'd like to see you try, sweetheart."

Benedictus stepped toward them, fists clenched. "Stop this," he demanded.

Gloriae swung Per Ignem at him.

So fast she barely saw him move, Benedictus raised a dagger and parried. With his other hand, he shoved her back. She fell two paces, snarled, and prepared to attack again... but Kyrie reached out a foot, tripping her.

She fell. Benedictus placed a boot on her wrist and yanked her sword free. Kyrie leaped onto her back and held her down, pressing her head into the mud.

"Take her crossbow too," Benedictus said. "And there's a dagger on her thigh. Grab it."

As Gloriae struggled, Lacrimosa took her weapons. She screamed and floundered, but Kyrie and Benedictus held her down. Mud and hair filled her mouth, but she managed to scream.

"Cowards! Fight like men. I will kill you, weredragons."

"Stars, she's dumb," Kyrie said, his forearm on the back of her neck, holding her head down. "Are you sure she's your daughter, Lacrimosa? Maybe she was actually born to a warthog. She does smell like one."

Gloria screamed into the mud. She felt Kyrie pull her arms back and bind her wrists. She kicked, but Benedictus grabbed her legs and tied them too.

No, no! I cannot fall prisoner to weredragons. Cannot. Tears burned in her eyes. First she had failed to kill them. Then Lacrimosa had infested her with the curse. Now the nightshades she had freed were destroying the empire, and the weredragons had captured her. Her world crumbled around her, and she screamed and wept and shouted curses.

Once she was tied up, they placed her on her back beside Agnus Dei. Kyrie stuffed an old sock into her mouth and smirked.

"I've been wearing this sock for two days," he said. "It should be nice and stinky now, and perfect for keeping you quiet."

Gloriae ceased struggling. It was pointless. The sock tasted foul in her mouth, and she glared at Kyrie with a look that swore she would kill him. Most men would cower under that glare; she had killed men after staring at them thus. Kyrie, however, only snorted and rolled his eyes again.

What will they do to me? Gloriae wondered. Would they torture her, or would the death they gave her be quick? She suspected the former, but she was ready for it. She could endure it.

Lacrimosa knelt over her, and Gloriae clenched her jaw, prepared for whatever torture the weredragon planned. But Lacrimosa only held out her bluebell pendant, clicked a hidden clasp, and it swung open. The insides of the locket were painted with a delicate hand. The right side held a painting of a brown-eyed baby with black curls. The left side featured a baby with green eyes and golden locks.

"The black-haired baby is Agnus Dei," Lacrimosa said, voice soft and sad. A tear ran down her cheek. "The golden baby is you, Gloriae. That's how you looked before Dies Irae kidnapped you."

She tried to speak, but could not. The sock still filled her mouth. Lacrimosa reached for the sock, but paused and said, "You must promise not to scream if I remove it. Do you promise?"

Gloriae glared at the weredragon woman and nodded. Lacrimosa removed the sock from Gloriae's mouth, but left her arms and legs tied.

"Dies Irae is my father," Gloriae said, letting all her fire and pain fill her voice.

Lacrimosa nodded. "Maybe. Maybe not. He raped me, Gloriae. I don't know who your father is, Benedictus or Dies

Irae. But I know that I gave birth to you and Agnus Dei." She gestured at the girl, who stared unblinking into space. "She's your sister."

Gloriae looked from weredragon to weredragon. "I... I remember harps. And... columns among birch trees. I remember walking with my mother and sister through courts of marble."

Lacrimosa nodded. "You remember the courts of Requiem. Dies Irae toppled them with his griffins, and burned the birches, and stole you from me. You were only three years old. He left Agnus Dei, because she could shift into a dragon already; Dies Irae thought her cursed."

"I can shift t--" Gloriae began, then bit her lip. Suddenly she was crying and trembling. "You cursed me," she said, tears on her lips. "You infected me. The day I met you in the dungeon, when you told me I could shift, I... I turned into a dragon that day. A golden dragon. I'm horrible now, diseased."

Lacrimosa leaned down and hugged her. Gloriae squirmed, but Lacrimosa would not release her. "Gloriae, my beloved. My sweetness. You are not cursed. You are blessed with beautiful, ancient magic that flows from starlight. I knew you could shift too. You bloomed into this magic late, but the Draco stars shine bright in you. Do not fear your magic, or be ashamed of it. It is beautiful. You are not diseased, Gloriae. You are perfect and beautiful and blessed."

Gloriae wept onto Lacrimosa's shoulder. She wanted to scream, to bite, to struggle, but only trembled. Her head spun. She was not cursed? Not diseased?

"I'm so confused," she said, speaking into Lacrimosa's hair. "Dies Irae told me that you murdered my mother."

Lacrimosa nodded, weeping too. "I know, child. But I am your mother. Don't you remember me? Do you remember nothing of your first three years?"

Gloriae sniffed back tears. "I remember you, but... I thought you had planted those memories in me. With foul magic."

Lacrimosa shook her head. "Those are your real memories, Gloriae. That is who you are. Do not doubt it, and do not fear it. I love you."

Gloriae shook her head too. "It makes no sense! Why would Dies Irae lie to me? He loves me. He... he's my father."

Benedictus knelt beside them. He placed a large, calloused hand on her shoulder. "Dies Irae is my brother, and he hates me. He hates our father. He is Vir Requis too, and mostly he hates that he lacks our magic. So he killed our father, destroyed Requiem, and hunts us. He trained you to kill us, but he cannot hide the truth from you. Not any longer." Benedictus seemed overcome with emotion. His eyes were moist. "Welcome home, daughter. Welcome back to our family."

Gloriae gazed at him, this rough man, her tears blurring his hard lines. "You are my real father?"

He touched her cheek. "I don't know. But I think so. I'm almost certain." He smiled, and Gloriae could see from the lines on his face that he smiled rarely. But it was a warm smile. A good smile.

He does not hate me, Gloriae realized. *He does not try to kill me. He truly loves me.* How could he? He was a weredragon! He was evil! Wasn't he?

A twinge yanked her heart.

Gloriae froze.

Again, something tugged her chest. It felt like a demon had wrapped a noose around her heart, and was pulling it tight.

"What are you doing to me?" she demanded, breathing heavily. Were the weredragons casting a spell upon her? Her head spun. She had heard of warriors stepping into battle, then clutching their chests and dying without a scratch, their hearts stilled. Was this happening to her? Again something tugged inside her, invisible hands.

"What are you talking about?" Kyrie said. "We haven't touched you."

Gloriae clenched her jaw. Something was crawling inside her chest, pulling, whispering, calling to her.

"Sister," it spoke. "Sister, hear me."

Gloriae thrashed in her bounds. "You cast a spell upon me! Stop this black magic."

The invisible hands wrapped around her heart, her soul, her mind... and tugged. It felt like a nightshade, but nightshades pulled souls out of the body. Whatever spell infested her, it was pulling her soul inward, deeper into her body, into a world that pulsed far in memory. Gloriae resisted, gritting her teeth, clenching her fists, and kicking.

"You will not--" Gloriae began to shout... and her breath died.

"Sister, hear me!" the voice inside her cried, and pulled harder. White light flooded Gloriae.

That was it, she thought. She was dead. This black, weredragon magic was killing her. She tried to scream, to roll around, to fight it, but could not. She drowned in the light. The force pulled her. She felt herself sucked into a tunnel, and she tumbled down, deep, far, streaming into nothing. She flowed like water down a drain.

Nothing but white light.

She floated.

Sunlight fell upon her eyelids.

Gloriae opened her eyes, and saw birch leaves. They rustled above her, kissed with sunlight, the green of spring. Their shadows danced upon her, and Gloriae saw that she wore a white dress. She no longer had the body of a woman. Her body was small now, the body of a toddler, no more than two or three years old. She wore no leather boots, but soft shoes. She wore no armor, but a cotton dress.

"Where am I?" she whispered. Her voice was that of a child.

She was lying on her back, and pushed herself onto her elbows. Marble columns stood before her, their capitals shaped as dragons. *A temple,* she thought. But not a temple to the Sun God. No golden dome topped this temple. It had no ceiling, and birch leaves scuttled along its floor.

Roars sounded above her. Gloriae raised her eyes and gasped. Dragons! Dragons flew there! Not scattered refugees, but a herd. There were hundreds. Green dragons, and blue, and silver, and red, and black. They did not fly in war. They did not burn or bare fangs. They would not hurt her, Gloriae knew. She felt only warmth and love from them.

"Do you remember, Gloriae?" somebody spoke beside her. "Do you remember this place?"

Gloriae turned her head, and saw a ghost sitting beside her. It seemed the ghost of a girl her age, but Gloriae could not be sure. The ghost was near transparent, flickering in and out of sight.

"Who are you?" Gloriae whispered.

The ghost smiled. Her hair was like black smoke, a mop of curls. "I'm your sister. I'm Agnus Dei. A part of her, at least. A whisper and a speck."

"Are you a ghost?"

Agnus Dei shook her head. "I'm a figment. A shard of a soul. I live inside you now, Gloriae."

Gloriae rose to her feet. It felt strange to stand this way. She was used to standing tall and strong, powerful in her steel-tipped boots, a warrior. She was so short now, her limbs so soft, her voice so high.

"What do you mean? Why am I a child here? Is this a spell?"

Agnus Dei shook her head. "It's a memory. A memory that still lives inside me, and inside you. Do you remember being inside the nightshades?"

Gloriae nodded. "I... I flew with them, yes. I saw through their eyes. I smelled through their nostrils of smoke. My body sat upon the Ivory Throne, but my soul was scattered, hunting with a thousand nightshades."

Pollen glided through the ghostly girl. "And now my soul is shattered. The nightshades broke me into a hundred pieces. Ninety-nine of those pieces are trapped now. Nightshades devoured them. But one piece, Gloriae... the hundredth piece... that piece went into you. When you flew inside the nightshades, you claimed that piece for yourself. Maybe you didn't mean to. Maybe you didn't even know it. But that piece of my soul is trapped inside you. That piece is me, who speaks to you here."

Gloriae shook her head. Her hair whipped side to side, slapping her face. "I don't understand."

"Neither do I. But I've looked inside you, Gloriae. I've seen our past together." The ghostly Agnus Dei spread her arms around her. "Look at this place, Gloriae. This is a memory I found within you. It's no spell. It's no trick. This place is yours."

Gloriae looked around her, at the marble columns, the birches, the herds of dragons.

"It is Requiem."

Agnus Dei nodded. "Requiem sixteen years ago--when you and I lived here, twin girls."

Dapples of sunlight played across the grass. The air smelled of bluebells, trees, and life. Robins, starlings, and finches chirped in the trees. Home. Was this truly her home? Gloriae had always lived in Flammis Palace, in a room full of swords, lances, and armor. She had never lived among flowers, trees, and birds. And yet... this felt real to her. Agnus Dei spoke truth. Gloriae could feel it. This was no spell, but a memory that filled her nostrils, her ears, her eyes, and her soul.

"I remember," she whispered. "I had a cat here, a gray cat with green eyes. We lived beyond that hill, in a palace of marble. You and I shared a room. There was a fireplace for the winters, and flowers on the walls, purple ones." Her eyes moistened. "This is where I'm from. This is where I was born. But... how did I leave this place? What happened to me?"

Agnus Dei smiled sadly. She flickered more weakly now, appearing and disappearing.

"Look," she whispered and pointed skyward.

Gloriae looked, and ice flowed through her.

Griffins.

Hundreds of the beasts swooped upon Requiem. They shrieked, lashed claws, and their wings bent the trees. Riders rode them, clad in white and gold. Dies Irae rode at their lead, bearing a lance of silver and gold. His banners flapped around him, the red griffin upon a golden field. A jewel glowed red around his neck. The Griffin Heart.

"Run, Agnus Dei!" Gloriae said. She tried to grab her sister, but her hands passed through the ghostly girl.

Agnus Dei smiled sadly. "Watch, Gloriae. They cannot hurt you now."

Gloriae stood and watched the skies. The dragons crashed against the griffins, blowing fire. The griffin riders attacked with crossbows, lances, and bows. Flame and blood filled the sky. The trees burned. Feathers and scales rained. The war was like a painting of red, gold, and black, the colors swirling, mixing together, and tearing the canvas.

Gloriae wanted to fly, to fight, to kill. But... who was her enemy now? This was her home, and the griffins were destroying it. Their talons tore down trees. They crashed into columns, toppling them. Were they her warriors, or her enemy?

"Agnus Dei, what's happening?" she demanded, but she knew the answer.

Dies Irae had stolen the Griffin Heart. The war of Requiem had begun.

Flame and tears covered Gloriae's world. She fell onto her back, her eyes closed, and ash fell onto her like snowflakes.

She lay for a long time.

When she opened her eyes, it seemed like many days had passed. The griffins and dragons were gone. The fires had burned away. Requiem lay in ruin around her. The trees smoldered. The columns lay smashed. Bloodied bodies covered the field, vultures and crows gnawing on them. Requiem stank of rot, blood, and fire. Gloriae couldn't help it. She rolled over and threw up, then lay trembling.

For a moment she could only lie there, hugging herself.

"Agnus Dei?" she finally whispered. "Is this a memory too?"

Her ghostly sister still sat beside her. She nodded.

"Look, Gloriae. Stand up and look around you."

Gloriae stood on shaky legs. The ruin spread around her. She saw nothing but blood, ash, and destruction. She should be happy, she knew. Requiem was defeated! The evil of weredragons was wiped clean!

But Gloriae could not rejoice. Nothing seemed clean here. There was no Sun God light, only ash and smoke in the sky. There was no good, clean earth, only bodies and blood.

But no. Not all were dead. A group of dragons crouched behind the toppled columns. A few were warriors, tough male dragons with sharp claws and dented scales. A few were females. Some were children.

"Dragons of Requiem!" cried a burly black dragon. "Fly! Fly from here."

It was King Benedictus, Gloriae realized, but he was younger here, stronger, his voice clearer. Blood and ash covered him. He flapped his leathern wings and took flight, leading the other dragons into battle.

As Gloriae watched them fly away, she heard a new voice. "Daughters."

She turned toward the voice, and tears filled her eyes.

It was her mother.

Mother was beautiful, her hair silvery-gold, her skin pale, her eyes deep lavender. She wore a gown of white silk. Blood and ash covered her.

"Girls, come, we must leave," Mother said. She ran toward them, feet silent on the bloody earth.

Wings flapped.

A griffin landed before Mother.

Volucris. King of Griffins. And Dies Irae rode him.

"You will not touch them!" Mother screamed and shifted into a silver dragon. She lunged at Dies Irae, blowing fire.

Volucris leaped back. Dies Irae shot his crossbow, and the quarrel hit Mother. The silver dragon screamed, lashed her claws, and hit Dies Irae's armor. Dies Irae fell from his griffin, hit the ground, and swung his sword. Mother tried to bite him, but Dies Irae held her back with his blade. Volucris leapt onto the silver dragon. Shrieks tore the air. Fire rose. Blood splashed.

Gloved hands grabbed Gloriae. Somebody hoisted her into the air.

"Mother!" she screamed. Dies Irae had grabbed her, she realized. His fingers dug into her, so painful she could barely breathe.

"No!" Mother cried. "Not my daughter. Leave her, Irae!"

Dies Irae only laughed and shot his crossbow again. He hit Mother in the neck, and the silver dragon screamed and fell.

"She's my daughter too, lizard whore," Dies Irae said. "You can keep the dark one, the freak who shifts into a red dragon. Gloriae is pure. Gloriae is not cursed. She is mine."

Mother tried to rise, but Volucris kicked her down.

Gloriae screamed and cried and twisted. "Mother!" she cried. "Sister! Help me!"

Dies Irae's gloved hand covered her mouth. She could not scream. She could not breathe. Stars floated before her eyes. She was so small, so weak, her arms so soft.

She thought she would die, and then a dozen dragons swooped upon them.

Fire. Claws. Pain and heat and blood.

Gloriae kicked and felt faint. Her lungs felt ready to burst. Her eyelids fluttered.

The world went black, then red, then blue. The next thing she knew, they were airborne. She sat in a griffin's saddle. Dies Irae sat behind her, his arm wrapped around her. Dragons chased them through the sky, and a thousand griffins screeched and flowed around them. The griffins and dragons clashed, and blood rained. The screams nearly deafened Gloriae.

"Daughter!" Mother cried somewhere in the distance. Gloriae could not see her through the smoke and fire. "Gloriae! Stay strong, daughter! I will save you."

Gloriae cried, and screamed, and kicked, but Dies Irae held her tight.

They flew from the battle. They flew from the smoke and fire, from her mother's cries. They flew over leagues of ruin, toppled temples, fallen palaces, burned forests, a million bodies. They flew to the east.

The world of ruin blurred.

She slept.

When she awoke, she saw a world of light and beauty. Forests and rivers. Farms of gold. Castles and walls. Dawn, sunset, stars, and dawn again. Still they flew, Dies Irae clutching her in the saddle. Finally she saw a city ahead, a great city of white stone, its towers touching the clouds, its banners white and gold.

"Our new home," Dies Irae said. "Behold the city of Confutatis." He stroked her hair. "I will raise you here, Gloriae. Away from the weredragons. I will raise you to be pure, and strong, and cruel. I will raise you in the light of the Sun God, to be a huntress of evil."

"I want to go home," she whispered, tears on her cheeks. He kissed her head. "We are home, daughter."

"Where is Mother? Where is Agnus Dei?" She trembled.

Dies Irae caressed her cheek. "The weredragons killed your mother. They killed your entire family. All but me, your father. I will teach you to fight back, to kill those who hurt us. Do you understand?"

She did not, but said nothing. He took her to this city, to a palace of light and gold. He took her to a room of blades, shields, and poison. She trained. She hated. She fought and she killed. She wore gold, steel, and fury.

"I am Gloriae the Gilded," she cried to the city, a woman, a huntress, a ruler. "The weredragons cannot hide from me."

She ruled, and she warred, and she killed. She freed the nightshades, and she lived inside them, and her soul shattered. She tore into the soul of the red weredragon, this Agnus Dei. She scattered the pieces into the worlds beyond this world... all but one shard, a whisper inside her, a voice and memories.

"Do you see?" Agnus Dei whispered, a ghostly child. She was fading fast, dispersing like smoke.

"I don't understand," Gloriae whispered.

But she did. She trembled, shook her head, and wanted to scream.

She understood. She remembered.

"Now you must help me, Gloriae," Agnus Dei said. She was nothing but smoke, her voice an echo. "Return this shard of me, this bit of soul, into my body. Breathe this smoke into my lips. Return me to my body, so that I may wake, and hold you, and see you in life."

Gloriae shook her head wildly. "How can I? You are but one piece. One of a hundred."

"I will find the other ninety-nine. I will reclaim them. Please, Gloriae! Please, sister. I love you. Please. Only you can save me now. Open your eyes. My body lies here beside you. Only you can wake it."

Agnus Dei flickered like a guttering candle. Her voice faded into nothing.

"Please, Gloriae. Please...."

Gloriae's eyes snapped open.

She took a deep, desperate breath like a woman saved from drowning.

"Agnus Dei!" she cried.

The weredragons crowded around her. She was back in the true world. She was captive in the night, her limbs bound.

"Mother!" she said. Her arms trembled. "Mother, help me. He's taking me with him. He's taking me from you. Mother!"

Above her, Lacrimosa and Benedictus looked at each other, and their eyes softened. Kyrie's eyes filled with confusion.

"She's lost her mind," the boy said. "I didn't think I hit her that hard."

Gloriae turned her head, and saw Agnus Dei, not the ghostly child, but the soulless woman. Her empty body still breathed, but her breath was shallow.

Please, the voice whispered inside her. *Please.*

Gloriae took a deep, shaky breath, then looked at Benedictus.

"I think I can cure her," she said to him.

"How?" the three Vir Requis asked together.

Gloriae lowered her eyes. "I was in... inside the nightshades. When they attacked Agnus Dei." She took a deep breath, prepared for a storm of anger. "I was controlling them. Well, not truly. Mostly they controlled me, but I could see through their eyes. I know where they hid Agnus Dei's soul. They did not claim all of it. They wanted to. I wanted to. But a piece still remains inside me."

Kyrie took a threatening step toward her, fists raised. "I'm going to kill you if she dies."

Lacrimosa placed a hand on Kyrie's shoulder, holding him back, and looked at Gloriae.

"What can you do to help her?"

Gloriae shuddered. "I don't know. I understand little of it. Agnus Dei fought well; I felt it inside the nightshade. She is strong. Her soul still remembers its name. When the nightshades sucked her soul, part of it went into them, and part into me. I think I can give it back. The jolt might cure her, suck in the rest of her soul, and wake her up."

Kyrie blew out his breath loudly. It fluttered his hair. "Fighting griffins was easy. You bit, you clawed, you blew fire. These nightshades... none of it makes any sense to me."

"I understand little too," Gloriae confessed. Her head still spun from the memories. "I feel more than I understand. Their world is so different from ours. It's not a world our language has words for. It's not a world of objects or flesh. It's of endless dimensions, of emotions rather than thoughts, of smoke and shadow and darkness, not material things. They don't understand our bodies. They only see our minds. Let me go to Agnus Dei. Can you free my hands?"

The Vir Requis glanced at one another, and Gloriae knew they didn't trust her. She herself wasn't sure what she'd do with free hands. Would she try to attack them? She had spent years wanting to kill them. But... her memory was true. She knew that.

This was a piece of her twin.

Benedictus untied her hands, and Gloriae knelt by Agnus Dei. She placed her hands on her sister's cheeks. Her flesh was cold, but she still breathed. Her eyes stared blankly. They looked alike, Gloriae realized, almost shocked. Their faces were identical. Agnus Dei had a mane of black curls, and Gloriae had a mane of gold. Agnus Dei had tanned skin and brown eyes, while Gloriae had pale skin and eyes of green. But otherwise they had the same face--the same full lips, high cheeks, straight nose.

"Agnus Dei," Gloriae whispered. "Once we were together. We were one being in the womb. We are one again and need to separate. Take your spirit, Agnus Dei. Sister. It is yours."

Gloriae leaned down and kissed her sister's lips. Mist fled from her mouth into Agnus Dei's mouth. A light glowed. Agnus Dei coughed.

"Agnus Dei!" Lacrimosa called.

Gloriae looked into her sister's eyes, still holding her cheeks. "Do you hear me, sister? You have a piece of yourself now. Call your other pieces. Summon them; they are there in the worlds, you can find them, grasp them. Wake up, Agnus Dei. Your time has not yet come. Return to your body and speak to me."

Agnus Dei's mouth opened wide, and she called out, wordless. Her eyes moved. Her body floundered, but still Gloriae held her cheeks, keeping her head still.

"Sister, can you hear me?" Tears streamed down Gloriae's cheeks to land on Agnus Dei. "I was lost from you for so long. For years I wandered the world without you. I didn't know. I was torn and broken. Now I'm back, and you are lost. You are torn. You must return too. You must return and be with me, with us. I love you, Agnus Dei." Her own words shocked her, but Gloriae could not stop them; they flowed from a deep, hidden place inside her, a place now broken and spilling its secrets. "I remember you, sister. I love you."

The tears fell onto Agnus Dei's face.

The girl took a deep, ragged breath.

"Gloriae!" she called. She hugged her sister. "Gloriae, I remember you too. I saw you in the worlds. I saw us as children. I loved you once. I remember. I love you again. You've returned to us."

And then the others were embracing them too. Lacrimosa wept, and even Benedictus and Kyrie shed tears. The five hugged one another, the fire burning around them. The Draco constellation shone above.

The nightshades could return any moment, Gloriae knew. The next time, she would not be able to heal the bodies they emptied. Dies Irae would lead them upon the Vir Requis with all his wrath and pain. But Gloriae could not fear nightshades, not tonight.

Tonight her world crashed around her. Tonight memories flooded her, making her fingers tremble, her eyes water, and her head spin. Dies Irae had banished her; the weredragons had welcomed her. Who was her family? Who was she now? Gloriae looked to the sky, swallowed, and closed her eyes.

BENEDICTUS

"Get up," Benedictus said to the others. "We move."

The twins still lay on the ground, embracing. Lacrimosa and Kyrie were hovering around them, hugging and laughing and crying. Benedictus too wanted to cry, to laugh, to hug them, but forced himself to his feet. He pulled a burning branch from the ring of fire, and held it as a torch.

"What do you mean 'move'?" Kyrie asked, tearing himself away from the twins. "It took us three hours to build this ring of fire. We're safe here for the night."

Benedictus grunted. He drew his dagger and pointed at the sky. "Safe from a scout nightshade, maybe. We have enough light to send one fleeing. But you heard Gloriae. Dies Irae controls the nightshades now, and whoever controls them can see through their eyes. Dies Irae knows we're here. There's likely an army of those creatures heading our way as we speak. Up! On your feet, everyone. Agnus Dei, you too. We move."

"Where will we go?" Kyrie demanded, clutching his own dagger. "Where can we flee that's safer than here?"

"Anywhere is safer," Benedictus replied, glaring at the boy. "We move until sunrise. There will be no safety this night."

They collected their things with numb fingers. They didn't have much--a few blankets, a pot and pan, some ale and bread and salted beef. Gloriae gave her dagger to Agnus Dei, and her crossbow to Lacrimosa. She kept her sword, holding it drawn.

"We should all be armed," she explained. Still, she kept eyeing her crossbow as if she missed it, or didn't trust Lacrimosa fully, or perhaps both.

"Grab torches from the fire," Benedictus told the others. "These will serve you better than weapons tonight."

Soon they were walking along the valleys and hills, burning branches in hand. They wrapped tattered bits of a blanket around the branches' tops, fashioning torches. Benedictus kept glancing around for nightshades, but it was hard to see in the dark. Once he thought he saw one, but it was only a pair of stars behind a cloud.

As he walked, he also kept looking at Gloriae. The others did too. They all walked near her, surrounding her, glancing at her. For so many years, Gloriae had hunted them. To have Gloriae the Gilded, the Terror of Osanna, walk among them.... It was surreal, Benedictus thought.

My lost daughter. Benedictus felt a lump in his throat. *She's back.*

She saw him gazing at her, and turned to look at him. Her eyes were quizzical. Little emotion showed on her face, and Benedictus guessed that she often looked this way. It was the look of a warrior, a killer trained to feel no compassion or pain.

"When you were three years old," he said to her, "you argued with Agnus Dei over a rag doll. You pulled one end of the doll, Agnus Dei the other, until it split. Agnus Dei ran to her room, crying. That evening you brought all your dolls to Agnus Dei, ten of them or more. You gave them to her. I was proud of you."

Gloriae's eyebrows rose. "I played with dolls? I was raised on swords, arrows, and shields. I don't remember playing with dolls."

Benedictus felt an ache in his chest. "I'm sorry, Gloriae. I'm sorry for how my brother raised you. To fight. To hate. To kill. For many years, I wanted to storm Confutatis, to steal you back, but... I knew that was impossible. I knew Dies Irae was raising you, looking after you. Not as I would, no. And cruelly perhaps. But you were alive. You were well. That comforted me. I'm sorry we couldn't save you, return you to us earlier."

Gloriae stared into the distance, and for a long time, she said nothing. Finally she spoke. "Let's not talk of my childhood yet. I'm still confused. I still don't know what to think of Dies Irae. Is he my father? Are you my father? I don't know." She looked at him. "I was raised to kill you, Benedictus. That was my purpose. Give me time."

He nodded. "I will. When you're ready to talk, we'll talk. For now, you're safe here, Gloriae. At least, as safe as I can make this world for you. That perhaps is not saying much, but know that we love you. Fully. Forever."

She nodded but said nothing more. She walked staring blankly into the night, the starlight in her hair.

They saw wisps of pink dawn in the east when the nightshades shrieked.

Benedictus spun around and stared to the west. An army of nightshades flew there. There must have been thousands--tens of thousands.

"Oh great," Kyrie muttered beside him.

Benedictus shifted into Black Fang, the great dragon. "Fly!" he said. "It's almost dawn. Fly to the sun!"

The others shifted too. Lacrimosa became a silver dragon, Agnus Dei a red one, and Kyrie blue. Gloriae, however, remained standing in the field, arms limp at her sides.

"Gloriae, can you shift too?" Benedictus asked. "Or should I carry you?"

The nightshades screeched. The world trembled. They were getting closer, crackling with thunder and lightning. Gloria stared at them, shivered, then looked at Benedictus.

"I shifted once," she said. "I didn't fly then, but... I can do it. I think so. I'll try."

"Well, you better get a move on, sweetheart," Kyrie said, tapping his claws. "We haven't got all night."

Gloriae nodded, clenched her jaw, and shifted. She did so slowly, hesitantly. Golden scales grew across her. Wings unfurled from her back, trembling, growing larger and larger. Fangs grew from her mouth, then claws from her fingertips. Finally a beautiful, golden dragon stood in the grass, her eyes emerald green.

"Now fly!" Benedictus bellowed as nightshades howled behind. "All of you."

They began flying to the east, even Gloriae. The girl flew slowly, wobbling, and Benedictus kept tapping her with his tail to guide her. The nightshades were gaining on them. When Benedictus looked over his shoulder, he saw them like a puddle of oil, covering the land. Countless eyes burned in their darkness.

"We're almost there," Benedictus said to Gloriae. She was growling and flapping her wings mightily. Her jaw was clenched. "You fly very well."

She snickered. "I spent my life on griffinback. This is surprisingly similar."

When they reached the dawn and flew into sunbeams, the nightshades screamed behind. A few flew into the light, then screeched and turned back. The Vir Requis turned to watch. The nightshades bellowed. Lightning flashed between them, and stars swirled. Finally they turned to flee, and soon disappeared into the west, back to darkness.

"Yeah, keep running!" Agnus Dei shouted after them. She blew fire.

The land here was rocky, strewn with pines and mint bushes. Benedictus led the others to a hilltop. They landed by an ancient oak tree and shifted back into human forms. Kyrie and Agnus Dei began arguing about who had flown faster. Lacrimosa busied herself dividing their meager food. Gloriae stood by the oak, one hand upon its trunk, and stared silently into the west.

Benedictus approached Lacrimosa.

"Both our daughters returned to us today," he said to her softly. "Our family is whole."

His wife smiled at him. "I knew it would be so some day." She lowered her eyes. "I just wish it were on safer days."

After long moments, Gloriae left the tree and approached her parents. Finally Benedictus saw her in daylight. Her leggings were torn, her boots were bloody, and ash covered her cheeks. And yet she walked with the stately, powerful stride of a warrior. Her armor still shone. Her eyes were steel, her face beautiful but cold and deadly. Gloriae the Gilded.

"Benedictus," she said to him. "I... I am to blame for this. The nightshades were entombed in the Well of Night, in a dungeon below Confutatis, and... I freed them. I thought I could control them, use them to... well, to kill you. I'm sorry. I will leave now, and return to Confutatis, and reseal these creatures in the Well of Night."

Benedictus lowered his head. *My daughter destroyed the world in an attempt to kill me; how could such darkness have befallen our family?* He sighed, her words stinging. "Daughter, you cannot control these creatures. Not anymore. How would you seal them in the Well?"

Gloriae lowered her head too. "I don't know." She looked up again, eyes flashing, pleading. "But I must do something. I caused this. I must fix it."

The others stood around them, watching silently. Lacrimosa gazed with moist eyes. Agnus Dei and Kyrie stood holding hands, silent. Benedictus looked over them, then back to Gloriae.

"How were they originally sealed?" he asked. "Do you know?"

Gloriae shook her head. "Father-- I mean, Dies Irae spoke of heroes sealing them in the Well of Night thousands of years ago. It sounded like there was a great struggle, that sealing them was a great triumph. But I don't know how it was done. Irae might be able to reseal them; he controls them now. But how are we to do it? I don't know."

Benedictus turned to the west. He gazed past the hills and valleys, as if seeking Confutatis and his brother. Finally he turned back to the others.

"It's time," he said, "that we hold council, and decide what to do. Sit down, we'll build a fire, and we'll talk."

Once they were seated around a campfire, eating the last of their rations, Benedictus spoke again.

"We must rebuild Requiem, our home among the birches. We must rebuild the Vir Requis race. But we cannot do so while these nightshades hunt us, as we could not while griffins hunted us. We freed the griffins, and now we must seal the nightshades in the Well of Night, as Gloriae said. First we must learn more about them. We know they steal souls. We know they fear light. But where are they from? How were they first sealed? How can one reseal them?"

Kyrie rolled his eyes. "So we're on a quest for knowledge now? I prefer a straight fight, like with the griffins. Bite, scratch, kill. That's my kind of mission."

Benedictus glowered at him. "Quiet, kid. Don't speak unless you have something smart to say. In other words, don't speak at all." He sighed and his voice softened. "When I was prince of Requiem, and the old kings still ruled in Confutatis, I would visit the city. I especially liked exploring the city library. I recall great chambers full of scrolls and books. Dies Irae has no use for books, but the kings he usurped had collected them. Gloriae, does the library still stand?"

She nodded. "Yes, I've seen it. The books are still there. Irae does not read them. Nor would I, or anyone else. But the library is a beautiful building, of marble columns and gilded ceilings, so Irae left it standing."

Benedictus grumbled. "Maybe if Irae spent more time reading books, and less time polishing swords, his empire would prosper. The library might contain books about nightshades. We might find the answers we need there." He placed a hand on Gloriae's shoulder. "Daughter, you know Confutatis better than we do. You know its alleys and secret halls. You will travel there, in disguise, and seek books about nightshades. We must learn how the elders sealed them."

"Great!" Kyrie said, rising to his feet. He seemed thrilled to get rid of Gloriae. "Gloriae will go read some books, and meanwhile, the rest of us will fight the nightshades. Right? Right, Benedictus?"

Benedictus shook his head. "Sorry, kid, but no. You're going with Gloriae--to protect her on her way."

Both Kyrie and Gloriae began to protest, voices raised and hands waving.

"I don't need some callow boy to protect me!" Gloriae said.

"I don't want to go to some dusty library, especially not with *her*!" Kyrie said.

Benedictus scowled. "I haven't asked what you want, or what you need. I tell you what to do. You obey. This isn't a request, this is a command." Then his voice softened. "Gloriae, you are strong and brave. But you sleep at night, don't you? You'll need a companion to guard while you sleep, at least."

"I am not a bodyguard," Kyrie said.

"No," Benedictus agreed. "You are a strong fighter. I've seen you fight, and I can tell you: You fight as well as the greatest warriors I've commanded. I need a good fighter like you for this quest."

Kyrie beamed with pride. His cheeks turned red, his chest puffed out, and he seemed to grow an inch taller. "Very well. When you put it that way, I suppose it makes sense. We'll go to Confutatis. We'll find books for you. But if I see Dies Irae, I'm going to kill him."

Benedictus nodded. "If you see him, you have my blessing to do so."

Agnus Dei had sat silently throughout the meeting, chewing a piece of dried meat. Now she stood up, shook her black curls, and snorted. "So Kyrie and Gloriae go on a quest. What about the rest of us? What, we just wait here and hope the nightshades don't kill us?" She shuddered. "I don't want to meet those nightshades again. Not after what they did to me."

Benedictus shook his head. "You have a task too, Agnus Dei. You will join me. We go to Requiem."

The others gasped.

"Requiem?" Agnus Dei whispered. "Dies Irae will know to seek us there among the ruins. He knows we want to rebuild our courts. The place will be swarming with his men, and probably with nightshades too."

"Maybe," Benedictus said. "But we must seek knowledge there too. Not only Osanna has books. The Vir Requis elders were wise. They wrote much of their wisdom onto scrolls. They did not keep the scrolls in libraries, but in underground tunnels. Those tunnels might have survived the fall of Requiem. They might still contain scrolls. We will seek knowledge of nightshades there."

Agnus Dei shuddered again. "Tunnels beneath ruins, in a land swarming with nightshades. Lovely."

For the first time, Lacrimosa spoke. The dainty woman, Queen of Requiem, stood up. She wrapped her cloak around her, shivered in the wind, and said, "And I will fly to seek the griffins."

They all gaped at her. Kyrie rubbed his eyes.

"It's official now," the boy said. "Lacrimosa has gone mad."

"My love," Benedictus said to her. He walked to his wife and held her hands. "Are you sure? The griffins still hate us. They no longer serve Dies Irae, but they remember centuries of servitude to Requiem's kings. They were slaves to my father, as they were slaves to Dies Irae. They hold no love for Requiem, even now."

Lacrimosa nodded. The wind played with her pale hair. "I know. But we need them, Benedictus. Not to be our slaves. To be our allies." Wind blew, and she shivered again. "If we're to rebuild Requiem, to raise her from the ruins, we'll need allies. We cannot face Dies Irae alone, just the five of us. Even if we seal his nightshades, he'll still have men, horses, armies. The salvanae are our allies, but they live far in the west, and might not readily fight with us again. The griffins hate us? Maybe. But they will hate Dies Irae more. I will speak to Volucris, the prince of griffins. He served as Irae's mount. He will hate the man. I will have him join our war."

Benedictus embraced her and kissed her forehead. "The griffins live many leagues beyond the sea. They dwell on islands no Vir Requis has visited in centuries, maybe millennia."

Lacrimosa nodded, staring into the east. Geese flying south for winter reflected in her eyes. "I know. I will find them."

Benedictus pulled Agnus Dei into the embrace. After a moment's hesitation, Kyrie and Gloriae joined too. The five Vir Requis, the last of their race, held one another, huddling together in the cold. The grass and trees moved in the cold autumn winds.

"The moon is full tonight," Benedictus said. "In two more moons, we meet in Fidelium Mountains. We meet in the cave where Agnus Dei and Lacrimosa hid throughout the summer."

They nodded, embraced again, and whispered teary goodbyes. Benedictus hugged and kissed Lacrimosa.

"Come back to me," he whispered.

She nodded and caressed his rough, stubbly cheeks. "Now and always."

Kyrie and Agnus Dei embraced too, and when they thought nobody was looking, they shared a kiss. Benedictus pretended not to see. He wanted to grumble and throttle the boy, but he only grunted and looked away. Agnus Dei had found a good man, he knew. Kyrie was a man now, seventeen this autumn. As much as Kyrie irked him, Benedictus knew his heart was true.

"It's time," he said softly after the goodbyes were said. "We go. Keep to human forms. Shift into dragons only when nobody can see, and only when you must. The skies are watched. The ground is safer. Remember that."

They nodded. Everyone but Gloriae had moist eyes; hers were cold, almost dead.

Kyrie and Gloriae began moving downhill, armed with dagger and sword. Lacrimosa, holding the crossbow, headed east.

Benedictus held Agnus Dei's hand. "We go north, daughter. We go to the ruins of Requiem."

They began walking. The winds moaned, ice cold. Winter was coming.

KYRIE ELEISON

"First thing we'll need is a good horse," Gloriae said.

Kyrie rolled his eyes. They were only minutes away from the hill they'd camped on, and already she was complaining.

"Walking not good enough for you, princess?" he asked.

Gloriae glared at him. Her eyes flashed with green fire, and blood rushed into her cheeks. "Watch your tongue, boy. You are not my family. I owe you no fealty, and if you speak out of line, I will bash respect into you."

Kyrie snorted. "Spare me. You might have been high and mighty in Osanna. But if I recall correctly, Dies Irae banished your backside. Out here on the run, you're no more important than me."

She gritted her teeth. "I am the daughter of King Benedictus, Lord of Requiem, am I not? You are Vir Requis. I am your princess. You will show me respect, and you will obey me."

Kyrie couldn't help it. He burst out laughing, which seemed to only further infuriate Gloriae. Her cheeks were deep pink now.

"My princess? Oh, pardon me, Your Majesty," Kyrie said. He sketched an elaborate bow. "How shall I serve the princess? Shall I fetch thee thy slippers? Perhaps some tea and pastries?"

She tried to slap his cheek. Kyrie caught her wrist, blocking the blow. They stared at each other. Gloriae was thinner than him, but almost as tall, and her eyes blazed. Golden flecks filled her green eyes, he noticed, like sparks from fire.

"Release my wrist," she said.

Kyrie shook his head. "Depends. Will you slap me again?"

"Maybe."

"Then I'm not letting go."

She kicked his shin. Kyrie yelped and released her arm, and she punched his chest. He couldn't breathe. She kicked him again, and he fell to the ground.

He grabbed her leg and pulled.

Gloriae fell, and before she could recover, Kyrie was atop her. He pinned her arms down and snarled.

"Do I have to tie you up again, princess?"

She tried to bite him. He pulled his head back, narrowly missing her teeth. She spat at him instead, hitting his eye.

He grunted, rolled off her, and rose to his feet. She stood up too, eyes now icy, fists raised.

"Had enough, boy?" she asked. A crooked smile found her lips.

Kyrie wiped her spit off his face. "I think I'm going to be sick."

Gloriae shook her mane of golden hair. "Look, kid. I don't like walking. I don't like blisters. I like riding. If I can't ride a griffin, and if Benedictus said we can't shift into dragons, I want a horse." She pointed to a town a league away. "They'll have horses."

Kyrie looked at the town. He couldn't see much from here, only stone walls and chimney smoke. "And I suppose you'll walk in and demand they give you one, because you are Gloriae the Gilded, Maiden of Confutatis?"

She shook her head and sighed. "Those days are behind me. But I have gold in my pouch. Not much, but enough to buy a horse and some food. We'll buy disguises too. Come, Kyrie. We go to town."

Kyrie grunted. He doffed his cloak and handed it to her. "Wear this. You don't want people seeing that gilded, jewelled armor of yours. You'll stick out like a golden thumb."

Gloriae took the cloak and sniffed it. "This thing stinks, and there are moth holes in it. God, don't you ever wash it?"

"Sorry, princess, but when you're on the run from griffins and nightshades, laundry isn't exactly a priority."

Wrinkling her nose and groaning, Gloriae donned the cloak. She coughed. "Now I think *I'm* going to be sick."

"Just don't throw up on my cloak."

"Not that it would make it any dirtier or smellier."

They walked downhill toward the town, pebbles crackling beneath their feet. Ant hives and mole burrows littered the earth. Crows and geese flew above. The wind kept blowing, rustling the sparse grass and mint bushes. When they were closer to town, Kyrie noticed that something was wrong.

"That smoke... it doesn't look like chimney fire."

Gloriae shook her head. "This place is burning."

They found a dirt road leading to the town walls. They followed it to the gates, which were open. The guards lay slumped by them, eyes staring blankly, chests rising and falling, mouths open and drooling.

"Nightshades were here," Kyrie whispered.

Gloriae rolled her eyes. "Sir Obvious saves the day again."

Kyrie glared. "Why don't you show some respect? People died here."

Gloriae shook her head and hitched the cloak around her. The wind moaned, scattering ash. "No, they're not dead. They probably wish they were, though."

They entered the town and walked along its streets. Many of the buildings had burned down. Some still smoldered, flames crackling within them. Bodies littered the streets. Some were burned. Some had fallen upon swords. Most were still alive, but soulless.

"They must have realized the nightshades hate light," Gloriae said, walking down a cobbled street between smoldering shops. She coughed and waved smoke away. "They knew firelight scares them. They ended up burning down the town."

Kyrie shuddered. "Lovely creatures, the nightshades. Let's get out of here."

Gloriae shook her head. "We came for horses. We'll find them."

Kyrie wanted to throttle her. "Horses? How can you think of stealing horses from this place? This is a graveyard, Gloriae. I don't like it here. Let's leave."

Her eyes flashed with rage. "If there are horses here, they'd die alone. Would you leave them to starve? Let's find a stable."

They kept walking. The devastation worsened as they walked deeper into town. When they reached town square, they found a hundred bodies on the cobblestones, twisting and drooling. The shops surrounding the square smoldered. Many had shattered windows and doors; people had looted them.

Kyrie pointed with his dagger. "That temple is still standing."

It looked like an old building, round and crumbling. Kyrie guessed it had once been an Earth God temple, now converted to Dies Irae's new religion. A bronze Sun God disk crowned its dome.

"Do you think the priests are alive inside?" Gloriae asked.

"I don't know, but I have an idea. Follow me."

They entered the temple and winced. Hundreds of people were crammed inside. Many were dead and stinking. Others were alive, but soulless. Ash and smoke clung to the walls, as if nightshades had rubbed against them.

Gloriae covered her nose. "God, it's awful."

Kyrie pointed at two priests, a man and woman, who lay slumped upon a stone altar. "White cloaks. White masks. Disguises."

Gloriae glared at him. "Stealing from dead Sun God priests? You're mad, Kyrie."

He snorted. "The Sun God can go kiss Dies Irae's wrinkled old backside. And besides, those priests aren't dead. They're just... missing their souls. Look, Gloriae. We can't just saunter into Confutatis as we are. Dies Irae knows my face. He'd recognize you too, even in that smelly old cloak. But if we enter with the robes and masks of priests, well... the city will be ours. Nobody would try and stop us."

Gloriae sighed. "Fine, but I hope the Sun God forgives us." She closed her eyes and muttered a prayer.

Kyrie groaned, rolled his eyes, and went to the priests. Soon he and Gloriae were walking down the town streets, clad in white silk. They kept the white masks in their backpacks; there was no point wearing them now, not with the whole town soulless. They walked until they found stables by a manor. Half the stables were burned and smoking.

"Think there are any horses alive in there?" Kyrie asked.

"Let's see," Gloriae said.

They stepped into the stables to another ugly scene. Many horses had burned. Others had died in the smoke, or maybe the nightshades had attacked them too. The beasts lay on the ground, buzzing with flies. Only one horse lived, a chestnut mare with a white mane.

"There there, girl," Gloriae whispered to the horse. It whinnied and bucked, but Gloriae kept patting its nose and whispering soothing words into its ears. Finally it calmed, and Gloriae kissed its forehead. "Good girl, good girl."

"If only you were so sweet with people," Kyrie muttered. As Gloriae kept patting the horse, Kyrie couldn't help but stare at her. She looked so much like Agnus Dei, the girl he loved, and it confused him. True, Agnus Dei had tanned skin and black curls, while Gloriae was all paleness and golden locks, but otherwise, the two were identical. Even their tempers and the fires in their eyes were the same.

Kyrie shook his head to clear it. *Cool it, Kyrie,* he told himself. Gloriae might be beautiful, achingly so, but she was Agnus Dei's sister. And he loved Agnus Dei more than anything. He didn't want anyone else. *So stop thinking about Gloriae like that right now,* he told himself. He didn't care if she was the most beautiful woman in the world; she was a snake, and he didn't trust her. For all Kyrie knew, Gloriae still worked for Dies Irae.

Kyrie remembered that day at Fort Sanctus. The Lady Mirum had raised him there since Dies Irae had murdered his parents. For ten years he had lived with her at the seaside fort... until Dies Irae and Gloriae arrived. Until they murdered Lady Mirum. To be fair, Kyrie told himself, Dies Irae had landed the killing blow. But Gloriae had been there. She had watched, smirking. Kyrie vowed to never forgive her for that. Benedictus and Lacrimosa might have forgiven Gloriae, but they had to; they were her parents. Kyrie, however, was unrelated. He knew that once a killer, always a killer; he would always hate Gloriae.

"All right, stop cooing to that horse, and let's go," he said. He ached to leave this town. The whole place stank of blood and fire.

Gloriae saddled the horse and mounted it. She patted the half of the saddle behind her. "Well, come on, little boy. I thought you wanted to leave. Up you go."

Kyrie raised an eyebrow. "I'm not riding that thing. I'll walk."

She snorted. "I intend to gallop today. You would not keep up walking. Into the saddle. You're not afraid, are you?"

Kyrie had never ridden a horse, and in truth, he was a little afraid. But he refused to show it. "All right, all right," he muttered. He tried to mount the saddle, slipped, fell, cursed, and tried again. Gloriae watched, silent, eyes never leaving him. Kyrie cursed and grumbled and struggled. Finally he pulled himself into the saddle and sat behind Gloriae.

"Comfortable?" she asked.

He wasn't. His legs felt stretched, and the saddle pushed him against Gloriae. His torso was pressed against her back, and her hair covered his face.

"I'm fine," he said.

"Then we ride."

Her boots were spurred, and she nudged the horse. Soon they were riding through the town. Kyrie had never felt more uncomfortable. The saddle hurt his legs. He felt ready to fall off any moment. He kept sliding around, and had to wrap his arms around Gloriae's waist to steady himself. The vertigo and wide saddle were bad enough. Worse was feeling Gloriae's body. To have her bouncing up and down against him, her hair in his nostrils, was just... wrong. It felt intoxicating and horrible.

"You okay back there, kid?" she asked, leading the horse out of town and into the countryside.

"I wish we could just fly," he muttered.

"You heard Benedictus. Too dangerous. Irae's men would see us for leagues."

He snorted. "I'd prefer they saw us. I'd prefer a fight to this slinking around. Can you please take your hair out of my face?" He spat out a lock of the stuff.

"I could wear my helmet, but it would bash your nose in. I think you would prefer my hair."

Kyrie moaned. The horse clipped down a road, wilted willows and elms at their sides; the nightshades had flown here too. "Why did I have to go with you?" he lamented.

Gloriae looked over her shoulder at him. Her cheeks were pink with wind. "Because Benedictus doesn't want two young female Vir Requis together. He wants me and Agnus Dei apart."

Kyrie glared. He hated those green eyes of hers. He hated every freckle on her nose. "Why? You two are sisters. Doesn't your dad want you two to bond or something?"

"Kyrie," she said, "you really are dense. I hope your dagger is sharper than your mind."

Kyrie bristled. He opened his mouth to speak, but Gloriae cut him off.

"There are only three Vir Requis females left," she said. "We can bear children. We can continue the race. You think Benedictus wants to place all our eggs in one basket? What if only death awaits in Confutatis? Then Agnus Dei and Lacrimosa can still bear more children. What if the underground below Requiem collapses, killing Agnus Dei? Well, then maybe you and I will survive, and can have children."

Kyrie felt hot in the face. He was keenly aware of Gloriae's body pressed against him, bouncing in the saddle, and of the smell of her hair in his nostrils. He cleared his throat. "Well, why didn't he send Agnus Dei with me, then?"

"You know why. Agnus Dei doesn't know Confutatis. She wouldn't find the library. I know the city."

Kyrie wanted to say more, but could not. To bear children with Gloriae? He hated himself for it, but couldn't help imagining Gloriae naked, lying against him, her breasts in his hands, and--

No. He pushed the thought aside. He loved Agnus Dei. And he hated Gloriae. Didn't he?

"Do you think we'll find anything in Confutatis Library about how the elders sealed the nightshades?" he asked. "Lady Mirum had a library too, at Fort Sanctus, but it was all prayer scrolls and--"

He bit his words back, realizing what he'd said.

Gloriae looked over her shoulder at him. Then she halted her horse and dismounted. She stood in a patch of grass under an elm. Hills rolled around them.

"Off the horse," she said to Kyrie. "Talk time."

"Look, Gloriae. Forget it. All right? We both know what happened, and--"

"Off. The. Horse."

He dismounted, fingers shaking slightly, and stood before her. Gloriae stared at him, eyes icy, cheeks pinched. The wind streamed her golden locks. What she did next shocked Kyrie so badly, he lost his breath.

Gloriae the Gilded, the Light of Osanna, the Killer of Vir Requis... hugged him.

"Kyrie," she whispered into his ear, "I know you're always going to hate me. Maybe someday I will hate myself too. You were an enemy to me. You and the Lady Mirum. I was raised to hate my enemies. To crush them. That is what we did at Fort Sanctus. I show no mercy; you already know that about me. That was true then, and it's true now."

"Gloriae, forget it, really," Kyrie said. He squirmed out of her embrace. "Can we not talk about this now?"

"Fine, Kyrie. Just remember that I didn't know I was Vir Requis then. I thought the Vir Requis were monsters, that they killed my mother. That's what Dies Irae told me. You may hate me and judge me harshly. I just ask that you remember that. Do I regret what I did? I don't know. I'm still confused. Just promise me I won't wake up one night with a knife in my throat."

He groaned. "I was going to make you promise the same."

"I promise. I won't kill you, Kyrie."

Her words sounded both comical and chilling. He nodded. "I won't kill you either. And... I understand. About Dies Irae. At least, I'm trying to. That doesn't mean I don't hate you. I'll always hate you, Gloriae. But I won't kill you in the night. Deal?"

She shook his hand. "Deal. Now back on the horse."

They kept riding, soon moving into a forest of old oaks. Kyrie felt hopelessly lost, but Gloriae seemed to know the way. "I would normally fly over these lands on griffinback, but I can find my way on horseback too," she explained.

In the evening, they reached a crossroads, a tavern, and a well. They heard no sounds of life, but smoke rose from the chimney. The tavern's iron sign read "Oak Cross"; it swung in the wind, creaking.

Kyrie sniffed the air. "I smell beef stew." His mouth watered and his stomach grumbled. "Think there's anyone alive in there?"

"What do you think, Kyrie?"

He sighed. "You know what I think. But I don't care. I'm hungry enough to dine among bodies."

They dismounted, led their horse to the tavern stables, and found no stableboy or horses. They tethered their horse, fed it hay, then stepped toward the tavern.

Gloriae drew her sword, Kyrie drew his dagger, and they stepped inside.

Kyrie grunted.

"I knew it," he said.

Bodies lay slumped against the tables and bar. They were not dead, merely soulless, but that didn't stop two rats from gnawing on one's face. The man had only a bit of cheek and forehead left. The rats screeched, teeth bloody, and fled. Kyrie covered his mouth, nauseous.

"Lovely," Gloriae said, looking a little green. She gestured with her sword to a doorway. "The kitchen would be back there. Let's eat."

Kyrie hesitated. "It's almost night. Do you think the nightshades will return?"

Gloriae shrugged. "They might. But I'd rather face them here, with a burning fireplace and food in my belly."

Kyrie wanted to argue, but he could smell beef stew and bread, and that overcame all other thoughts. They stepped into the kitchen to find a cook slumped on the ground. They propped him up against a wall, found a pot of simmering stew and bowls, and returned to the common room to eat. They filled mugs from a casket of ale at the bar. As they ate, Kyrie kept looking outside the windows. It was getting darker. Soon night fell.

"Let's add some logs to the fire," he said.

Gloriae nodded. Soon the fireplace blazed. They found oil and lit the tin lamps around the common room. Wind rattled the shutters, and the lamps swung on their chains, swirling shadows like demons.

"It's still not very bright in here," Kyrie said. He clutched his dagger, as if that could stop the nightshades. *As if anything could stop them*, he thought.

"No," Gloriae whispered. She was pale. The firelight danced against her face.

They returned to their table and sat silently, weapons drawn.

"At least we had one good, last meal, huh?" Kyrie said.

Gloriae regarded him with eyes that were clearly not amused.

A log in the fireplace crackled.

Lamps swung.

Outside, nightshades shrieked.

Gloriae stiffened, and her hand tightened around the hilt of her sword. Kyrie bit his lip and struggled not to shiver. It was a horrible sound, so high pitched it raised his hackles. Even the bodies on the floor and tables shivered, as if they could still hear.

"Glor--" Kyrie began.

"Shh!" she hushed him. Her face was a mask of pain and rage.

The nightshades kept shrieking, and soon Kyrie could see them out the windows. They swirled around the inn, rustling the trees, creaking the walls. *Please, Draco stars, send them away*, Kyrie prayed. *Let them leave this place.*

Had nightshades found Agnus Dei too? What about Lacrimosa? Kyrie clenched his jaw. Would they all die this night?

A window smashed open in the kitchen.

A nightshade shrieked, its shadow spilling into the common room.

Gloriae slumped onto the tabletop, her arms sprawled at her sides.

No! Kyrie thought. *The nightshades got her.*

"Gloriae," he whispered and clutched her.

She glared at him. "Down, you idiot!" she whispered. "Play dead."

Kyrie slumped across the table too, closing his eyes to slits. Just then the nightshade burst from the kitchen into the common room. It was a huge thing, twenty feet long, maybe thirty. It snaked around the room, sniffing at the bodies. When it neared the fireplace, it shrieked so loudly, the casket of ale rattled and shattered. Ale spilled across the floors.

Kyrie wanted to shift. He wanted to blow fire. He wanted to flee. But a thousand nightshades filled the forest outside. He knew that if they attacked too, he would die. He kept lying against the tabletop, not moving, peeking beneath his eyelids. Gloriae was slumped against him, her hair once more tickling his face, her hand under his.

The nightshade moved from body to body, sniffing. It cackled, a sound like the fireplace. It then moved its great, wispy head of smoke to Kyrie and Gloriae.

The head hovered over them. Kyrie had never seen one so close. He had often thought them made of smoke, but he saw that was false. They were made of black, inky material that swirled. Stars seemed to shine inside them. Their eyes were glittering stars, so bright they burned him.

Go away, he prayed. *Leave this place.*

The nightshade sniffed him and Gloriae and seemed to be considering. It had passed over the other bodies quickly, but it paused over them.

It knows we're alive, Kyrie thought. *Stars, it knows.*

The sound of hooves sounded outside.

"Back, demons!" cried a voice outside. Several other voices screamed. "Back!"

The nightshade over Kyrie and Gloriae screamed. It was so loud, Kyrie's ears thrummed. With a jerk, the nightshade left them and flowed outside the window.

Kyrie raised his head an inch. Gloriae did the same, staring at him. Her eyes were ice, as if she felt no fear.

"Is it gone?" Gloriae whispered.

Kyrie nodded. "For now. But they'll return. It smelled a ruse. Let's move upstairs, it might be safer there."

They hurried to the tavern's second floor and entered a bedroom. They found a single bed, two bodies within it.

"Under the bed," Kyrie whispered. "They might not find us there."

"Kyrie, these are nightshades. They're smart enough to look under a bed."

Kyrie glared. "If you have any other ideas, I'd like to hear them. I don't think they're that smart. If they were smart, they'd have caught us in the common room. We leave the bodies in the bed. We hide beneath them. If a nightshade enters the room, it'll see the bodies and leave."

Gloriae sighed. "Well, I don't have any better ideas, so we'll try it."

They crawled under the bed. It was dusty, dark, and cold. They crept into the middle and huddled together. The nightshades shrieked outside, and soon the screams of men died. Kyrie could hear the nightshades smash tables and plates in the common room below. He pushed himself deeper into the shadows under the bed, close to Gloriae.

As Gloriae huddled against him, Kyrie found himself cursing the endless circumstances he found himself pressed against her. First there was the horse, then the table, now this. He tried not to think about her. He tried to ignore the smell of her hair, the curve of her body, the beauty of her eyes. But damn it, how could he ignore all that when he kept finding himself huddled against her?

Cool it, Kyrie, he told himself again. *This is hardly the time or place. And it's Agnus Dei you love. Only her. Not Gloriae.*

As the nightshades screamed downstairs, Kyrie thought of Agnus Dei. He remembered the softness of her lips against his, the warmth of her hands, her mocking eyes. He missed her so much, he ached. He couldn't wait to get back to her, to get away from Gloriae.

Someday you and I will live together in a reborn Requiem, he thought, willing his thoughts to travel into her mind. *We'll be together forever, Agnus Dei. I love you.*

The door burst open, and two nightshades flowed into the bedroom. Kyrie froze, not daring to breathe. Gloriae clutched his hand so tightly, it hurt.

The nightshades screamed and swirled across the room. The curtains swung, and the lamp on the bedside table guttered. The nightshades sniffed the bodies on the beds, screeched, and then they were gone.

"It worked!" Gloriae whispered.

Kyrie nodded. "Let's stay under here for tonight. We might be safe here if they return. You sleep for a few hours, and I'll watch. I'll wake you for your watch."

He had barely finished his sentence before she was asleep, her face on her hands. Kyrie could barely see her in the darkness. Once, when the moonlight flowed through the window, it touched her cheek. Kyrie marvelled at how soft and white it looked.

Then shadows covered the moon, and the night fell into long, cold darkness.

LACRIMOSA

She walked through the country, watching leaves fall from wilted trees. They glided before her, danced around her feet, and reminded her of the birch leaves that would fall in Requiem. *My home.*

She smiled sadly as she recalled the light that had shone between Requiem's columns, and the harpists who walked in white silk, and the birches she would play among as a girl. Those columns were smashed now, and the birches burned, and so did Osanna now lie in ruin.

Everywhere she looked, Lacrimosa saw the nightshades' work. Smoldering houses. Fallen temples. Bodies lying along the roads. When she saw these empty shells, she wiped the sweat and dirt off their faces, and closed their eyes lest flies nest within them, and prayed for them. She no longer knew if the stars heard her prayers, if they still lit the world. How could such horrors exist in realms where stars still shone? Perhaps their light was not holy, but mere memories of old gods, dying flames.

Icy wind blew, ash fluttered, and Lacrimosa felt coldness spread inside her.

"All the world has fallen. Can I still find starlight under the sky? Can I still find joy here for my family?"

Two more leagues down the road of ruin, and Lacrimosa came upon the soulless body of a knight. He was middle aged, his face weathered, his beard rustling with insects. A swooping vulture was emblazoned on his shield. House Veras, she knew, and lowered her eyes. Her heart felt colder, the world darker. She had seen this coat of arms before. Griffin riders bearing these banners had descended upon her home once; it seemed a lifetime ago. The blood of her parents and siblings had splashed these vulture shields.

"Are you the man who killed my family?" she asked the body.

For once, no tears found her eyes. The pain seemed too great for tears; it froze them dry. Had her stars truly abandoned her? Or worse, did they mock her by showing her this knight, this murderer?

A glint caught her eye, and she stared down. The knight bore a jewelled sword. Sapphires shone upon its hilt, arranged as the Draco constellation. The scabbard was filigreed with silver birches. This was no sword of Osanna. Now tears did fill Lacrimosa's eyes, and streamed down her cheeks. She smiled through them. She fell to her knees and raised her eyes to the sky. She laughed and trembled.

"You have not abandoned me, my stars," she whispered. She laughed again and clasped her hands together. "I will never more lose hope in your glow."

She reached gingerly toward the sword, as if reaching for a holy relic. It hissed as she drew it, and its blade caught the light. It shone upon her face like the Draco stars, like the souls of her slain family. This had been her father's sword.

"I will never more lose faith, Father," she whispered. She took the scabbard and hung it from her belt. "I will never more fear, not with your sword on my waist. I will never more walk in darkness, for I know that your light shines upon me. Thank you for this gift."

Vir Requis fought as dragons; their swords were beacons of honor, of ceremony, of beauty. Stella Lumen, her father had named this blade. The light of stars. The light of her soul.

"I will carry your honor. I still fight, Father. For your memory. For your grandchildren. For our lost home. I love you forever."

She kept walking through swirling ash and dead leaves, her hand on the hilt of her sword.

That evening, she found a farmhouse among burned fields. *The peasants burned their crops to ward off the nightshades,* she thought. The sunset red around her, Lacrimosa entered the farmhouse, and found a family there. The nightshades had robbed them of their spirits. The parents huddled over three children, eyes still wincing, mouths still open as if in screams.

Silently, Lacrimosa moved the bodies away from the hearth, and laid them side by side. She gave them water from her wineskin, closed their eyes, and covered them with blankets.

Night was falling. Lacrimosa scanned the room and saw a chest by the wall. She hid inside, closed the door, and waited.

She did not have to wait long.

The nightshades emerged as the sun set, howled, rattled the house, and shook the chest. Lacrimosa shivered inside, hugging her knees, prepared to leap out if she must, to shift into a dragon and breathe fire. But the nightshades did not sense her. Perhaps they saw the soulless farmers, and knew they had already claimed this house, and moved on.

She slept fitfully inside the chest, and emerged at dawn with stiff muscles.

She missed her family. It ached in her belly. Hunger ached there too, but there was no food in this house. If there had been any before the nightshades, looters had taken it. Lacrimosa moved on. Once more she walked through desolation. She wore her father's sword on her hip, and kept her hand on its pommel.

In the afternoon, she saw the place she sought. The sea, and the port of Altus Mare, lay before her.

She had never been to Altus Mare, but she knew it from stories. Poets sang of its crystal towers that gazed upon the sea; its thousand ships of wood, rope, and canvas; its wharfs where sailors, peddlers, and buskers crowded for space. In the stories, it was a place of exotic spices; shrimps cooked on seaside grills and served hot in fresh bread; dancers from distant lands, clad in motley; and a hundred bars where patrons told ten thousand stories of pirates, sea monsters, and adventure.

Today Lacrimosa saw no life here. Smoke rose from the city, and vultures circled above it.

She walked the road toward Altus Mare, and found that its walls had fallen, and no guards defended it. She walked in and saw looted shops, children cowering in a gutter, boarded windows, and everywhere--soulless bodies.

She walked through the narrow streets, hiding her sword under her cloak. There were survivors here, but they huddled indoors. Lacrimosa could see them peeking between shutters, daring not speak to her. She kept walking, found a tavern, and stepped inside. It was empty, and she ate and drank from the pantry, then resumed her walk to the sea.

When she reached the wharfs, she found that most ships were gone. The poets had spoken of a thousand ships here. Lacrimosa saw only four, and between them--row after row of empty wharfs.

"They fled this city," came a voice behind her.

Lacrimosa spun around, drawing her sword.

She found herself facing a man with rough stubble, a shock of brown hair, and dark eyes. He appeared to be her age-- somewhere between thirty to forty--and his weathered face spoke of years at sea.

He nodded at her sword. "A fine weapon," he said, "but it won't help you here. Not against the creatures who sent these ships fleeing."

Lacrimosa nodded, fingers trembling, and sheathed her sword. "Forgive me," she said. "I startle easily these days."

The man squinted and gazed over the empty wharfs. The soulless bodies of several sailors lay there. Vultures were eating them alive.

"This place is a graveyard, my lady," the man said. "Flee into the countryside. Hide in the hills. Or better yet, fall upon that pretty sword of yours. The death it will give you is kinder than the vultures." He gestured his chin at the birds, then lifted a rock at tossed it at them. They scattered, hissed, then returned to feast.

Lacrimosa gave the man a closer look. He was dressed as a sailor, she saw, in canvas pants and a leather tunic. A short, broad sword hung from his belt.

"Why do you not flee then?" she asked. "Why don't you fall upon your sword?"

He drew that sword, and pointed the blade to one of the remaining ships. She was a small cog, smaller than Lacrimosa's dragon form, with a single mast. She sported the wooden figurehead of a griffin, its paint faded.

"My ship," the man said. "I sail east today, seeking lands where no nightshades fly. Her name is Leo, after the star." He bowed his head to her. "And my name is Marcus."

She examined the ship. She creaked as the wind rocked her. Lacrimosa turned back to Marcus and raised her eyebrows.

"Marcus," she said, "the stars shine upon us. I have five copper coins, and one of good silver. Would you accept this payment? I would sail with you."

"When ruin covers the world, what could coins buy?" Marcus said. "Smile for me instead; smiles are worth more these days."

An hour later, they sailed the sea.

A ship bearing a griffin figurehead, to sail to the land of the griffins. A ship named Leo, to sail to Leonis. Surely she was star blessed, Lacrimosa knew, standing on the ship's bow, gazing into the horizon. The wind whipped her hair and caught Leo's sails.

She did not know much about sailing, but she learned, and she followed Marcus's orders, and the ship cut through the waters. They sailed east. East to Leonis. East to hope. East where the sun rose, and griffins dwelled, and perhaps Lacrimosa could find aid.

Marcus joined her at the prow, and placed a calloused hand on her shoulder, and gazed into the sea.

"You think the griffins can truly fight nightshades?" he asked, squinting.

Lacrimosa saw old pain in his eyes. For so many years, she had lived the pain of Requiem's loss. Did Marcus feel the same now, his own home destroyed?

"Do you have a family?" she asked him softly.

He scratched his cheek. "A wife," he said, voice low. "Once."

He turned away, entered the ship's belly, and soon returned with a bottle of wine. He opened it, drank, and passed the bottle to Lacrimosa. She drank too. It was strong and thick, and only several sips made her head fuzzy.

"I'll teach you a song," he said, and began to sing a song about randy sailors, and buxom maidens, and unholy deeds that made Lacrimosa laugh and feel her cheeks burn.

"You should not sing such songs to a lady!" she said, but could not stop laughing. The song got ruder and ruder as they drank, and soon Lacrimosa sang along, voice loud, singing words she'd normally blush to utter.

She had not laughed in so long.

When the bottle was empty, and Marcus had taught her several more songs, she finally fell silent. She gazed into the sea, wrapped her cloak around her, and whispered.

"The sun is setting."

Marcus's eyes darkened. "Would nightshades fly this far out to sea?"

Lacrimosa clutched the hilt of her sword, remembering Marcus's advice. *Fall upon it.* She shivered. "I don't know."

Soon they sailed in darkness. It was a quiet night. Lacrimosa heard nothing but the water, gently lapping against Leo, and the creaking of wood and rope. The breeze was soft, and the stars shone above. She saw the Draco constellation in the north, and smiled sadly. Requiem lay beneath those stars.

Marcus stood beside her, hand on his sword's hilt. For a long time he was silent. Finally he spoke, voice soft.

"My wife's name was Aula." He stared into the night. "I buried her at sea with my unborn child. I loved her. I don't know why I tell you this. I want to tell someone before...."

He froze.

He spun around.

Lacrimosa followed his gaze and felt her insides wilt.

Two stars moved toward them from the night. Eyes. Nightshade eyes.

The creature screeched, and the ship rocked, and Lacrimosa bit down on a scream.

"Did it see us?" she whispered.

Ten more pairs of eyes opened in the dark. Screeches jostled the boat, and this time Lacrimosa did scream. Marcus drew his sword, grabbed her arm, and pulled her.

"Into the hull!" he whispered, pulling her downstairs. "We hide."

They raced into the shadows, and leaped behind caskets and a roll of canvas. A lamp hung from the ceiling, swaying madly.

Lacrimosa's heart pounded and cold sweat drenched her. The shrieks grew louder, and the ship rocked, nearly capsizing. Barrels, rope, and jugs rolled across the floor.

Marcus gripped his sword. "I won't let them take us alive." His eyes were dark, his jaw tight.

The ship jolted.

Splinters flew.

Lacrimosa screamed, and the ship swayed, and something slammed into it again. More splinters flew. The lamp fell and shattered, and the floor began to burn. A third time, something crashed into the ship, and wood shattered. The head of a nightshade burst into the hull, screaming, eyes blazing. Water followed it, crashing into the ship. A second nightshade slammed into the hull, and the world became fire, water, and smoke.

The nightshades began tugging her soul, and Lacrimosa howled and fought them. Through the fire and darkness, she saw Marcus draw his sword. He was burning.

"You will not take us alive!" he shouted.

He thrust his sword into his chest.

Lacrimosa screamed.

Tears filled her eyes.

With a howl, she shifted.

Her body ballooned, until she was forty feet long, and the ship shattered around her. Tears in her eyes, anguish in her chest, she dived into darkness. She swam into the black water, seeing nothing, trembling, Marcus's cry echoing in her mind. Her tail flapped behind her, driving her deeper and deeper.

The nightshades screamed behind her.

Lacrimosa swam until her lungs ached, and she hit the seabed. She would need to breathe soon. When she looked above, she saw nightshade eyes scanning the darkness, a dozen pairs.

Do I die here, at the bottom of the sea? Do I die alongside Marcus?

Her lungs screamed. She trembled. The nightshades swarmed above, and in the light of their eyes, Lacrimosa saw Marcus's sword. It sank slowly, hit the sand beside her, and was still.

Daniel Arenson

AGNUS DEI

"Father, please, will you *stop* doing that?" Agnus Dei said. She snorted, blowing back a curl of her hair.

Father growled. "Doing what?"

"Humming. You've been humming for days."

He scowled at her, the legendary scowl of King Benedictus. "I do not sing. I do not dance. And I definitely do not *hum*."

Agnus Dei shook her fist. "Stars, are you stubborn!"

They walked in silence for long moments. Their boots rustled weeds that grew from the road. A stream gurgled at their side, and oaks swayed around them, their leaves red and yellow. Blue mountains soared to the east.

"There!" she suddenly said, wheeling toward Father. "What was that?"

Benedictus raised his eyebrows. "What?"

"That sound! That sound that left your throat. That hum."

He snorted. "That was no hum. That was just me clearing my throat."

"You clear your throat to the tune of Old Requiem Woods?"

He sighed and shook his head. "Agnus Dei, do you have something against Old Requiem Woods?"

She jumped up and down in rage and kicked a rock. "Oh, it is a lovely tune... if you're eighty years old. And you have a lovely humming voice... that is, if you're a toad. But since I'm nineteen, and not a toad, I would dearly appreciate it if you *stopped* humming. Okay? You've been humming Old Requiem Woods for three days. Three days. I've had enough of Old... Requiem... Woods. For a lifetime."

His eyes twinkled, and King Benedictus, the Black Fang himself, began to sing. "Old Requiem Woods, where do thy harpists play, in Old Requiem Woods, where do thy dragons--"

Agnus Dei gave the longest, loudest groan of her life. "Father!"

He laughed, a sound like stones rolling. "Okay, Agnus Dei, but tell me one thing. How did your Mother ever handle you?"

She stared at him. "Maybe you'd know, if you were with us."

He sighed. "Daughter, we've been over this. You know it was dangerous. You know we had to stay separate. I wanted to see you more often, but--"

"But yes, we couldn't keep all our eggs in one basket, griffins were hunting us, this and that. I've heard it all before. Let's just walk in silence, okay? I don't want to talk. I don't want singing or humming. I just want some silence."

Father winced. *Good*, Agnus Dei thought. She wanted to hurt him. The man might be the King of Requiem, a warrior and leader of legend, but he was intolerable. Agnus Dei couldn't understand how Mother could love him so much, or how Kyrie could worship him. He scowled all the time. He hummed. He snored. When she did try to talk to him, he was about as interesting as a log. He looked a bit like a log too, if you asked Agnus Dei.

She sighed. Though she'd never admit it aloud, she missed Kyrie. He was a pup, of course, but a cute pup. She missed seeing the anger in his eyes when she taunted him. She missed kissing him, and.... Blood rushed into her cheeks. Yes, she even missed those things they did in darkness, when nobody was there to see. Lovemaking. Loud, fiery, sweaty and--

Agnus Dei shoved the thought aside. This was no time for such thoughts. They would soon be in the ruins of Requiem and delve underground. Agnus Dei shuddered.

"Father," she said, "what do you know of the tunnels under Requiem? Where the scrolls are?"

Benedictus seemed to be looking inward, and a soft smile touched his lips. "They are where Requiem began. Before we learned how to build homes of stone, we lived in those tunnels. We painted murals on their walls, and carved doorways and smooth floors. After we moved overground, they remained holy to us, dry and dark. I loved them as a child. I would explore them with lamps and candles, and read all day."

"What did you like to read?" she asked. It was hard to imagine Father as a child. The man was so gruff, all stubble and muscle and leathery skin, his hair like iron. What would he have looked like as a child?

"I read everything I could find, from prayer books to stories of trolls and maidens and heroes."

Agnus Dei sighed. Maybe Father wasn't so bad after all. She slipped her hand into his. "What happened to the tunnels after... after Dies Irae?"

Benedictus looked to the sky and rubbed his chest, where Dies Irae's spear had cut him in Lanburg Fields. "We fled there at first. We sought safety from griffins underground. But Dies Irae sent poison into the tunnels."

"Ilbane?" Agnus Dei asked. Dies Irae had attacked her with ilbane once; the stuff burned like fire.

"Worse," Benedictus said.

"Worse than ilbane?" She shuddered.

"Evil smoke, sickly green. I don't know where he found the magic. Thousands of Vir Requis fell ill in the tunnels, and... changed. Scales grew on them."

"You mean they shifted into dragons?"

He shook his head, eyes dark. "No, they stayed in human form. And these were no dragon scales, but clammy scales, gray and white, like those of a fish. People's eyes bulged from their heads, bloated and yellow, and their fingers became webbed."

Agnus Dei shivered and felt ill. "What happened then? Did they die?"

Benedictus lowered his head. His voice was low. "No. They lived. But they hated daylight, hated life. We burned them. We killed them for mercy. Some escaped deep into the tunnels, and we couldn't find them. But before we fled into the skies, and to Lanburg Fields, we made fires and--"

"Stop," Agnus Dei whispered. She felt the blood leave her face, and cold sweat trickled down her back. Her fingers trembled.

Benedictus nodded. "Those were dark days."

They walked in silence for several hours, first down cobbled roads, and then down dirt roads, and finally through open country. At first trees rustled around them, but as they walked, the trees dwindled and vanished. Burned logs and ash littered the ground. Soon they saw toppled columns, strewn bricks, broken statues, and scattered bones.

They had arrived in Requiem.

They walked silently through the ruins, daggers drawn. Vultures flew under the overcast sky, and bugs scurried around their boots. Nothing else lived here. A cold wind ruffled their cloaks. As they kept walking, more bones littered the earth, thousands of Requiem's skeletons. *Once this place rustled with birch trees, and marble halls rose here, filled with laughter and harp songs,* Agnus Dei thought. *Once we sang here in temples and played in forests. And once we died here; all of us but five.*

She wanted to talk to Father. She wanted to ask about the old life here. Her memories were vague; she had been only three when Dies Irae destroyed this place. But she dared not speak.

This place was holy, the graveyard of their kind. Any words would defile it, she thought. She looked around at the skeletons and wondered if any were her cousins, uncles and aunts, childhood friends. The skeleton of a mother huddled the skeleton of her baby. The spines were broken.

Tears filled Agnus Dei's eyes. She hugged herself, and Father placed an arm around her. Finally she dared speak.

"I want to be angry," she whispered, tears in her eyes. "I want to hate Dies Irae. And I do, but... I don't feel hatred or anger now. I feel sadness."

Benedictus held her as they walked, but said nothing. She continued speaking.

"I'm sad to see the bones, and the broken columns, and the ash. All the ruin. But mostly, I'm sad to see the living Vir Requis. I can see them in my mind. The columns still stand, and the trees still rustle. I can hear the songs and harps, the prayers to the Draco stars. It is those visions that make me sad, the lost life more than this death. Does that make sense, Father?"

He nodded and kissed her head.

She looked up to the western horizon. The sun was low, a blob of red like blood. "Night is almost here," she whispered.

They found three columns that had fallen over one another, forming a huddle between them. They sat there in the shadows, hugged their knees, and waited for darkness.

When the sun vanished, the nightshades emerged.

Agnus Dei shivered and hugged her father. He held her and whispered, "Do not move, do not speak. We will be safe. Same as last night. I'll watch first."

She nodded silently, shivering. She could not sleep. The nightshades screamed above, and several times, she saw them dip to swirl among the ruins, then fly into the sky again. Agnus Dei hated those creatures. Hated them with such fire, she wanted to fly at them and torch them all.

"Do you think we'll find answers in the tunnels?" she whispered to Father. "Instructions for how to reseal them?"

He stared grimly out of their huddle, where nightshades swarmed and screeched. "I don't know."

Finally Agnus Dei found fitful sleep, her head against Father's shoulder. Whenever a nightshade shrieked, she started and woke, then slept again. Benedictus watched all night; he let her sleep as best she could.

Finally dawn rose--cold, gray, scented of fire and death.

They continued to walk, cloaks wrapped tight around them. The wind blew, scattering ash. Agnus Dei wondered if the dead Vir Requis had become this ash that stained her clothes, covered her face, and filled her hair. They passed communal graves, some which hadn't been covered. Hundreds of skeletons filled them. Bugs scuttled between the bones. Once they stepped over marble tiles, smashed and crooked, half-buried in dirt. This had once been the floor of a temple or palace. One wall still stood, three skeletons propped against it, staring with empty sockets.

"Why were they not buried?" Agnus Dei whispered, fiery tears in her eyes. "They were just... left here."

Benedictus nodded. "We fled. Griffins and men chased us. We fled into the fields, but died there too. We buried most, whoever we could. We burned others. For every skeleton you see above the earth, we buried a hundred, maybe a thousand."

Agnus Dei covered her mouth. She felt sick. "But there are thousands of skeletons here. That means... Dies Irae must have killed...." She tried to do the math, and felt the blood leave her face.

Benedictus nodded, his own face pale. "A million Vir Requis once lived here, maybe more. Dies Irae murdered all but five. You, me, your sister, your mother. And Kyrie."

Agnus Dei shivered. She had been to Requiem once before, stopping here in dragon form. It was the place she had fought

Gloriae. But this was the first time she explored it on foot, seeing all this death, this loss.

"Did we fight well?" she asked. "How many of Osanna's men did we kill?"

"We fought well. We killed many. We toppled their walls, and crashed their forts, and tore into their armies with fangs and claws and fire. We killed countless of Osanna's sons. But they outnumbered us. Twenty to one, or more. They had griffins and ilbane. We could not win."

"But we will win," Agnus Dei said. "The war is not over yet. Not while I draw breath." She clutched Father's hand. "We're going to find scrolls here, and they'll tell us how to seal the nightshades. And Mother will align us with the griffins. And then Dies Irae will fall. Then we'll rebuild this place, and bury the dead, and Requiem will shine again." Tears ran down her cheeks.

Benedictus pointed to a pile of scattered bricks, a fallen gateway, and cracked tiles. "There, Agnus Dei. It's an entrance to the tunnels."

They approached, and pushed aside a burned bole, and saw stairs leading underground. Agnus Dei shivered. Icy wind blew from below, and she could see only ten or fifteen steps down, before the stairs disappeared into darkness.

"What do you think is down there now?" she asked and tightened her grip on her dagger.

"Hopefully some information."

Agnus Dei shivered to remember the stories of the poisoned Vir Requis, the fish scales that grew across them, and their eyes that bulged. "Do you think... do you think the Poisoned are still down there?"

"I don't think so, Agnus Dei."

She took a deep breath. *I don't think so.* Not *no*. Not *of course not, don't be foolish, Agnus Dei.* Only... *I don't think so.* It wasn't comforting.

"Let's go," she said. "We'll grab scrolls about nightshades and get out of here. I don't like this place."

She grabbed a broken lance from the ground, tore a strip off her cloak, and fashioned a torch. Benedictus did the same, then lit the torches with his tinderbox.

Daggers and torches held before them, they stepped down into darkness.

LACRIMOSA

She hid underwater in dragon form, lungs ready to burst. Nightshades swarmed above, dipping their heads into the sea, screeching, then emerging into the air again. Lacrimosa felt ready to faint. Stars glided before her eyes.

She flapped her tail, forcing herself through the water. When she thought no nightshades saw, she peeked her nostrils over the water, took a breath, and dived again. She kept swimming.

It's almost day, she thought. *Please, stars, make it be almost day.*

But it was not. The night was still long, a night of nightshades over water, of aching lungs, of stolen breaths. Several times the nightshades saw her. They swooped at her, screaming, sending her deep underwater. There she would swim, rise to the surface as far away as she could, and breathe again.

It was perhaps the longest night of Lacrimosa's life.

When finally dawn rose, the nightshades fled. Lacrimosa rose to the surface, lay floating on her dragon back, and wept. She wept so many tears, she could fill another sea.

She was thirsty, hungry, and bone tired. But she saw no islands, no place to rest. She took flight, wings aching. She flew over the sea, travelling east. How far was Leonis, the realm of griffins? It was a place of legend. Perhaps Leonis did not exist at all.

At noon, Lacrimosa could fly no longer. She floated on her back. She dived into the water several times, caught fish, and ate them. She was still thirsty, but there was nothing to drink but seawater. Then she flew again.

When evening began to fall, she saw an island in the distance. She hoped it was an island of Leonis, but it was only a desolate rock. Fatigued, she climbed onto the island and collapsed.

As she waited for nightfall, it began to rain. Lacrimosa drank from the rain puddles. She shivered in the cold and watched the thunder and lightning. No nightshades emerged this night. Perhaps Lacrimosa was too far now from Osanna. Was there any end to this sea, or was it only water and rocks? Thunder rolled and the rain intensified. Lacrimosa huddled against a boulder, wrapped her wings around her, and shivered until dawn.

She flew again over the sea. She flew into the east.

"I will find the griffins," she whispered into the wind. "I will find Volucris, their king. I will bring them back as allies. We will rebuild our home, Ben. We will rebuild our life and love among the birches."

Her wings stirred clouds. She could see nothing but sea on all horizons.

GLORIAE

Gloriae rode into the city of Confutatis, her sword drawn, her eyes narrowed.

The place lay in ruin.

"Stars," Kyrie muttered. He sat behind her in the saddle, arms wrapped around her waist. "This place is a graveyard."

Gloriae nodded, riding the horse at a light clip. The city gates were smashed open. Guards lay strewn around them, dead or empty shells. Their swords were drawn in their hands, but clean of blood. Past the gates, bodies littered the streets. Vultures, crows, and rats were feasting upon them, tearing off skin, fingers, faces. Blood and sewage flowed across the street. Stray dogs slunk in shadows, growling.

"I hope the library still stands," Gloriae said. Many buildings had fallen. Others burned. Wind shrieked through the streets, billowing smoke.

Kyrie pointed his dagger to a statue of Dies Irae, twenty feet tall and gilded, that stood in a square. "If that statue still stands, the library better too."

Gloriae gestured with her chin toward a distant wall. Soldiers moved there, crossbows in hands.

"Not all here are dead," she said. "Masks on."

She placed her priestess mask on. It was a blank mask, expressionless, formed of white wood. Kyrie did the same. With the white robes they already wore, she hoped nobody would recognize or trouble them.

A child came running toward them. Gloriae raised her sword.

"Halt!" she said. "Do not approach us, or you'll meet my blade."

The child, his clothes tattered and his face ashy, froze.

"Gloriae!" Kyrie said. "He's only a boy. Lower your blade." He looked at the child. "Are you hungry, kid?"

The child--he looked eight or nine years old--nodded. "There is no food here," he said meekly. "The people took what they could. They left the city." He had a black eye and was missing a tooth. "The ink monsters drove them away. They'll be here soon. They'll kill you too. The Light of the Sun God does not shine on them."

Kyrie rummaged through his things, found walnuts and an apple, and tossed them to the boy. The child caught the food, turned, and ran into an alley.

"You shouldn't have done that," Gloriae said, watching the dark alley. She wondered how many more children hid there. "This city must be swarming with beggars, and beggars are like stray cats; feed one, and they'll pester you in numbers. We need our food."

"You are sweet and caring as always, Gloriae. Your reign must have been a fabulous time for the city. Dies Irae the Benevolent and Gloriae the Kindhearted, they must have called you two." He snorted.

Gloriae frowned. "The reign of Dies Irae has not ended yet, Kyrie Eleison. I may be banished from his favor, but he rules still."

Kyrie snorted again. "Rules what, a pile of rocks, bodies, and looters? Aside from a few soldiers on those walls ahead, I see nobody. And in case you forgot, I freed the griffins."

Gloriae turned to face him. She gave him a blank, cold stare. "Dies Irae rules the nightshades now, and they are greater than any soldiers or griffins. Their worlds are greater than any cities of stone."

Kyrie stared back at her, eyes flashing. Then he turned his head, spat, and grunted. "Let's find this library."

Gloriae kneed her horse, leading it up the cobbled street, past the statue of Dies Irae, and up Market Lane. She wasn't used to travelling the city this way. Usually she flew over these streets on Aquila, her griffin, or rode in a procession, surrounded by guards and banners and horses clad in splendor. Riding alone with Kyrie, robes hiding the gold and jewels of her armor, she felt like a commoner.

As they rode deeper into the city, they saw more people. Most were beggars and outlaws and other commoners, those too poor to have fled the city. Gloriae wrinkled her nose at their filth and stench. There were soldiers too, their faces gaunt and their eyes sunken. All who saw Gloriae and Kyrie bowed, reached out dirty hands, and begged for prayer and favor. Even the soldiers dropped to their knees and pleaded.

"Pray for us, Sun God priests. Bless us. Shine your light on these dark days."

Behind her mask, Gloriae gritted her teeth. Soldiers bending the knee, forgetting their post? She was half tempted to pull back her cloaks, reveal her identity, and send them to the stocks. She forced herself to keep riding, shoving through them.

Kyrie muttered impromptu blessings to them. He obviously knew nothing about the Sun God; his blessings were probably botched translations of Dragontongue prayers.

Once they had moved through the people, and were riding down Blacksmith Road, Gloriae turned in the saddle to regard him.

"Kyrie," she said, "teach me to speak Dragontongue."

He raised an eyebrow. "Gloriae, this is hardly the time to request tutoring in dead languages."

"Firstly, I am not requesting; I am telling you. Secondly, it's not a dead language. It's what you speak with the other Vir

Requis. I just realized that. You were all speaking High Speech for my benefit, but you probably speak Dragontongue amongst yourselves."

"Well, yes," Kyrie said. "But you probably used to speak it too. When you were three. Before Dies Irae kidnapped you from Requiem and took you to Osanna."

"I want to learn again."

Kyrie sighed. "Gloriae, first let's learn how to defeat these nightshades, or ink monsters as folk here seem to call them. All right? Now where's that library?"

"I'm taking us there. Be patient."

They kept riding deeper into the city. Gloriae couldn't help but frown at the devastation. Statues of Dies Irae lay toppled in every square. Most of the buildings were nothing but rubble, and blood seeped from beneath them. Several times, Gloriae saw hands, heads, and legs peeking from the rubble. They were rotting and raising a stench. Around one fallen column, she saw several survivors huddling around a fire, eating what seemed to be a dog. Gloriae covered her mouth, looked away, and rode by.

Soon they rode by the palace. A colossus of Dies Irae had stood here once, marble and gold, gazing over the city. Today the statue's head lay on the road, ten feet tall. As Gloriae rode around it, she wondered where the real Dies Irae was. Did he still sit on the Ivory Throne, encased in nightshades?

She looked up to the palace. Several of its towers had fallen. The main hall's walls were cracked, but still stood. Gloriae stared, feeling a chill.

"Dies Irae is in there," Kyrie whispered, echoing her thoughts.

Gloriae nodded. "Yes. How did you know?"

"I can feel it. Let's not go there. I don't want to get anywhere near Irae. At least, not until we figure out how to hurt his nightshades."

"Agreed. The library is behind the palace. We're almost there."

As they rode around the palace, they saw guards manning the walls and remaining tower. More guards patrolled the streets, crossbows in hand. Kyrie and Gloriae muttered prayers at them, raising their hands as if to bless them. The guards bowed their heads, whispering prayers in return. Their eyes swam with fear.

What has happened to my home? Gloriae thought. She felt close to tears. She had spent years in this palace, since she was only three. Here she had trained with blade, arrow, and fist. Here she had lived with May, her handmaiden and sweet friend. Where was May now? Did she still live in this palace, or had she fled the city? Gloriae had never had a friend but May.

"We must enter the palace," Gloriae whispered.

Kyrie groaned. "What? You're crazy, Gloriae. There's no way I'm going in there."

"So stay here. I... I must look for somebody."

"Who, Dies Irae? I thought we were going to avoid him."

"No. My... friend."

Kyrie snorted. "*You* have a friend? What, your favorite sword? A man-eating tiger? An iron maiden? Forget it, Gloriae. Benedictus sent us to the library."

"We'll go to the library. It'll only take a moment."

Kyrie moaned but said nothing more. Gloriae led her horse under a gateway, nodding to the guards.

"We've come to bless the palace with the light of the Sun God," Gloriae said to them.

They nodded and bowed their heads, and Gloriae and Kyrie rode through. They drew rein in a courtyard. Gloriae remembered that Dies Irae had once chained Lacrimosa here and tortured her. Pushing the memory aside, Gloriae dismounted, helped Kyrie off the horse, and they entered a back door into the palace.

The palace interior had fared scarcely better than its exterior. Suits of armor, tapestries, and swords had fallen. Bloodied prints covered the floor, and ash coated the walls. A servant lay soulless by a doorway, drooling, eyes staring.

"Not the best house guests, nightshades," Kyrie muttered.

Gloriae stared at the servant, a chill claiming her. Would she find May like this too, mindless and drooling?

"Come, Kyrie. Quickly."

They walked down several hallways and up three sets of stairs. Here, the third floor of the eastern wing, was Gloriae's domain, the place she had ruled for fifteen years. Almost running now, her boots clacking, Gloriae headed to the corner by the tower staircase, where May had a small room.

The door was closed. Gloriae paused outside it. She placed her hand on the knob, but dared not open it.

Kyrie caught up with her, muttering and glancing around nervously. When he saw her hand on the doorknob, his eyes softened. He sighed.

"Do you want me to look?" he said quietly.

Gloriae looked at him. His eyes, normally angry, now seemed concerned for her. Caring. Gloriae gritted her teeth. She needed nobody to care for her. She could do this. Whatever she found behind this door, she would deal with it.

She opened the door to May's room and stepped inside.

May lay nude on her bed. Her skull was broken; the wound looked like a mace's work. Her arms were bound.

"Stars," Kyrie whispered.

Gloriae stared at the scene, eyes dry. "She was raped," she said. Her voice sounded dead to her ears. She examined the wound on May's head. "A mace did this. My father's mace."

Kyrie placed a hand on her shoulder. "Gloriae, I'm sorry. Was this girl close to you?"

Gloriae spun to face him. He had removed his white mask. She saw herself reflected in his eyes.

"She was my best friend. My only friend. She... she was with me since childhood."

Kyrie tried to embrace her, but Gloriae shoved him back.

"No," she said. "Spare me your pity. I need no pity. I am Gloriae the Gilded, even now." She drew Per Ignem. "My father did this to her. When I was a child, and did poorly at a lesson of daggers, or at target practice, Dies Irae would be furious at me. He never beat me, though. He would beat May and make me watch. I watched. And I cried. And I knew that he desired May. I could see him staring at her, especially when we grew older." She looked back to the girl, and her voice softened. "But he can't hurt you anymore, May. Wherever you are now, you are safe from him."

Kyrie covered May with a blanket and looked at Gloriae, his eyes haunted. "I'm going to kill Dies Irae," he said.

Gloriae shook her head. "No, Kyrie. You will not. I will kill him."

They took May out of the palace, and built a pyre in the courtyard using firewood from the kitchens. They watched as the pyre burned, the fire drying her tears. *You're with the Sun God now,* Gloriae thought, staring into the flames. Pain like she had never felt filled her. The world entire was on fire. *I'll avenge you, May. I swear. I love you.*

She turned from the fire and lowered her head. Her fists clenched at her sides.

"Come," she said to Kyrie. "The library is near."

They walked silently around the palace, past a cobbled yard, around several toppled statues, and across a bridge. Gloriae breathed out in relief. The library still stood. It was an ancient building, three stories tall and round, topped with a bronze dome.

She and Kyrie climbed the stairs, opened the doors, and stepped into a shadowy chamber.

For a moment they froze, gaping.

"Wow," Kyrie finally said, finding his voice.

Gloriae nodded. "Indeed."

She had never been inside the library. Only monks and priests would go here, not maidens of sword and shield. Gloriae had always imagined some dusty chamber full of moldy parchments. What she saw spun her head. Rows and rows of shelves lined the walls, rising all the way to the domed ceiling. Tens of thousands, maybe millions of books covered the shelves, all bound in leather. Gloriae's head spun. Dies Irae never read, but the old kings of Osanna must have loved the written word. She had never imagined so many books could exist.

"Look at the ceiling," Kyrie said, pointing with his dagger.

Gloriae raised her head, and a gasp fled her lips. That ceiling was painted with scenes of stars, clouds, and griffins. Filigree and jewels made the figures glitter.

One part of the ceiling was chipped away. It looked like somebody had painstakingly chiseled at the artwork, as if to efface a scene. The chisel-work resembled the shape of a dragon.

"A Vir Requis was once painted there," Gloriae said. "I'd bet anything. Dies Irae must have ordered it chiseled off, but you can still see the shape."

"I'd like to chisel something of his off," Kyrie muttered. He shook his head, as if to clear it. "So, Gloriae my dear. How in the name of the Draco stars are we going to read all these books?"

She looked at him, placed her hands on her hips, and raised an eyebrow. "Never learned how to read, little boy?"

He groaned. "I can read faster than you."

She gave him a crooked smile. "You're on."

They began attacking the books, and soon realized the shelves were organized by category. One shelf was devoted to herbalism; they felt that shelf safe to ignore. Same for the shelf on astrology and theology. That left an entire wall of books on history, magical creatures, black magic, and warfare. Gloriae figured that information on nightshades might exist in one or all of these sections.

"I'll search the magical creatures shelves," she said to Kyrie. "You peruse the history section; there might be books about how the nightshades were sealed."

Kyrie nodded. They began pulling down books, opening them on the floor, and turning the pages. The books were heavy, ancient tomes, two feet long and often ten inches thick. Bound in leather, their pages sported delicate calligraphy. The scribes had treated these codexes as works of art not inferior to the ceiling. Every letter was a masterpiece, and every page featured colorful illustrations.

"Look at this book," Kyrie said. He sat cross-legged beside her, frowning into a dusty tome. "It's called *Early Kings of Osanna* by a monk named Lodinium." He scratched his chin. "Somebody's tampered with this book."

"What do you mean?" Gloriae asked. She looked up from a book called *Elder Beasts*, which was open to an illustration of a warty roc.

He pushed the book closer to her and sat beside her. "Take a look at this. See these pages at the front? They're frail, tattered, crumbling. Now look. Around the middle of the book, the pages are new. This parchment isn't ten years old, I'd wager."

Sitting on her knees, Gloriae leaned down and scrutinized the book. Kyrie was right. Some pages looked a thousand years old, the others new. "Could it be the author, this Lodinium, added older pages into his book?"

Kyrie shook his head. "No. The binding is old too. It's falling apart. And Lodinium lived over seven-hundred years ago;

his date of birth appears on the first page." He looked up at her over the pages. "Somebody changed this book. Recently."

"Why would anyone do that?" Gloriae asked.

Kyrie shrugged. "I reckon there was information they didn't want people to find. Here, look. The first pages tell of Osanna's early days, before there were kings. There were just ten tribes here then. Look how old these pages are--tattered with faded ink. Now look." Kyrie flipped the pages. "Just around the time the first king is crowned...."

"New pages," Gloriae whispered. The parchment was flawless, the ink dark and clear. The handwriting was different too. She read aloud. "In the year 606, Taras Irae built the Ivory Throne of Osanna, and founded the Irae dynasty. The old tribes united under his wise rule." She flipped more pages, tracing the ancestry of the kings. They led from Taras Irae, to Theron Irae, and to many more kings, until finally the last page featured Dies Irae. She looked back to Kyrie and shrugged. "So what? I know this story already. I had to study the Irae dynasty as a child; I myself am... *was* heir to it."

Kyrie snorted so loudly, it blew dust off the pages. "Don't you get it, Gloriae? Dies Irae, the man who claims to be your father, is the first emperor of his line. I mean, the man's a Vir Requis. Sure, he lacks the magic. He can't shift into a dragon. But he's still from Requiem. He's still Benedictus's brother. He killed Osanna's old kings and only pretends to be her son."

Gloriae understood. "He doesn't want people to know he's Vir Requis. Of course. He hates the Vir Requis. He wants people to think his family has always ruled here." She slammed the book shut. "The bastard rewrote history."

"Or threatened the scribes to rewrite it, to be more exact," Kyrie said grimly. He shoved the book aside. "*Early Kings of Osanna* is useless now. Let's keep looking."

Kyrie drew another book off a shelf, and Gloriae returned to *Elder Beasts*, which still lay open on the floor. As she flipped the pages, searching for nightshades, she noticed oddities with this codex too. There were no replaced pages, but some existing pages seemed modified. When she reached a page featuring the Vir Requis, she narrowed her eyes and leaned down, so that her nose almost touched the parchment.

Gloriae gasped. Some words had been scraped off, it seemed. The parchment was thinner and rougher here. New words, their ink deeper, overwrote the old ones.

The weredragons are hideous beasts, the book read. But it seemed like the words "weredragons" and "hideous" were new, replacing older words, which had been scraped off. For all Gloriae knew, it could have once read, *The Vir Requis are noble beasts.*

She read the next line. *They murdered the sons and daughters of Osanna, and destroyed their halls.* Only it seemed like "murdered" and "destroyed" were new words. When Gloriae leaned close and squinted, she could see scratches where the older words had been effaced.

Meanwhile, an entirely new sentence was scrawled in the bottom margin. The ink was darker, the calligraphy similar but not identical. *Dies Irae, noble king of Osanna, defeated the weredragons and banished their darkness from his kingdom of light.*

"Well," Gloriae said, pushing the book aside in disgust, "*Elder Beasts* is useless too. Dies Irae rewrote this one too."

Kyrie groaned. "Stars. Will we find nothing useful here? Was the whole library rewritten to glorify Irae?"

Gloriae sighed. "The entire city was remade to glorify him. Maybe the entire empire. What's one library? But let's keep looking. We've come all the way here. I don't want to give up yet."

The afternoon sun cast long shadows into the library. They found candles between the shelves, lit them on the floor, and rummaged for new books. In every book, they found similar alterations. Some books had pages torn out. Others had new pages sewn in. Some were like *Elder Beasts*; their original pages still existed, but somebody had carefully scraped away some words, then replaced them with others. Gloriae and Kyrie read all afternoon, but found nothing about nightshades. The entire library painted a picture of a heroic Dies Irae, the defeater of weredragons, a noble hero whose line had ruled Osanna for two thousand years.

Finally Kyrie tossed aside a book in disgust. It crashed into a corner, raising a shower of dust. "Great," he said. "Just great. You know, that Dies Irae of yours is a real griffin's backside."

Gloriae scrunched her lips and stared at the Magical Creatures shelves. She tapped her fingers against her thigh. "He is, but we can still find information here."

Kyrie clutched his head. "How? We can't trust anything these books say. Even if we do find a book about nightshades, what's the use? It would probably just tell us that Dies Irae, ten feet tall with muscles of steel, single-handedly tamed the nightshades over breakfast, using nothing but his butter knife."

Gloriae allowed herself a small smile. "Funny, Kyrie. But one can still read between the lines."

They searched the books until they found one called *Mythic Creatures of the Gray Age*. Gloriae wasn't sure what the Gray Age was, but she was certain it was not during Dies Irae's reign; his reign was nothing but white, gold, and blood red.

"Let's try this one," Gloriae said. She opened the book and began reading.

This book, like the others, had been modified. For the first time, however, Gloriae found a chapter speaking of nightshades.

"Look, Kyrie!" she said. She grabbed his arm and pulled him over. They leaned over the book. On the parchment, a drawing of three nightshades stared up at them. The artist had skillfully captured the smokiness of their bodies, and the glint in their burning eyes. Bodies were drawn beneath them, mouths open, eyes blank, limbs limp.

"Those are our boys, all right," Kyrie said.

Calligraphy appeared on the opposite page. The text wasn't far off from what Kyrie had imagined. It didn't quite speak of Dies Irae taming the nightshades with a butter knife, but it did describe a fictional ancestor of his--Lir Irae--taming the nightshades with something called "The Beams".

Gloriae frowned over the calligraphy. "See here, Kyrie. Some of these words are old--the original text. Others are new."

In some areas, the ink looked old, cracked, fading. In other places, bits of parchment had been scraped clean, and new letters appeared here. These letters weren't as cracked and faded. It was truly a masterwork; Gloriae had to turn the pages in the light, squint, and touch the parchment to distinguish the old words from the new.

"This part about these Beams is the original text," Kyrie said. "But what are they?"

"Great rays of light, it seems," Gloriae said. They turned the page to see another illustration. It showed a man holding something--what, they could not see, for drops of ink had fallen there, obscuring the drawing. Whatever the man held, a ray of light shot out from it, and seemed to slay a nightshade. The hero's original face had been scraped away, and replaced with a face that resembled that of Dies Irae's.

"Great!" Kyrie said. He rose to his feet. "So all we need to do is find these Beams, and point them at the nightshades, and kill them. Seems easy enough. So where do we find them?"

Gloriae sighed. "That's the complicated part. Look what it says here. According to this text, the Sun God created the Beams. Which is utter nonsense. The Sun God didn't even exist back in those days; the religion is only a hundred years old. According to the cover, this book is a thousand years old."

"So who did make the Beams?" Kyrie asked. "If we can find whoever made them, they can make us new ones."

Gloriae groaned. "Think, Kyrie! The book is a *thousand years old*, remember? Whoever made the Beams must be long dead."

"Fine, fine! Well, does it say how to make new Beams?"

Gloriae glared at him. She wanted to throttle him. "I'm trying to read, but it's hard with you talking so much. Do shut up. Honestly, I don't know how my sister puts up with you."

Kyrie grumbled, but otherwise remained silent and let her read. *Mythic Creatures of the Gray Age* spoke more about the nightshades and their powers, and offered gory illustrations of nightshades devouring people's severed heads, but didn't explain more about the Beams.

"The Beams are definitely the key," she muttered. "It speaks of them again here." She read aloud. "'Lir Irae rode against the nightshades, wielding the Beams of power, and he blinded the nightshades, and drove them into the Well of Night, and sealed them there.'" She scratched her cheek. "But it says nothing about who made the Beams, or how they're used."

She slammed the book shut, stood up, and went to the Black Magic section of the library. She climbed a ladder to the tallest, dustiest shelf. It lay cloaked in shadows and cobwebs. She blew the dust away, brushed the cobwebs aside, and rummaged through the shadows. Soon she found an ancient codex, bound in red leather, titled *Artifacts of Wizardry and Power*.

She returned with the book to the floor by the window. The sunlight was fading outside. Soon it would be dark and the nightshades would emerge.

"We better hurry," Kyrie said, looking out the window. He clutched his dagger.

"I know, Kyrie. One last book." Gloriae opened *Artifacts of Wizardry and Power* on the floor, blew more dust away, and began reading. The first chapter spoke of glowing "Animating Stones", which could let statues, suits of armor, and even corpses walk. The second chapter was titled "Summoning Stick"; it showed a golden candlestick decorated with emeralds, which when lit could summon others to aid. The third chapter described the Griffin Heart--"we already know about that one," Gloriae muttered--and the fourth chapter made her gasp and slap the page.

"Here," she said. "The Beams. We found what we need."

Kyrie turned from the window, face pale. "Great, Gloriae. But I think reading time is over."

Outside, the nightshades screeched. Night had fallen.

Gloriae tucked *Artifacts of Wizardry and Power* under her arm, then looked around.

"Where can we hide here?" she whispered. Her eyes narrowed as she scanned the library.

"The fireplace," Kyrie suggested and pointed. "You'd reckon nightshades would hate fireplaces. Firelight and all."

Gloriae considered. If cornered, they'd be stuck there. Then the nightshades screamed closer, and she saw them swirling outside the window, and she nodded.

They raced to the fireplace and climbed inside. The chimney led into darkness above, two feet wide.

"Into the chimney," she whispered. "Side by side. We'll be hidden there."

She and Kyrie wiggled into the chimney. Soot covered Gloriae's white robes, filled her hair, and tickled her nostrils. Kyrie coughed beside her, pressed against her, and she elbowed him.

"Shh!" she whispered. "No coughing. And keep your feet inside the chimney. They're dangling into the hearth."

He grumbled and pulled his feet up. It was a tight squeeze. Gloriae's back was flat against the chimney bricks. She was pressed against Kyrie, his nose against her cheek, his breath against her mouth.

"Gloriae," he whispered.

"Shh!" She elbowed his stomach--hard--and he grunted and fell silent. *Artifacts of Wizardry and Power* almost slipped from under her arm, and she tightened her grip on it.

For a moment there was silence. Then Gloriae heard the library doors swing open, and the nightshades swarmed in.

Their shadows danced even inside the chimney. The candles she and Kyrie had lit blew out, leaving them in darkness. The nightshades screamed, the sound echoing in the chimney, making them wince. Gloriae shut her eyes and prayed to the Sun God to save her... though she suspected the book under her arm would provide more succor.

Kyrie slipped an inch.

His foot dangled into the hearth.

The nightshades froze, then shrieked so loudly, the library shook. Gloriae heard books fall off the shelves.

She grabbed Kyrie and pulled him up. The nightshades howled and swirled.

"Climb!" she whispered to Kyrie. "Quickly."

They scurried up the chimney, wriggling into the darkness.

A nightshade's head emerged into the fireplace beneath them.

119

Gloriae froze. Were they high enough? Were they dark enough?

She peeked down. The nightshade's head was huge; it filled the fireplace. It looked left, right, and then up into the darkness. Its glittering eyes narrowed, as if it tried to peer into the shadows.

It can't see us, Gloriae thought. *It may hate light, but it needs some light to see.*

The nightshade began to sniff. Its head wasn't solid, merely wisps of darkness and stars, but it seemed to have nostrils. Gloriae scratched the chimney wall, so that ash fell down the chimney. The nightshade sniffed the ash, snorted, and shook its head wildly.

It left the fireplace.

Gloriae and Kyrie breathed out shakily. They dared not speak or move, not until the nightshades gave a final screech, swirled, and seemed to leave the library. Finally, when they were sure the library was empty, they crawled back into the fireplace and onto the floor.

Nightshades still swirled and screeched outside, but the library seemed safe for now.

"I'd wager they do a nightly patrol," Kyrie said, "scanning the buildings they haven't toppled yet. That's probably why we found no people in the library. Nobody wants to hide here, not if the nightshades come here at night."

Gloriae nodded. "I hope they only scan the place once a night. We better stay near the fireplace, just in case we have to scurry in again. And this time please do not cough in my face, Kyrie."

He bristled. "Well, don't elbow my stomach. I don't wear a breastplate like you do, and your elbows are bonier than a skeleton's backside."

Gloriae lit one candle--she would risk no more light--and sat cross-legged at the hearth. She opened *Artifacts of Wizardry and Power*, flipped to the chapter on the Beams, and sighed.

"Wonderful," she said. "We finally find the right book, and Dies Irae modified this one too."

In the candlelight, she could see that more words had been effaced, new words replacing them. She read out loud. "'Lir Irae prayed to his father, the Sun God, for light to tame the nightshades. The Sun God, of infinite wisdom and power, created the Beams and filled them with his light and fire, so that Lir Irae might tame the nightshades in his name.'" She scrunched her lips and pointed at words. "'Lir Irae' is new; there used to be another name written here. The stuff about the Sun God is also new. But some of these words, such as 'created the Beams' and 'tame the nightshades', are the original text. You can see how the parchment is thicker, and the ink more faded."

"So let's get this straight," Kyrie said. "We've spent hours in this library, and what have we learned? That thousands of years ago, somebody used something to tame the nightshades." He groaned. "Gloriae, we knew all this already."

She glared at him. "Not *something*. We learned we must seek the Beams. We know there is an artifact that can help us, or was one. We know somebody created it, and it wasn't the Sun God."

Kyrie sighed. He looked out the window at the nightshades that still swirled outside. "We'll learn nothing more here. Let's get some sleep, Gloriae. We'll head to Fidelium Mountains tomorrow, and see if the others learned anything better."

Gloriae sighed too and closed the book. "All right, Kyrie. Good night."

They huddled into the fireplace, under the chimney should they need to climb, and Kyrie took first watch. Gloriae leaned against the cold bricks, but could find no rest. She was cold, and the bricks hurt her head. Finally, silently, she shifted so that her head lay against Kyrie's shoulder, and so his arm draped over her. She did this as if in sleep, so he wouldn't object. She heard him sigh, but he let her nestle against him. His body was warm, and Gloriae felt safe against him.

Visions of sunrise over clouds filled her mind, and the flapping of wings, and Gloriae slept.

LACRIMOSA

After seven days of flying over the ocean, Lacrimosa saw islands ahead.

Tears sprung into her eyes. Her wings ached, but she forced herself to keep going. It had been days since she'd seen land--endless days of flying, floating on her back when she rested, drinking rain when it fell, eating fish when she could catch them. Lacrimosa had not felt such weariness since fleeing the griffins last summer.

So do the fates taunt us, she thought. *I drove myself to agony fleeing the griffins; now I do the same seeking them.*

The islands were still distant, mere specks on the horizon. As Lacrimosa flew closer, she saw that cliffs drove the islands up from the water, dangling with vines. Trees crowned the islands like bushy green hair. Gulls and hawks flocked among those trees, calling over the water.

She saw dozens of islands. She flew to the nearest one. Palm trees grew from it, and a waterfall cascaded down its western facade. Lacrimosa was a league from the island when griffins shrieked, took flight from the trees, and began flying toward her.

The sound made her start. For so many years, the shrieks of griffins had meant running, hiding, praying for life. For so many years, Dies Irae had ruled the griffins, driving them against the Vir Requis, destroying the world with their talons and beaks.

But I no longer need fear them, Lacrimosa thought, watching three griffins approach. *They no longer serve Dies Irae. They no longer hunt Vir Requis.*

Still her heart hammered. The griffins flying toward her were young, burly, twice her size. They shrieked and reached out their talons.

"Griffins of Leonis!" Lacrimosa called. "I come as ambassador of Requiem. I come in peace. Will you let me land on the islands of Leonis, and speak with your king?"

The griffins flew around her, cawing. Lacrimosa shivered. Golden fur covered their lion bodies. White feathers covered their eagle heads. Their beaks were large and sharp; Lacrimosa had seen such beaks kill so many dragons. Memories of the war assaulted her; Dies Irae and his men riding griffins, swooping upon Vir Requis children, cutting them down--

She forced the thought away. "Requiem will be reborn," she said to the griffins. They were circling around her, shrieking. "I am Lacrimosa, Requiem's queen. I seek Volucris, your king."

They shrieked with new vigor. They clutched her limbs, and Lacrimosa cried and thought they would bite her. But they began to fly to the island, dragging her with them.

"Let go," she said, frowning. "I can fly myself."

They cried and kept dragging her forward. Lacrimosa remembered how Volucris had once carried her to Confutatis. She felt a prisoner again.

Soon they flew over the island. The foliage was so thick, she couldn't see the ground. Mist hovered over the trees. Pillars of stone thrust out from the greenery, bedecked with vines. Griffins covered these pillars, nesting in eyries. For leagues in the eastern ocean, Lacrimosa saw other islands--hundreds of them-- griffins flying above them.

Lacrimosa wriggled in the griffins' grasp. "Where are you taking me?"

Of course, griffins could not utter the language of men or Vir Requis; they only shrieked, cawed, and squawked. They flew with her to a jagged stone pillar. It seemed a league high, towering over the island, taller than the highest steeple in Osanna. A nest crested the tower, shaking in the winds.

The griffins flew to that nest, and placed Lacrimosa upon the branches, grass, and leaves. They tilted their heads at her, cooed, and one took flight.

"Does he go to call Volucris?" Lacrimosa asked the remaining two griffins. They nodded.

She waited. The winds blew, and the nest shook, teetering on the pillar. She remained in dragon form, should she fall and need to fly. Once she tried to stand up, to peer down the pillar, but the griffins shoved her back down.

"Am I your prisoner?" she asked, baring her fangs. "I am Queen of Requiem. Do not hold me down if I wish to rise."

They shrieked and tilted their heads, and when Lacrimosa tried to rise again, they pushed her down a second time.

Lacrimosa swallowed her pride. She would let them win this battle. She would have to impress Volucris, king of these islands, not these griffins.

An hour passed, maybe two, and finally Lacrimosa saw ten griffins fly toward her. Volucris flew at their lead.

The King of Leonis landed before her. He was the largest of the griffins, fifty feet long and burly. Lacrimosa stared into his eyes, ice in her heart. She remembered Dies Irae riding this griffin. She remembered Volucris hurting her, biting her, carrying her to pain and torture. She bowed her head to him.

"Your Majesty."

Volucris walked toward her, and at first Lacrimosa feared he'd hurt her again. Once more she could feel that old pain, his talons that cut her.

Volucris bowed to her, and nuzzled his beak against her head. He cooed.

Lacrimosa touched his cheek, its soft feathers, the tear that flowed down them. "I'm sorry, Volucris," she whispered. "I'm sorry for what Dies Irae did to you, how he enslaved you with his amulet. I'm sorry for what he forced you to do."

Volucris nodded, and his tear fell into the nest.

"And I'm sorry for what the Vir Requis elders did," she whispered. "We created the amulet with the blood of griffins. We enslaved you too. We forced you to guard our skies, before Dies Irae stole the Griffin Heart."

Volucris stared at her, silent.

Lacrimosa too was crying now. "Requiem was punished for her sins, mighty Volucris. We enslaved you. We paid for that. Dies Irae made us pay. He turned you against us, turned our slaves into our destroyers. But we are reborn now. We rise from our sins and destruction with purer hearts, kinder souls, stronger spirits. Will you forgive us? Will you befriend our new nation?"

Volucris looked to the west, as if he could see over oceans to the distant realms of Osanna, where he was slave to Dies Irae, or to the lands of Requiem, where the Vir Requis kings had bound him. He looked at her and said nothing. Then, so fast that she gasped, he took flight.

His wings flapped, rattling the nest. He gestured with his head for her to follow.

She took flight too. Surrounded by griffins, they flew across the waters, over the islands, heading further east. Lacrimosa gazed in wonder below her. The islands were beautiful; waterfalls cascaded from them, trees rustled upon them, and griffins flocked in all directions.

They flew for an hour, over many islands, until Lacrimosa saw a great island ahead, three times larger than the others. A mountain grew atop it, all stone and vines. Many griffins flew there, and nested in alcoves across the mountainsides.

Volucris led the group to the mountaintop, where Lacrimosa saw a great nest, a hundred yards wide. A harem of two dozen females brooded there. Lacrimosa saw many griffin eggs. Among the eggs lay a golden candlestick decorated with emeralds.

Volucris gestured with his head to the back of the nest. Lacrimosa looked, and saw a griffin cub lying on his side. He was so small, the size of a pony. His eyes fluttered, and his breath was shallow. Sweat matted his fur.

"Your son," Lacrimosa whispered to Volucris. "He is ill."

Volucris nodded. With his beak, he nudged Lacrimosa toward the cub.

Lacrimosa stepped forward, still in dragon form. Two female griffins were tending to the child. They backed away, and Lacrimosa knelt before him.

"Hey there," she whispered. "Good morning, sweetness."

The cub blinked at her. He tried to coo, but the sound was weak. His leg was wounded, Lacrimosa saw, sliced from heel to knee. Maggots and pus filled the wound, and lines of infection ran from it. Lacrimosa winced.

She turned to Volucris. "I'm sorry," she whispered. "How can I help him?"

Volucris gestured back at the cub. He lowered his head, raised it again, and pointed at the child with his talons. *He's trying to tell me something*, Lacrimosa knew. But what?

"Do you want me to do something to him?" she asked.

Volucris nodded.

"Do you think I can heal him?"

Volucris nodded again.

Lacrimosa returned her gaze to the child. How could she heal this? She knew some herbalism, some home remedies. But even if she had herbs, alcohol, and bandages, this wound was beyond her. This wound meant death. Lacrimosa had seen many such wounds during the war. They ended with fever and a grave.

She whispered into Volucris's ear. "His leg is beyond me. We could try to amputate it, but... I don't think that would help.

The infection runs through his whole body now." A tear rolled down her cheek. "I cannot heal this."

Volucris cawed and gestured at the cub. He nudged her back to him.

Lacrimosa looked at the child again. She shook her head, and another tear fell. "I'm sorry. I cannot heal him."

Volucris nudged her again, mewling. He pushed her toward the child, almost violently. Lacrimosa wanted to object. She wanted to flee.

"Please," she said. "Don't shove me. I can't heal him."

He placed his foot on her head, and pushed it toward the child. He forced her face near the wound. It stank of rot. The maggots in the blood swirled. Lacrimosa grimaced and tried to pull away, but Volucris held her face up to the wound.

"Please, release me," she said.

The child was shifting, trying to caw. His eyes fluttered.

"Ma," he seemed to say. "Ma. Caw! Ma."

Lacrimosa closed her eyes, the stench of the wound in her nostrils. The child would die, she knew. Son of Volucris, prince of griffins, heir to these islands. An innocent child, perhaps the first griffin born in freedom. Lacrimosa thought of all those griffins born into slavery—first in Requiem, then in Osanna. How could she let this one die? She bore responsibility to them. As she wanted to rebuild Requiem, she owed Leonis a debt too.

"Ma," the cub cawed again. "*Caw*. Ma. Ma."

He was in pain. He was weeping. Suddenly it no longer mattered that he was a prince, that Lacrimosa's fathers had enslaved his people. All that mattered was that he was a child. A child in pain, a child dying. Wasn't that the entire gravity of it?

She felt tears gather once more in her eyes. One tear fell, splashed into the wound, and raised steam.

Volucris and the other griffins all cried. The cub yelped and tried to move, but was too weak. Another tear fell from

Lacrimosa, hit the wound, and more steam rose. *My tears hurt him,* she thought, but she could not curb them. They fell into the wound, hissing and steaming, as the griffins shrieked.

And then Lacrimosa noticed that when the steam cleared, the wound looked better. The pus drained from it. New blood filled the wound, and then it scabbed over.

"Ma," the griffin cub said, and his voice was relieved, some of the pain cleared from it.

Volucris released her, and Lacrimosa raised her head. She looked at the cub in amazement. The infection had left him! He looked up at her, his eyes clear.

"Dragon tears," Lacrimosa whispered. "They heal griffins."

Volucris nodded. Then he tossed back his head and cried in joy. The other griffins did the same. The young prince rose to his feet, limped, and then flapped his wings. He flew a few feet, landed, and squeaked.

Lacrimosa laughed and cried. *Requiem enslaved you,* she thought. *With our tears we find some salvation.*

The cub embraced his parents. Then Volucris moved toward Lacrimosa. He knelt before her, bowed his head, and looked into her eyes.

Lacrimosa smiled.

"Will Leonis be our ally? Will Requiem and Leonis fight together, fight against Dies Irae?"

Volucris gave her a long stare. He looked to the west. He looked at his son. Then he walked to the eggs, and retrieved from between them the candlestick. He placed it at Lacrimosa's feet.

She shifted into human form and lifted the candlestick. It seemed made of pure gold, and when she turned it in the sun, its emeralds glinted.

"It's beautiful," she said. "Is this a gift for saving your son?"

He squawked and pawed the nest. There was more he wanted to tell her. Lacrimosa examined the candlestick more closely. When she turned it over, she saw words engraved into its base. *Summoning Stick.* Lacrimosa gasped.

"I've heard of the Summoning Stick," she said. "Only two were ever made, one of silver, one of gold. When lit, they call for aid."

Volucris nodded. Lacrimosa embraced his great, downy head.

"Thank you, Volucris, King of Griffins," she said. "When I need your aid, I will light the candlestick." She drew back and gave him a solemn stare. "When we rebuild Requiem, there will be war with Irae. We will need your wings."

Volucris nodded, staring at her, and she saw the answer in his eyes.

Our wings are yours.

AGNUS DEI

At the bottom of the staircase, Agnus Dei froze. The tunnels under Requiem stretched before her, all darkness and moaning wind. She held her dagger with one hand, her makeshift torch in the other.

"How deep are the scrolls?" she whispered. She wasn't sure why she whispered. Surely the Poisoned--those Vir Requis turned scaly and webbed with Dies Irae's black magic--no longer dwelled here. But Agnus Dei found it difficult to speak any louder. *Just in case.*

"They were buried deep in the darkness," Father said, "to protect them from snow, fire, rain... or war."

Agnus Dei glanced at him. She reminded herself that Father was more than just an annoying, gruff old man who hummed and creaked and scolded her whenever she growled. He was King Benedictus, the Black Fang. He had once ruled these lands and worn fine silk and steel. He had once led this land to war and seen it destroyed. He had once fought in these tunnels and watched as others burned, and drowned, and became creatures of fish scales and bulging eyes and--

Enough, Agnus Dei told herself. *Don't dwell on it. Get the scrolls. Get out. Learn about the nightshades. Let the past remain in this darkness.*

She took a step deeper into the tunnels.

The winds from below moaned, rustling her cloak. She clenched her jaw and kept walking, Father at her side. Their torches crackled, and shadows danced like demons. The walls were black stone, hard and smooth, too close to her. Agnus Dei hated enclosed spaces. There was no room to shift into dragons here. What if creatures attacked--ghosts, or... the Poisoned? Could she fight them in human form, with only her dagger? Agnus Dei growled.

Her feet hit something. A clattering sound echoed. Agnus Dei lowered her torch and grimaced. She had kicked a skeleton, scattering its bones. Several more skeletons lay within the sphere of light, covered in dust and cobwebs and tatters of leather. The flickering torch made them seem to shiver.

"Irae's men," she said. They bore chipped, wide blades in the style of Osanna, and one wore a breastplate engraved with a griffin.

Father nodded. "Many of them died here too."

They walked over the skeletons, careful not to further disturb their bones. The tunnel plunged deeper, its slope steep. Shattered swords, arrowheads, and helmets littered the floor. At one point, the skeleton of a griffin cub blocked their way, and they had to walk between its ribs. A rusty helmet topped its skull. The air grew colder and the wind moaned. Once, Agnus Dei thought she heard a cackle from deep below, but when she froze and listened, she heard nothing more.

Around a bend, she saw a new skeleton. She paused and grunted. This skeleton was strange. It was shaped like a man, but the skull was too long, the eye sockets too small. Its fingers were twice the normal length, and its femurs were twisted like ram's horns. At first Agnus Dei thought it an animal--an ape, like those drawn in picture books--but this skeleton held a sword, and wisps of a tunic clung to its ribs.

"A Poisoned," she whispered.

Father nodded.

As they walked around the Poisoned, Agnus Dei couldn't help but stare into its eye sockets. Even in death, it seemed in agony. She could imagine it being a Vir Requis like her once, maybe a girl, poisoned until her bones twisted, and her eyes popped, and--

No. No! Don't think of it. Agnus Dei gritted her teeth and kept walking.

Soon she and Father reached a staircase. The steps were chipped and narrow. Agnus Dei's boots stepped on old arrowheads, a dagger's blade, and a skeleton's hand. Once she kicked a helmet. It clattered down the stairs, echoing. She winced, and Father grumbled, and they froze until the clacking stopped.

Past the staircase, they found a crossroads of three tunnels, and Father led them down the left one. Their torches guttered. Agnus Dei tore fresh strips off her cloak, and wrapped them around the stick she carried, so that it blazed with new light.

In the firelight, she saw many more skeletons. The main battles must have been fought here. Bones covered the floor. Shattered shields, swords, crossbows, and arrowheads lay everywhere, threatening to cut her boots. The air here was so cold and dry, skin and hair remained on the bodies, shriveled and white. Their fingernails were yellow and cracked like rotten teeth.

"How much farther are the scrolls?" she whispered.

"Not far," Father said, his voice low, his eyes watery. Agnus Dei looked at him, and all her irritation and anger at her father faded. She realized that he'd known many of these fallen Vir Requis. Some had been soldiers under his command. Others must have been his friends, cousins, uncles.

They stepped gingerly over the skeletons, and plunged deeper into the darkness. The tunnels kept sloping down; Agnus Dei could not guess how far underground they were. As horrid as the burned forests of Requiem were, with their ash and bones and fallen columns, she longed to return there now, to see the sun, and to see life, even if life meant only vultures and bugs.

Soon they reached the remains of a doorway in the tunnel. Once it had sealed the passageway beyond; today it was but splinters of wood and old hinges. They stepped through it, and found themselves in a towering chamber.

Father pointed with his torch. "There, in the alcoves."

It was hard to see in the darkness, but it seemed like hundreds of alcoves covered the walls, maybe thousands. Rolled up scrolls nested in them.

"Here lies the wisdom and knowledge of Requiem," Father whispered.

They walked deeper into the chamber. Agnus Dei tried to walk lightly, but her boots clanked and echoed despite her best efforts. The walls rose thirty feet tall. *So many scrolls!* She thought it must have taken a thousand years to write them all, and would take a thousand more to read them. She moved her torch left and right, scattering shadows.

"Which scrolls do we need?" she asked.

"In the back, near that tunnel," Father said. "You see where--"

A cry pierced the darkness.

Agnus Dei and Father froze. The only movement was the fire of their torches.

The cry sounded again, coming from the second tunnel, the tunnel that led beyond the chamber of scrolls. It sounded hurt, mournful.

"What--" Agnus Dei began, and then a shadow leaped at her from the ceiling.

She cried, thrust her dagger, and heard a scream. Blood splashed her hand. She had cut something, something of dangling eyeballs, of webbed fingers with cracked nails, of clammy pale flesh. And then it was gone, scurrying into the shadows.

"The Poisoned!" she said. She raised her torch, hand sticky with blood. The firelight reflected in a thousand eyes and fangs.

"Friends!" Father said, voice trembling slightly. "We can end your pain. Do not--"

The Poisoned lunged at them.

"Stay back!" Agnus Dei shouted. She waved her torch and dagger before her. A hundred Poisoned reached with cracked claws. Some of them stared with eyeballs that bulged, bloodshot. Others had eyes that dangled down their cheeks, but even those eyes stared with hatred. Agnus Dei slammed her torch into one; it screamed and fell back, burning. She cut another with her dagger. One cut her, slicing claws down her arm. The cuts blazed and raised green smoke.

"Back, friends!" Father called, slamming at them with his torch. Their scales flew. "We can help you."

But they could not, Agnus Dei knew. There was no cure for these Vir Requis. With a growl, she shifted into a dragon. The Poisoned shrieked, strings of saliva quivering between their teeth. A dozen raced at her, and Agnus Dei blew fire.

"No, Agnus Dei!" Father cried. "You'll burn the scrolls."

Agnus Dei was beyond caring. Blood roared in her ears. She blew flames again. A dozen Poisoned caught fire. They fled into the tunnels, blazing.

Father shifted too. Soon the burly black dragon was kicking Poisoned, biting them, clawing. Tears sparkled in his eyes as he fought. "You'll feel no more pain, friends," he said.

Suddenly, in her mind, Agnus Dei didn't see creatures of scales and claws. She saw men, women, children. Her cousins, her schoolyard friends, her uncles and aunts. How many of these Vir Requis had she known before Dies Irae malformed them? How many had Father known? She blew fire, weeping now, until the Poisoned all burned. They writhed on the floor, screaming, clawing the air. The sound was like steam from a kettle. The stench of their burning flesh filled the air, the stench of rotten fish.

"The scrolls!" Father said. Agnus Dei saw that they too burned. Across the chamber, fires filled the alcoves. The scrolls were curling, smoking, and burning away.

Still in dragon form, Agnus Dei began pulling the burning scrolls from the alcoves. She dropped them to the floor and stepped on them. But the fire was spreading. Smoke filled the chamber. A thousand Poisoned blazed; some dead, others screaming and dying. Father too was collecting scrolls, but soon there was no place to extinguish them. The entire chamber became an inferno, all flame and smoke and screams.

"Let's get out of here!" Agnus Dei cried.

"We must save the scrolls," Father shouted back. She couldn't even see him behind the fire and smoke.

Agnus Dei coughed. "We'll die in here! It's time to go!"

She scooped up what scrolls she could, shifted into human form, and raced into the tunnel they had entered from. A moment later, Father joined her, also in human form, also carrying smoldering scrolls. Smoke and ash covered him.

They raced through the tunnel, smoke and fire and screams chasing them. One Poisoned, who had somehow survived the inferno, ran behind them. He rose in flame, screamed, and reached out crumbling fingers. Agnus Dei stabbed him with her dagger, weeping, and kept running.

When they finally reached daylight and burst into the ruins of Requiem, Agnus Dei fell to her knees. The scrolls fell from her arms, rolled across cracked cobblestones, and sizzled in the rain. Agnus Dei lowered her head, sobbing. Thunder rolled, and mud flowed around her.

Father knelt beside her, breath ragged. The rain streamed down his face. He embraced her, and Agnus Dei clung to him, weeping against his shoulder. He smoothed her hair.

"Their torture is over now," he whispered to her. "They are now among our forefathers in our halls beyond the stars."

Agnus Dei trembled. "There were so many. So many remained...."

Father nodded. "They bred in the tunnels."

Agnus Dei pulled her head back from his shoulder. She stared into his eyes, still holding him. "Papa, are they all dead now?"

He nodded. "They are. I promise."

It was long moments before she could stop trembling. She could still imagine those screams, the hisses, the eyeballs. Finally the rain softened, and she saw a rainbow over the ruins. Even here, in this land of ruins, skeletons, old curses and pain... even here there was beauty. She looked at the rainbow, and calmed her breath, and pulled herself free from Father's embrace.

"I burned most of the scrolls," she said quietly. "I'm sorry."

He squeezed her shoulder. "But we recovered a few scrolls. Let's look at them."

They pulled the scrolls from the mud and cleaned them as best they could. Several yards away, they found a mosaic floor. Most of the floor lay buried in mud. Bones, ash, and dragon teeth covered the rest. They brushed an area clean, revealing part of the mosaic; it showed a scene of dragons flying in sunset. Agnus Dei and Father unrolled the scrolls there and examined them.

They were badly burned. Several crumbed in their fingers. Others were burned beyond reading. A few had survived the fire, but they contained no knowledge of nightshades; one was a prayer scroll, three others contained musical notes, and another two traced the lineage of Requiem's kings and queens.

"We might have come all this way for nothing," Agnus Dei said, head hung low. She hugged herself in the cold and stared, eyes finally dry, at a broken statue of a maiden holding an urn.

"Here, daughter. Look at this." Father brushed off one scroll and unrolled it. At the very top, in delicate ink, appeared a drawing of a nightshade.

Agnus Dei gasped. "You found it, Father! You found the right scroll."

He gave her a wan smile. She wanted to jump onto him, to hug and kiss him, but froze. Father looked so tired. His eyes were sunken, his cheeks stubbly and haggard. For the first time, Agnus Dei realized that Father was growing old. He was no longer the young man who'd led Requiem to war. Gray filled his black curls, wrinkles appeared on his brow, and the cares of the world and a fallen race filled his eyes. She gave him a small kiss on that rough, prickly cheek.

"Let's see what it says," she said.

When they unrolled the scroll further, revealing its calligraphy, Agnus Dei frowned. Burn marks covered the parchment. Some bits had burned away completely. The scroll had more holes than a suit of chain mail. She groaned.

"There's not much left," Father said with a sigh.

They huddled over it, blowing ash and dirt away, brows furrowed. Only one paragraph was legible, and even that one was missing half its text. Agnus Dei read it over and over, but it made little sense as it was.

"In the days of the Night Horrors, King T_____ite journeyed to the southern realms of G____nd sought the Loomers o_____olden pools. The Night Horrors stole the souls of Osanna, and cast them into the d___ness, and Ta_____omers, who were wise above all others in the land. He spoke with the Loomers, and prayed with them, and they crafted him th_____e returned with th_____anna, an_____m upon the Night Horrors. He tamed them, and drove them into Well of Night in the Marble City, and sealed it. He placed guards around it, armed wit_____cape."

"What do you make of it, Father?" Agnus Dei asked, raising her eyes from the scroll. After reading it several times, it still made little sense to her.

He scratched his chin. The wind blew his cloak, which bore as many burn marks as the scrolls. "I think you'll agree that Night Horrors refers to nightshades."

Agnus Dei nodded. "That must be how the ancient Vir Requis called them."

"And Marble City refers to Confutatis," Father said. "That one is easy enough. Even today we sometimes call it that."

"So we know that some king, whose name began with T, tamed the nightshades, and sealed them in Confutatis. Which king began with T?"

Father sighed deeply. He rubbed his neck, joints creaking. "Most of Osanna's kings had names that began with T. There were several kings named Tanith, and two named Talin. There was a King Talon too, I believe, and a few named Thoranor. Before Dies Irae took over, the letter T denoted royalty."

"So we have no idea which king tamed the nightshades."

"No," Father agreed.

Agnus Dei also sighed. "So this scroll isn't much help. I'm sorry, Father. I burned it. Now it's useless."

Father shook his head. "Not useless. Some information is missing, yes, but we have clues. The scroll tells us to seek the Loomers of these 'olden pools'. The Loomers crafted something for the king. What was it? Great weapons?"

Agnus Dei bit her lip. "Probably. Weapons that could defeat nightshades. The scroll says the olden pools are in a southern realm that starts with a G. What place is that?"

Benedictus said, "Well, for one thing, we know it's in the south."

Agnus Dei raised an eyebrow. "Father, did you make a joke? That's a first."

Father watched two crows that flew above. "Let us go to Fidelium Mountains. We'll meet Mother, Gloriae, and Kyrie there. Maybe they'll have found better information."

Kyrie. The word sent fire through Agnus Dei. Her mind flashed back to that day at the Divide, the border with Salvandos, where they had first made love. A day of fire, heat, and sweat. Agnus Dei bit her lip to quell the thought. It was ridiculous. Did she miss Kyrie now? She snorted. The boy was a mere pup.

She rolled up the scroll, rose to her feet, and nodded. "Let's go."

They walked through the wet ruins, between the bones, cracked statues, fallen columns, and old weapons. The rainbow stretched before them across the horizon.

KYRIE ELEISON

After riding all day behind Gloriae, Kyrie was ready to throttle her.

"Gloriae, for pity's sake, my legs feel like they were dipped into lava. Can you please stop that horse of yours?"

Gloriae didn't bother turning to face him. She kept directing the horse down the dirt road, bouncing before Kyrie in the saddle. "Not until we cross the Alarath River. If we're to reach Fidelium by the new moon, we have a schedule to keep."

Kyrie groaned. "Gloriae, seriously. My thighs and backside have blisters growing on their blisters. How can you ride so much? The horse is exhausted, and so am I." He pointed east. "I see a village. Let's go find an inn, eat, and rest."

Gloriae nodded. "You're right, Kyrie. Let's go to town."

Kyrie raised his arms in triumph, then wobbled in the saddle, and wrapped them around Gloriae again. "Great. Finally you're seeing some sense."

They rode toward the village. A small fort rose upon a hill-- merely a tower, wall, and stables. A score of cottages nestled below the hill by a temple and tavern. Fields of wheat and barley surrounded the village, fluttering with birds.

"Do you think anyone's alive in this one?" Kyrie asked. At the last few towns they'd passed, everyone was dead, soulless, or hiding.

Gloriae nodded. "I bet we can find a new, living horse." She rode past the cottages, heading toward the fort and stables.

"What? Gloriae! Stop it. Stop it! Turn this horse around right now, and take us to that tavern." He moaned. "Oh stars. I can smell beef stew from here, and bread, and beer."

Gloriae sniffed the air. "I can smell fresh horses ahead. You were right, Kyrie. This horse is exhausted. We'll find a fresh one."

Kyrie cursed to high heavens, and would have jumped off the horse, were he not terrified of breaking his neck. Gloriae was deaf to him, and Kyrie could do nothing but cling to her, arms around her waist, as she rode past the village. Once they reached the fort and stables, Gloriae finally stopped the horse and dismounted.

"Now you may get off the horse," she said.

Kyrie dismounted and moaned. His thighs were so chaffed and stiff, he could barely walk. He rubbed them.

"I'm going to that tavern," he said. He began limping downhill, leaving Gloriae behind. After a few yards, he regretted walking. Walking now hurt just as much as riding. Kyrie sighed. He wished they could have flown. Flying was the way to travel. But how could they? At daytime, anyone would see two flying dragons. And at night, well... he wasn't going anywhere in the open at night, not anymore.

He reached the tavern, stepped inside, and found more soulless people. They lay on the tables and floors, drooling. Kyrie tried not to look at them and stepped into the pantry. His eyes widened, his nostrils flared, and he sighed contentedly.

"Lovely," he said to himself, admiring the smoked hams, biscuits, jars of preserves, turnips, and best of all--caskets of ale. He licked his lips, prepared for a solid few hours of dining and drinking.

Hooves sounded outside. "Kyrie Eleison!" came Gloriae's voice from outside the tavern. "Are you in there? Come. I have a fresh horse. We ride."

Kyrie snorted. "You ride, I eat."

Her voice darkened. "Don't make me come in there to get you."

Kyrie took a bite of ham, chewed lustfully, and called out with his mouth full. "I'd like to see you try."

Not a minute later, Gloriae was dragging him by the hair out of the tavern.

"Ow!" he cried, sausages and bread rolls falling from his arms. "Let go, I'm carrying food and drink here, for stars' sake."

She glared and gave his hair a twist. He groaned. "You're lucky I'm dragging you by the hair, not your ears... or worse. On the horse. Now."

She finally released him. Muttering, Kyrie collected the fallen food. He hadn't grabbed much--the sausages, the rolls, two jars of jam, and a skin of ale. He stuffed them into the saddle's side bags.

"Gloriae, this new horse stinks," he said. "Hasn't anybody washed it?"

Gloriae mounted the horse and settled herself in the saddle. "No, Kyrie. The stable boys were gone. I reckon they fled into the countryside when the nightshades arrived. The horse is dirty, but it's rested, and has been eating leftover hay. I released our old horse into the farms; it's too weary to keep journeying."

Kyrie muttered and climbed onto the saddle behind Gloriae. His thighs protested, but he drowned the pain in curses and grumbles. Gloriae kneed the horse, and they left the village and resumed journeying north.

"So how many more horses are you going to break today?" he asked.

Gloriae shrugged. "As many as it takes. Benedictus gave us a time and place to meet him. I expect to be there."

"Benedictus can go eat a toad's warts," Kyrie said. He sighed. "I wonder if the old man found anything. Stars know we haven't found much at Confutatis. Unless you count the fact that Dies Irae is obsessed with glorifying himself, which I think everyone has sort of figured out by now."

Gloriae turned in the saddle and glared at him. "Kyrie, do you mind not whining and complaining so much? Do I have to hurt you again?"

Kyrie rubbed his neck. He sighed deeply. "You're right, Gloriae. It's just... I miss your sister. And I'm worried about her, and Lacrimosa, and yes, even Benedictus. I know I've been snapping at you a lot. I also haven't been sleeping much, what with those nightshades shrieking all night, which isn't helping."

As Gloriae bounced in the saddle, pressing against him, Kyrie knew he was speaking only half-truth. True, the nightshades kept him up a lot. But half the time, maybe *most* of the time, it was Gloriae who kept him awake. Gloriae's hair in his nostrils. Her body close to his, sometimes pressed against him. Her green eyes, cruel and mocking, and those freckles on her cheeks, and the curve of her--

Kyrie gritted his teeth. *Stop that,* he told himself. It was bad enough that thoughts of Gloriae filled his mind all night. He didn't need to think of her--not like *that*--during the daytime too. He forced himself to think of Agnus Dei again, and his heart melted like butter on hot bread.

Agnus Dei. As beautiful and tempting as Gloriae was, Kyrie knew that Agnus Dei was his true love. He thought of her brown eyes, her mane of bouncing curls, the softness and fullness of her lips. He thought of her pride, her strength, and the softness she showed only to him. Her heart was pure and good, even if she kept it wrapped in fire. Kyrie missed her. Badly. It ached more than his blisters.

"Are *you* okay, Gloriae?" he asked her. "You seem so strong. As if you feel no pain. If you ever want to talk, we can--"

"Kyrie, save it for my sister. I'm Gloriae the Gilded. I feel no pain."

Kyrie nodded. He remembered how Gloriae had wept over May's body. How much pain that one must carry... to have grown up in Confutatis, under the iron fist of Dies Irae.... Kyrie couldn't even begin to imagine it. He suddenly felt such pity for Gloriae, that his arms around her felt less like an attempt to keep from falling, and more like an embrace. If she felt the change in his grasp, she gave no note of it.

They rode silently for a while, Gloriae's curls bouncing as always against Kyrie's face. He occupied himself by looking at the landscapes--hills dotted with oaks, deer, and the occasional fort and village. Every once in a while, peasants, beggars, soldiers, or other motley travellers greeted them on the road. A few seemed hungry enough to attack, but Gloriae and Kyrie merely flashed their blades, and the hungry folk moved on.

"Come nightfall, most of them will be with the nightshades," Gloriae said.

Kyrie nodded. Every day, they saw fewer people on the roads, and more bodies in the gutters.

"At this rate, Osanna won't be much better than Requiem within a week," he said.

Gloriae turned her head and snarled. "Don't say that," she said. She clenched her fists. "Never say that again."

Kyrie glared back at her. "Why not? It's true. You released the nightshades, Gloriae. Take a long, hard look around you. The bloody things are turning the world into a--"

Suddenly she was crying. Kyrie stopped speaking. He had expected her to fume, scream, maybe even attack him. He had not expected this. She turned to face him. Her tears flowed down her cheeks, her lips trembled, and her eyes turned red.

"Kyrie," she whispered.

He didn't know how to react. He hated Gloriae. He wanted her to feel pain. Didn't he? Yet somehow--Kyrie couldn't figure out how--they found themselves standing on the roadside, embracing. She wept against him.

He patted her head awkwardly. "Gloriae, it's okay. We're going to trap the nightshades, and bring things back to normal."

She spoke into his shirt. "I'm scared, Kyrie. I'm so scared all the time. During the days, during the nights. I did this. I know it. I tried to kill you, and I destroyed the world instead. I'm so sorry." Her fingers dug into him. "I want to go home, Kyrie. I want to ride my griffin again, and live in my palace, and be strong. Be brave. Be certain of my way. I hate being so lost, so confused."

Her body trembled against him. She leaned back and looked at him with watery eyes, her lips quivering. Strands of her hair covered her face, and Kyrie drew them back, and tucked them behind her ears.

"Gloriae, have I ever told you about Requiem?" he asked. She shook her head.

"I don't remember much of it," Kyrie continued. "But I know it was beautiful. I remember a stone temple, where chandeliers hung, and monks played harps and sang. The place glowed at night with candles."

The memories flowed back into him, so real he could almost see them. Gloriae clung to him, staring with those moist eyes.

"Keep going," she whispered.

"I would sneak outside of services with my brothers. There were these trees outside the temple. I don't know their name, but they grew hard, green berries. We'd collect the fruit, and have wars, pelting one another from behind logs and benches." He laughed softly. "Requiem is still there. It's ruined now. That temple is gone. The people who prayed there are dead. But you and I are still here, and we have our memories. Once we defeat the nightshades, we'll go back there. We'll rebuild." He held Gloriae's hands. "And then we won't be lost anymore. We'll have our home. We'll have our purpose. We'll have Requiem again. You, me, and the others."

Gloriae looked to the west, as if imagining those old temples. "That doesn't sound so bad," she said, voice almost a whisper.

"Not at all," Kyrie said. But he wondered. Was it an empty dream? Could they truly defeat the nightshades? Even if they did, could they stop Dies Irae and his men? He sighed.

"Let's ride," Gloriae said. "We'll be at Fidelium soon."

They hid that night in a hollowed out log, which they first emptied of mud, twigs, and mice. The log was just wide enough for them, its bark rough and sticky. The nightshades screeched outside all night, and they could see their shadows and lightning, but they remained hidden and safe.

In the morning, they emerged from the log with stiff muscles, and found that the nightshades had claimed their horse. The beast lay on its side, mouth foaming.

"Look away, Kyrie," Gloriae said and drew her sword.

"Gloriae, what are you-- Stop tha--"

Gloriae thrust down her sword, piercing the horse's brain. It died instantly, gushing blood. Kyrie covered his mouth, feeling sick.

Gloriae removed her sword, cleaned it with a handkerchief, and stared at Kyrie. Her eyes were emotionless.

"I put it out of its misery," she said. "Crows and jackals would've been eating it alive within the hour."

Kyrie couldn't help but stare at the blood, which was now trickling between his boots. He looked back up at Gloriae, and found no pity, no compassion in her eyes. Gloriae the Gilded. The Light of Osanna.

"Let's go," he said.

They walked down the road, weapons drawn. Their robes, once white and pure, were now grimy with dirt and blood. Mud covered their boots. They walked all morning, their supplies slung over their backs. At noon they saw Fidelium Mountains in the distance, capped with snow. Kyrie's heart leaped. *Agnus Dei will be there.* He ached to hold her, kiss her, never leave her again.

"We travel cross-country from here," Gloriae said. They left the dirt road and walked through a forest of elms, oaks, and birches. Ferns and bushes grew everywhere. Kyrie slashed at them with his dagger. Everywhere were roots to trip him and branches to slap him.

They emerged from the trees in the afternoon, stepped into a field, and moaned. Kyrie felt like a deflated bellows.

"The bastard," he said. "How did he know?"

The mountain was still distant, but they were close enough to see Dies Irae's banners flapping across it. Archers covered the mountainsides, crouching in the snow. Below the mountain, thousands of soldiers drilled, kicking up snow as they marched and clashed swords. Knights on horseback rode among them, armor glinting.

"Back into the forest, Kyrie," Gloriae whispered.

They stepped back and hid behind an oak. They peered between the leaves, watching silently as the armies ahead drilled.

Hundreds of tents spread below the mountain, Kyrie saw. Most were the simple, squat tents of soldiers. One tent was large as a manor, its walls made of embroidered, golden cloth; Dies Irae would be in that one. Three other tents were even larger, their walls black. Those last tents bulged and fluttered, as if beasts swarmed inside them. Kyrie could hear nightshades shriek, and he shuddered.

"Agnus Dei hid here for a year once," he said. "And you and Dies Irae never thought of seeking her here. How did he know to come here now?"

Gloriae bit her lip, considering. "Remember when the nightshades claimed Agnus Dei?"

"Of course."

"They must have seen her memories. They must have learned of this hideout. And they told Irae. Now he's here, waiting for us."

A thought struck Kyrie, and he shivered. "You don't suppose that... the others got here before us? That Irae caught them?"

Gloriae looked at him. Fear filled her eyes. "I don't know."

Kyrie looked back at the mountain. He watched the golden tent's door open, and saw Dies Irae emerge. He wore his gilded, jewelled armor; it glinted like a small sun. As Kyrie and Gloriae watched from the trees, Dies Irae walked toward the dark, fluttering tent and stepped inside. The tent fluttered more wildly, and the nightshades inside screeched.

"Dies Irae is having fun with his new pets," Kyrie muttered. "Now we know where he keeps them during the daytime."

When he looked at Gloriae, he took a step back. She was pale, trembling, her fists clenched. She bared her teeth. She looked like a cornered wolf.

"I'm going to kill him," she said and took a step out of the trees.

Kyrie grabbed her shoulder. She spun toward him, snarling. "Let go!" she hissed.

He pulled her back into the brush. "Gloriae, Irae banished you. He disowned you. If you walk up to him now, he'll kill you."

She snorted, sword drawn. "He won't kill his daughter."

"You're not his daughter. You know that now, don't you? And Irae must know it too, or suspect it. Gloriae, please. We'll find a better way."

Her eyes narrowed, and blood rushed into her cheeks. Suddenly she was the old Gloriae, horrible and merciless. "What other way?"

Kyrie thought fast. "Look at that camp. Irae has been here for a while, I'd wager; at least a couple days. The full moon is tonight. If your family already arrived here--your real family-- they'd have seen Irae and backtracked."

Gloriae's freckles seemed to flash with rage. Golden flecks danced in her eyes like flames. "Where would they go?"

"To Requiem," Kyrie said. He didn't know if that was true. He knew, however, that he had to get Gloriae away from here--as far as possible. If they lingered, she'd march to Dies Irae, confront him, and die. "We've talked of rebuilding Requiem; they'd know to go there, realizing we'd think the same thing."

Gloriae considered him, head tilted, as if she were a bird of prey deciding when to swoop. Kyrie wasn't sure why he cared about her welfare. He hated Gloriae almost as much as he hated Dies Irae, didn't he? So what if she confronted Dies Irae and he killed her? And yet... Kyrie didn't want her to die. She was a Vir Requis. She was his companion. And she was Agnus Dei's sister. He would do what he could to save her.

"Why don't we hide in these woods?" she asked. "We might have a better chance of finding the others here, if they're still on their way."

A gruff voice answered behind them. "This is why."

Kyrie and Gloriae spun around to see five soldiers charging at them, swinging swords.

Kyrie snarled and raised his dagger. He deflected the sword of a sallow-faced soldier with a missing tooth. The soldier grunted and swung his sword again. Kyrie ducked. The sword whistled over his head. Kyrie thrust his dagger and hit the soldier's chain mail; his blade did the armor no damage.

He leaped back. From the corner of his eye, he saw that Gloriae had killed one man, and was battling the others. The soldier swung his sword at Kyrie again. He parried with his dagger, grabbed a branch, and yanked it. He ducked, and the branch slapped the soldier's face.

Kyrie thrust his dagger. It sank into the soldier's cheek, scraped along his skull, and entered his eye. The man screamed. Kyrie pushed the dagger deep, twisted it, and pulled. It came free with blood and eyeball juices.

A second soldier swung his sword at Kyrie. Kyrie jumped back, tripped over a root, and fell. The soldier raised his sword. Kyrie threw a rock at his face. The sword came down. Kyrie rolled and buried his dagger in the soldier's thigh. He twisted and pulled the blade. The man fell, and Gloriae's sword slammed into his head.

Kyrie panted, glancing around. The five soldiers were dead.

"Stars," he muttered, heart pounding and fingers trembling. "I only killed one, and you killed four, Gloriae. And you're not even out of breath."

She pointed her bloody sword to the mountains. "But I can't kill four thousand."

The sounds of battle had alerted the army. Soldiers were leaving the camp and running toward the trees.

Gloriae wrenched a sword out of a dead soldier's hands. "Ever use one of these?" she asked Kyrie.

"Of course," he lied.

Gloriae shoved the hilt into his hand.

"Good," she said. "Now run!"

They ran between the trees, branches lashing their faces, roots and pebbles threatening to trip them. The sounds of soldiers came behind--clanking armor, shouts, hissing swords.

"We go to Requiem, you say?" Gloriae asked as they ran.

Kyrie nodded. "To the old palace, where Benedictus and Lacrimosa lived. Where you were born."

They ran, sap on their faces, until night fell, and the shrieks of nightshades shook the forest. They hid in darkness, huddled in an abandoned wolf's den, under a hill behind the dangling roots of an oak. As nightshades screeched, Kyrie and Gloriae held each other and shivered.

BENEDICTUS

"Well, here's a pretty sight," said the soldier. He reached for his sword. "A father and daughter weredragon out for a stroll."

Ten other soldiers stepped out from the forest. They wore helmets and chain mail, and carried shields emblazoned with Dies Irae's coat of arms. They stepped onto the road, eyes narrowed.

Benedictus grunted. "We're simple travellers," he said to the soldiers. He took Agnus Dei's hand. "Let us be."

The soldiers surrounded them. They drew their swords as one, the blades hissing.

Benedictus glanced at Agnus Dei and nodded.

She nodded back; she knew the signal.

Together, they shifted into dragons and swung their tails.

Benedictus hit one soldier. He drove the spikes of his tail through the man's armor, and slammed him against another man. Agnus Dei took down two more men.

The remaining soldiers charged, blades swinging. Benedictus blew fire. The flames hit three men. They screamed and fell. Agnus Dei shot flames too, hitting two more soldiers.

Three soldiers remained. They were foolish enough to attack. Benedictus lashed his tail and knocked two down. Agnus Dei clawed another. With a few more swipes of their claws, the soldiers all lay dead.

Panting, Benedictus and Agnus Dei shifted back into human forms. They stood staring at the bodies.

"We made a bloody racket," Benedictus said. He panted and wiped sweat off his brow.

Agnus Dei nodded. "And raised smoke and fire." She spat onto the roadside. "If there are more soldiers a league around, they'll know we're here."

Benedictus glared at her. "Agnus Dei, you are a princess of Requiem. Do not spit."

She rolled her eyes. "Father, spare me. Let's go. Off the road."

They stepped into the forest just as the sound of boots came around the bend. Benedictus raced between the trees, Agnus Dei at his side. Grunts and curses sounded behind them, and soon the boots were thumping through the forest in pursuit.

"This whole forest is swarming with Irae's men," Benedictus said. He pointed his sword ahead, where between the trees, they could see an army mustered beneath Fidelium Mountain.

Agnus Dei uttered a curse that could make a sailor blush. "There were no soldiers when Mother and I hid here. Irae discovered our hideout."

They rushed around a boulder and shoved their way between brambles. The sounds of pursuit came between the trees.

"Wait," Benedictus said. "Let's load our crossbows. I want us to fight as humans--for as long as we can. We'd be tougher to find."

They stopped, panting, and loaded quarrels into their crossbows. Benedictus's lungs burned, and his heart thrashed

"Okay, go, quickly."

He heard a stream ahead and headed toward it. Curses and shouts came behind.

"I see prints," a soldier shouted. "That way."

Benedictus and Agnus Dei splashed into the stream. They walked through the water until they reached a boulder on the bank. They left the water, climbed over the boulder, and kept moving.

"You think they'll lose our trail?" Agnus Dei asked. "I--"

Her voice died. Two soldiers stood ahead. They seemed surprised; Benedictus guessed they hadn't expected to find anyone during their patrol. The men barely had time to draw their swords before he and Agnus Dei shot quarrels into their chests.

"Do you think Mother is here?" Agnus Dei said after they reloaded and kept trudging through the forest. "What about Kyrie and Gloriae?"

Benedictus frowned. He stared between the trees at the mountain, at Dies Irae's banners upon it, at the army that camped below.

"I don't know," he said. "We're supposed to meet them today in the cave, but... I don't know how they'd get there. There's an army guarding the place."

They kept running. The sounds of pursuit gradually faded behind. But it wouldn't be long, Benedictus knew, before thousands of soldiers were combing the woods.

Agnus Dei pointed at the mountainside, where archers surrounded the opening of a cave. "That's the cave Mother and I would hide in. Irae is guarding the entrance. But there's a back entrance too. If you go behind the mountain, a small cave leads into a tunnel. You can travel through the mountain, and reach the main cave from there."

Benedictus grunted. "You think the others are inside the tunnels?"

A soldier burst from between the trees, sword raised. Agnus Dei shot him with her crossbow. "I don't know," she said. "If they were waiting in the cave, and Irae arrived, they might have crawled deep into the tunnels, and hid there. We should look for them."

Benedictus stepped toward the soldier Agnus Dei had shot. He was lying in the mud, clutching his chest, whimpering. Benedictus knelt and gave the man water from his canteen.

"Your comrades will be here soon," he said to the soldier. He turned back to Agnus Dei. "More tunnels. I hate tunnels. But fine. Let's go."

They raced between the trees, crossbows and swords in hand, and cut west. They travelled for several hours through the forest. The sounds of soldiers faded behind them.

In late afternoon, the land became hilly, and pines replaced the elms and oaks. They found themselves climbing slopes, moving higher with every step. Old bricks, smoothed by centuries of rain, lay scattered around them. Once they saw the head of a statue, smoothed to bare features, emerging from the dirt. The remains of a wall and aqueduct nestled between a hill, overgrown with moss and vines.

"What is this place?" Agnus Dei asked. "These ruins are older than the ones in Requiem."

Benedictus nodded. "Fidelium Mountain is named after an old kingdom named Fidelium. Two thousand years ago, it fought a war against Osanna, and lost. These are its remains." He pointed at a column's capital rising from leaves and earth. "Most of Fidelium is now buried."

It was evening when they emerged onto a rocky terrain, finding themselves on the north side of Fidelium Mountain. The mountainside soared above them, green with pines. Higher up, they saw snow and jagged black boulders.

"We'll stay here for the night," Benedictus said.

Agnus Dei surveyed their surroundings in the sunset. "Where will we hide?"

Benedictus pointed at a mossy, rain-smoothed pile of stones. "This was a mausoleum once," he said. "The kings of Fidelium would rest in these tombs, in the shade of their mountain. We'll find rest there too, at least for tonight."

Agnus Dei grunted. "You want us to sleep in a mausoleum?" she asked and spat again.

"I told you, Agnus Dei, do not spit. Where did you pick up the habit? And yes, we're going to sleep there. Unless you prefer to sleep outdoors and face the nightshades?"

Agnus Dei grumbled curses so foul, Benedictus thought the pines would wilt. She began tramping toward the mausoleum.

"And where did you learn such language?" he said. "Do not speak that way."

Agnus Dei made a sound like an enraged boar. "Father, really. Must you?"

Benedictus grumbled, and the two knelt by the mausoleum. Most of it was buried. Only the top of its entrance was clear, and they spent some time digging. Finally the entrance was large enough, and they crawled inside. Dirt and dust filled the mausoleum, and they coughed and waved to clear the air. The sunset slanted through the narrow opening, lighting old bricks and shattered pottery. They pulled branches and bricks against the entrance, concealing it.

A second doorway led underground to a dark, clammy chamber. They climbed down to find two old skeletons, perhaps an ancient king and queen, lying by coffins. The grave must have been robbed years ago; the coffins were smashed, the skeletons denuded of jewels.

"Lovely place to spend the night," Agnus Dei said. She sat down with a groan. "If I get cold or lonely, I can cuddle with skeletons."

Benedictus stood, sword raised. "Sleep, daughter. I'll take the first watch."

He had barely finished his sentence, and Agnus Dei was snoring. The skeletons lay beside her, glaring with empty eye sockets at the intruders. Benedictus watched her sleep for a while, and he felt his face soften, the scowl that usually adorned it melting off. During waking hours, Agnus Dei was a firestorm--

cursing, spitting, shouting, arguing, or crying. In sleep, she looked peaceful, even with the dirt and blood that still covered her.

Benedictus knelt and kissed her forehead. "You're still my baby," he whispered. "Even if you were cuter as an actual baby."

She stirred, her lips scrunched, but she did not wake.

Benedictus turned to face the doorway they had crawled through. The last light faded, and soon Benedictus heard nightshades screeching outside. The air became icy, and he grunted and rubbed his joints. Lately they always ached in the cold. He held his sword drawn, as if that could harm a nightshade. As if his sword could win any of his battles.

The vision of the Poisoned return to him, and he lowered his head and clenched his jaw.

"It wasn't her," he whispered. "It couldn't have been."

And yet the Poisoned that had scratched his shoulder, the creature he'd killed with claw and fire, had worn his sister's pendant. The golden turtle with emerald eyes.

Benedictus clenched his fists. "No. It wasn't her. She died years ago."

Still the memory floated before him in the darkness--her hissing, toothless mouth; her green claws; her left eyeball that dangled against her cheek, spraying blood....

"No," he said, jaw tight. The nightshades screeched so loudly now, he couldn't hear his own words. "Don't think of her. It's over. It's over now."

Agnus Dei was alive and pure. Protecting her was what mattered now, Benedictus told himself. He turned to look at her... and felt the blood leave his face.

Agnus Dei was gone.

Benedictus stared, frozen for a moment.

He raised his sword.

Gone!

He peered into the corners and coffins, but could not see her. A chill ran through him; the skeletons were gone too.

"Agnus Dei!" he called.

A scream answered somewhere below, distant.

Benedictus searched for a door, but found none. Where had she gone? Then he noticed that the dust had moved by one of the coffins, and he shoved it. It was heavy. Benedictus grunted, strained, and managed to shove it aside.

A tunnel gaped open beneath it.

"Let go!" came Agnus Dei's voice from below.

Cursing, Benedictus leaped into the tunnel.

He fell ten feet and crashed onto bones. He couldn't see them in the darkness, but Benedictus had heard enough snapping bones in his life to recognize the sound. He pushed himself up, fumbled for his oil lamp, and lit it. The light flickered to life, illuminating a pile of skeletons.

"This isn't a mausoleum," he muttered. "It's a mass grave."

A scream sounded down the tunnel, maybe two hundred yards away, followed by the sound of more snapping bones. Benedictus began to run over the bones, moving down dark tunnels. He held his sword in one hand, the lamp in the other. The bones crunched beneath his boots. Spirals and skulls were drawn onto the walls with what looked like blood.

"Agnus Dei!" he called. He heard distant laughter, a chorus of it, cruel laughter. He kept running, the shadows dancing.

He was nearing the echoing laughter when three skeletons rose from the bones on the floor. Dust and cobwebs covered them. They swung rusty blades.

Benedictus parried. The blade he blocked disintegrated into a shower of rust. He swung his sword, decapitating the skeleton. The other two skeletons clawed at him, tugged his clothes, and snapped their teeth. Benedictus slammed the hilt of his sword against them, crushing their skulls. He kicked them when they fell, and slammed his sword down, until they were nothing but shattered bones. The bones moved at his feet, as if trying to regroup. Benedictus stepped over them and kept running.

He raced down the tunnel until he reached an archway. Its stones glowed with golden runes, and Benedictus saw mist and darkness beyond. The laughter came from there. He ran through the gateway, sword and lamp raised.

He found an ancient, dilapidated throne room. The chamber was wide but low, and columns filled it; there was no room here to shift into a dragon. Old candlesticks filled alcoves in the walls, burning with green fire. A hundred skeletons stood between the columns, wearing patches of rusty iron, holding chipped swords.

"Agnus Dei!" Benedictus called.

His daughter stood at the back of the chamber. Two armored skeletons held her arms. Another skeleton stood facing her. This one looked like the king; he wore a crown and still had wisps of a long, white beard. He shoved Agnus Dei into a dusty throne, and tried to force a necklace of jewels around her neck.

"Leave me alone!" Agnus Dei said. She was struggling and kicking, but the skeletons held her down in the throne. "Find yourself a skeleton wife, not me."

Benedictus ran toward them, but a dozen skeletons leaped at him. He hacked at them, but his sword did little damage; it kept entangling itself in their ribs. One of the skeletons wielded a mace. Benedictus grabbed it, wrenched it free, and began to swing. Bones shattered and flew in all directions. For every skeleton he bashed dead, new ones appeared. They surrounded him, scratching and biting. One sunk its teeth into his shoulder, and he shouted and clubbed it off.

"Agnus Dei, I'm here!" he called.

In the chaos, she had broken free from the skeletons holding her. She held an old iron candlestick, and was swinging it left and right, breaking skulls.

Benedictus clubbed several more skeletons, drove his shoulder into two more, and barrelled his way toward his daughter. Finally he reached her. She was still battling skeletons. Scratches covered her shoulder and thigh.

"I'm here, Agnus Dei, it's all right now," he said.

Agnus Dei groaned and kicked a skeleton's face, snapping its neck. "I do not...." She clubbed a skeleton with her candlestick. "Need you...." She kicked another's ribs. "To save me!" She sliced a skeleton in half with her sword.

The king skeleton leaped at them, snarling. His beard fluttered, and fires blazed in his eyes.

"You looked like you needed some help," Benedictus said to his daughter, swung the club, and bashed the king's ribs.

"I was fine," Agnus Dei said with a snarl. She swung her sword, shattering the king's shoulder.

"You were fine like I'm a nightshade," Benedictus said, clubbed the king's face, and watched the skeleton fall.

The king's bones collapsed into moldy heaps. As if signalled by some unseen banner, the other skeletons fell where they stood. They crashed to the floor, their bones disintegrating. Dust flew and the columns shook.

Benedictus and Agnus Dei stood facing each other, panting. For a moment, Benedictus had to place his hands on his knees, lean forward, and breathe.

"Are you all right?" he asked Agnus Dei, raising his head to stare at her. His hair was damp with sweat.

"I'm fine, Father. You worry too much."

"Worry too much? There was an army of skeletons after you."

She snorted, blowing back a curl of her hair. "I was handling them. I've always handled myself fine, Father. Good thing you finally remembered to look after me."

"What are you talking about?" He straightened and tried to examine her wounds, but she shoved him back.

"You don't even know, do you?" she asked. She snarled, but her eyes were red, as if she were about to cry.

"No!" he said. "I never know anything about you, Agnus Dei. I don't know why sometimes you're happy, and sometimes you're sad, and sometimes you're angry at me. I don't know why one moment, you're noble and proud, and the next moment, you spit and curse. And I don't know why you look like you want to kill me now."

Tears flowed down her cheeks, drawing lines through the dirt. "Of course you don't know!" she shouted. She clenched her fists. "You don't know me at all. You never bothered to get to know me. I grew up with Mother in caves, in tunnels, in hovels. You were off in your forest. I saw you maybe once a month, for only a few hours--"

Benedictus growled. "You know why. I've told you many times."

She rolled her eyes, sniffing. "Yes, yes. We were safer away from you. You know what? That's griffin dung. I think you just enjoyed being away from us. Being away from the memories. Not having to remember how you saved us, while everyone else died, and--"

"Agnus Dei!" he roared, voice so loud the chamber trembled, and dust rained from the ceiling. She froze, fell silent, and glared at him. Her hair was damp, and she panted.

"Agnus Dei," he said again, softly this time. "I love you. More than anything. More than life."

She stared at him silently. Slowly her fists unclenched. "You never tell me that," she said. "You never told me growing up."

He embraced her. She squirmed and struggled, but finally capitulated.

"I'm telling you now," he said. "I love you, daughter. I love you and Gloriae more than anything. I've always only wanted to protect you."

She sighed. "I hate you sometimes, Father."

"I know. That's all right. I hate myself sometimes."

She raised her eyes. "Really? You shouldn't." She sighed. "You snore, and you hum, and you make an annoying sound when you eat. You grumble way too much, and you don't shave nearly often enough. But you're not that bad, Dada. I'm sorry."

He scratched his stubble. "I do need a shave, don't I?"

She nodded. "Let's get out of here," she said. "We have a mountain to climb in the morning."

GLORIAE

The road was long, winding, and full of sadness.

Gloriae saw the sadness of the land--the bodies in the gutters, the toppled temples, the burning towns. She saw hungry children peeking from logs, from trees, from holes in the ground. She saw the blood and mud that covered them, the hunger in their eyes. Wilted trees filled the forests; nightshades had flown by them. Forts lay as scattered bricks. The horror she had unleashed from the Well of Night covered the world.

She looked at Kyrie, who walked beside her. He was staring at the wilted trees, eyes dark. Gloriae slipped her hand into his. He tried to pull his hand back, but she held him tight.

"Don't let me go," she said to him. He sighed and let her hold his hand.

"I have a memory of Requiem," she said. "From when I was three. I remember our home. I think it was our house. I remember marble tiles, and birches, and harps. Kyrie, what do you remember?"

He looked at the wilted trees, lost in thought. Finally he said, "I remember the temple with the fruit trees outside. I remember the harps too. And... I remember seeing many dragons in the skies. Thousands of them, entire herds."

Gloriae tried to imagine it--thousands of dragons, the sun on their scales, the sky in their nostrils. She imagined herself among them, a golden dragon, gliding through the clouds, her true people around her.

She looked at the ruins around her, and thought of the ruins of Requiem, and Gloriae made a decision. She squeezed Kyrie's hand, and smiled to herself, but said nothing.

In the afternoon, the forest recovered. The trees were not wilted, but alive with golden, red, and yellow leaves. Birds flew and deer grazed. A sign on the road pointed to a town, and promised a tavern and bathhouse.

Kyrie sighed. "I supposed this is another town you want to avoid. Too dangerous, huh."

"Actually, I'd like to visit that tavern," Gloriae said. "I've had enough of sleeping in logs and burrows, haven't you?"

Kyrie raised his eyebrows. "Didn't you say just the other day, how nightshades are smart enough to search inns now, and how Dies Irae has informants in them, and how you're a maiden of steel or something like that, and don't mind sleeping outside?"

Gloriae wanted to glare and hurt him, but not today. Today she'd have to be nice, if her plan was to work. She forced herself to smile. She knew that she had a beautiful smile, a smile to melt men's hearts. "I think we've earned a rest."

He nodded and whistled. "All right! Tavern it is. Beer, stew, bread, and a soft bed."

He walked with new vigor, and Gloriae smiled. Soon they approached the town. A score of cottages with thatch roofs nestled in the hills. A temple and tower rose above them, and farms rolled around them. The tavern stood closer to the road, its sign showing a turtledove sitting upon a firkin. Gloriae saw no movement in the windows, and two peasants lay slumped in the yard, drooling. The nightshades had been here too. She and Kyrie entered the tavern, and found the usual scene of soulless travellers.

"Not only nightshades have been here," she said. "Outlaws too."

The soulless were missing shoes and jackets. When she stepped into the pantry, Gloriae saw that most of the food had been taken. Only a handful of turnips, onions, apples, and sausages remained.

"I was hoping for some bread," Kyrie said, "but I'll make do with what we have. We'll cook a stew of it."

Gloriae left the pantry and searched the bar. Luckily, the caskets of ale were attached to the walls; the outlaws had left them. Most of the other drinks had been taken.

"And I was hoping for some wine or spirits," she said, scrunching her lips. "Something stronger than ale."

She could see marks on the floor where barrels of wine must have stood. She rummaged behind the bar and found a small, hidden door. When she swung it open, she smiled.

"Ah, good rye," she said. She lifted a bottle. "In a glass bottle too. These things cost a fortune, you know. Must be good stuff."

"I didn't know you're a drinker," Kyrie said, already eating an apple.

"There are many things you don't know about me. But you'll find them out."

They cooked a stew of turnips, onions, and sausages. Gloriae kept pouring ale into Kyrie's mug, though she drank little herself. They ate well, and then Gloriae opened the bottle of rye. She stood up, solemn, and raised the bottle.

"To Requiem," she said. "May our wings forever find her sky."

Kyrie too stood up. He nodded and repeated the Old Words.

Gloriae feigned a deep draft from the bottle, but only allowed several drops into her mouth. The spirits were strong, so strong they burned. She handed Kyrie the bottle.

"Drink deep," she said. "Drink well. For our home and forefathers."

He nodded and drank deeply. His cheeks flushed, he coughed, and he slammed down the bottle. "Good stuff."

Gloriae realized that she still wore her white cloak, and her armor beneath it. She removed the cloak and placed it on her chair. Her helmet followed. Gloriae shook her hair free, and the golden locks danced. She saw Kyrie staring, and she smiled crookedly.

"Drink, Kyrie," she said. "Drink for Requiem."

"For Requiem," he said and drank again. He passed Gloriae the bottle, and she feigned another draft.

When Kyrie had drunk a third time, Gloriae removed her breastplate. She placed it on a table, and stood before Kyrie in her undershirt. The cloth was thin, white cotton, damp with the sweat of their journey. Gloriae knew it clung to her, that it showed the curve of her breasts. She undid the laces at its top, opening her shirt halfway down her chest, and shook her hair again.

"It feels good to finally take off my armor," she said. She moved near Kyrie, took the bottle from him, and this time she truly did drink. The spirits burned down her throat. She shoved the bottle at Kyrie, placed her hand on his thigh, and told him, "Drink."

He drank, and she played with his hair and whispered into his ear. "It tastes good, doesn't it?"

Kyrie looked at her. His eyes were watery, his cheeks flushed. "Gloriae. What are you doing?"

She trailed her fingers along his thigh, and saw his flush deepen. Smiling crookedly, she brought the bottle to his lips. "Drink, Kyrie. For Requiem."

When the bottle was half empty, Kyrie was wobbling in his chair. "I'm tired," he said.

She nodded. "Me too. Let's find a bed and get some sleep."

She led him upstairs, helping him climb. They found a room, and Gloriae laid him in a bed. It was not yet evening; she still had time.

"Gloriae," he said groggily. "What are you doing?"

"I'm taking my clothes off," she said. "They're sweaty and dirty, and I want them off me."

"You shouldn't," he said from the bed.

But Gloriae was already naked. She stretched by the window, the sun on her skin. It felt good to be free of her clothes; she felt like a nymph. She ran her hands through her golden locks, smiled at Kyrie, and stepped toward him.

"Gloriae," he said, frowning.

He tried to rise from the bed, but she pushed him back down. With deft movements, she unlaced his pants and straddled him.

"Don't move, Kyrie," she said. "Just lie still. I'll do everything."

He tried to push her off, but he was too drunk. She held his hands, leaned forward, and kissed his forehead. "It's all right, Kyrie," she said. "I know what I'm doing. It's for the best."

"I can't," he said, though she could feel his eyes on her breasts, feel his desire beneath her. Gloriae had never done this before, but she knew how to. She had grown up among soldiers; she was no innocent. She did the deed quickly, gasping and digging her fingernails into Kyrie, her head back. It didn't take long. He was done. She left him. She pulled on her clothes, leaned over him, and kissed his lips.

"Thank you, Kyrie," she said. "Now sleep. I'll take the first watch."

He confronted her in the morning. Gloriae was in the common room, setting bowls of porridge on the table. Kyrie came stumbling downstairs. He had sacks beneath his eyes, and a sallow look, and winced in the sunlight.

"Good morning, Kyrie," she said. "I found some oatmeal in the pantry and made breakfast."

He trudged to the table, sat down, and lifted a spoon. His eyes never left hers. He began to eat, frowning at her suspiciously. She sat down beside him and began to eat too. For a moment they were silent.

Then Kyrie slammed down his spoon. "Gloriae," he began, "you--"

"Hush, Kyrie," she said and took a spoonful of porridge. She swallowed. "I don't want to hear it."

He rose to his feet so suddenly, his chair crashed to the floor. He winced and rubbed his temples. "Last night, you--"

Gloriae stood up too and slapped his face, hard enough to knock him back two steps.

"Kyrie," she said, glaring at him, "I have killed Vir Requis. Many of them."

He stared at her silently, his cheek red with the print of her hand. He said nothing.

"I killed my first Vir Requis when I was six years old," she said. "I've killed more since, many more. Now there are only five left. Maybe fewer now; we don't know if the others survived."

"They sur--"

"Quiet, Kyrie!" She grabbed his cheeks and stared into his eyes. "I am Vir Requis too. I know that now. And I need a child. We all need one, a new life for our race. So yes. I will have your child. You might not like it. I don't care. I will have it. Remember what we drank for last night? For Requiem. For her will I bear new life."

He tore free from her. "I promised my love to Agnus Dei," he said.

She snorted. "Promised your love? Are you a poet now? Well, good for you and Agnus Dei. I'm happy for you two. And I know that once we all reunite, you'll marry her. When we rebuild Requiem, you'll build a house with her, and have children with her, and then my chance will be gone. I need your child before then. So I made one with you last night."

Kyrie glared at her, eyes red. For a moment it seemed he would yell, but then he simply righted his chair and sat down with a sigh. He placed his elbows on the tabletop and leaned his head down. "You don't know that you're pregnant. It can take more than one try."

She nodded and placed her hand on his head. "That's why we're going to repeat last night. Again and again, until we reach Requiem and you're reunited with my sister."

He looked up at her. "Gloriae, you're her twin sister. It's wrong."

"The whole world is wrong. We do what we can to right it. Don't we?"

He took her hands. "Gloriae, look. You're beautiful. Achingly beautiful; a goddess. You're strong, and intelligent, and... everything a man could want. But I love Agnus Dei."

"I'm not asking you to love me, Kyrie. I'm not asking you anything. I'm telling you. We need more Vir Requis. I did my part hunting the race to near extinction. I'll do what I must to rebuild it, to redeem myself. Even if it hurts you and Agnus Dei. The future of our race is more important than your pain." She shoved the porridge close to him and patted his cheek. "Now eat, darling. You're going to need your strength."

After breakfast, they left the tavern with fresh supplies, and walked down dirt roads. In the distance, they saw mountains of burned trees.

The ruins of Requiem were near.

AGNUS DEI

She climbed through the snow, fingers stinging, the wind whipping her face. Snow filled her clothes, hair, and mouth. She spat it out.

"Have I mentioned already that I hate snow?" she said.

Father grunted. He was climbing beside her, snow covering him. It clung to his stubble like a white beard. "Once or twice," he said. "Or a million times."

Agnus Dei looked behind her. They'd been climbing all morning, and the mausoleum of skeletons lay a league below, piny hills surrounding it. When she turned her head and looked above her, she saw Fidelium soaring, all black boulders and swirling snow. The wind howled.

"We're close," she said. "We'll reach the cave within an hour."

Father nodded and they kept climbing, shivering in the cold and wind.

Agnus Dei thought of Kyrie as she climbed. The thought of him made her feel warmer. What was the pup up to now? Was he tolerating Gloriae? Agnus Dei knew the two held no love for each other. *I hope they made it to the caves,* Agnus Dei thought. *I hope they're huddling inside, waiting for us. Maybe I'll see them again soon, in only an hour or two.* She promised herself that she'd give her sister a hug, and the pup a kiss that would knock his boots off.

And what of Mother? Had she found the griffins? Would she be waiting here too? Suddenly Agnus Dei felt fear, colder than the snow. What if they weren't here? What if the nightshades had caught them, or Dies Irae's crossbow, or the griffins had attacked, or--

Agnus Dei shook her head to clear it. There was no use worrying now. Soon enough, she would know.

The wind howled, and a strange sound--a twang--sounded above.

Agnus Dei froze and frowned.

"Did you hear that?" she said to Father.

He nodded and drew his sword. "Yeah, and I don't like it."

The twang sounded again, closer now. It sounded like a wobbling saw, metallic. Agnus Dei narrowed her eyes, staring up the mountain. Snow cascaded.

"What--" she began.

Something leaped above, emitted that wobbling twang of a cry, and disappeared behind snow.

"Griffin balls," Agnus Dei swore, narrowed her eyes, and aimed her crossbow. "What the abyss was that?"

"Don't curse!" Father said.

The creature had seemed large, the size of a horse. Agnus Dei had only glimpsed long limbs, white skin draped over long bones, and three eyes. Where was it now?

The creature burst from behind a mound of snow, flying toward them. Its mouth opened, revealing teeth like swords, and its eyes blazed.

Agnus Dei shot her crossbow into its head.

It crashed a hundred yards away, squealed, and came sliding down the snow toward her. Agnus Dei snarled. *It's hideous.* It had a knobby spine and six legs, bony, with large joints. White, wrinkly skin draped over it. Agnus Dei had once seen a hairless cat; this creature looked like a cross between that poor critter and a giant spider.

It squealed at her feet, black blood squirting from its wound. It snapped claws and teeth at her. Father shot his own crossbow, sending the quarrel into the creature's brain. It made a mewling, high-pitched sound that sent snow cascading down the mountainside, then lay still.

Agnus Dei looked down at it. She shivered. "Ugly bastard. And new to this mountain. These things weren't here in the summer."

"Dies Irae must have new pets," Father said grimly. "This is a snowbeast, a creature from the far north."

"Let's shift and fly the rest of the way up," Agnus Dei said. "I don't want to meet any more of these creatures."

Father shook his head. "No shifting, Agnus Dei. Your scales are red. Irae's men would see you from the forests leagues away. Let's keep climbing." He pointed his sword. "I see the back cave. We're almost there."

They stepped around the dead snowbeast and began climbing again.

With a chorus of twangs, a dozen snowbeasts appeared and leaped toward them.

Agnus Dei and Father shot their crossbows. Two snowbeasts crashed and slid down the snow, screaming. The others screeched, scurried on six legs, and jumped at them.

Agnus Dei swung her sword. The blade sliced through a bony, wrinkly limb. The limb flew, the snowbeast screeched, and its blood spurted. It snapped its teeth at her, and Agnus Dei fell onto her back. Snarling, she drove her sword up. It hit the snowbeast's teeth, knocked one out, and drove into its head.

The snowbeast fell onto her, drool and blood dripping. One of its remaining teeth scratched her cheek. Agnus Dei grunted and shoved it aside. She rose to her feet to see two more snowbeasts leaping at her.

She swung her sword left and right. Bony limbs flew. Black blood covered the snow, smelling like oil. All around, from behind boulders and snow, more snowbeasts were appearing.

"We can't kill them all," Father cried over their screams. Black blood covered his blade and arms. "Run to the cave!"

They began running uphill, swords swinging. The snowbeasts' limbs littered the mountainside, but new ones kept swarming. Even the wounded came crawling at them, screeching. One scratched Father's calf, tearing through his pants and skin. Agnus Dei ran screaming, sword and arms sticky with blood. A snowbeast jumped off a boulder, swooping toward her. She tossed her dagger at it, burying it in its head, and kept running.

When she reached the cave, she dashed in. Father was a few paces behind. Hurriedly, Agnus Dei loaded her crossbow. She shot over Father's head, hitting the snowbeast behind him.

"Hurry up, old man!" she said.

He dashed into the cave, breath ragged, the snowbeasts in hot pursuit. Father and daughter stood at the cave entrance, swinging swords. Creatures' limbs and heads piled at their feet.

"Get lost!" Agnus Dei shouted at them. "Away, find food elsewhere!"

Finally, her shouts and their blades convinced the snowbeasts to leave. They scurried away on their bony limbs, their white skin flapping in the wind.

Agnus Dei and Father leaned against the cave walls, breathing heavily. Her heart thrashed, and even in the cold, sweat drenched her.

"Nothing's ever easy," Father muttered, and she nodded.

When they had caught their breath, Agnus Dei said, "The tunnel passes through the mountain. It's dark, and it's narrow, but I've travelled it before. It's safe. After an hour's walk, we'll reach the south cave."

She checked her tin lamp, which she'd pilfered from an abandoned inn three nights ago. She still had some oil left; maybe an hour's worth. She lit the wick, narrowed her eyes, and stepped into the darkness. Father walked beside her, his sword raised.

A hundred yards into the cave, Agnus Dei grimaced. Her lamplight flickered across hundreds of eggs. The eggs were the size of watermelons, translucent and gooey. She could see snowbeast maggots inside, their limbs twisting, their mouths opening and closing. Mewls left their throats, the sound muffled inside the eggs.

"They're even uglier as babies," she muttered. "I'd hate to be here when they hatch."

Benedictus nodded. "We won't be. Let's keep walking."

As they walked down the tunnel, Agnus Dei tightened her grip on her sword. She hated narrow places like these. It meant she couldn't shift. She had mostly resisted shifting outside the tunnel, but at least the option had existed. Here, if she shifted into a dragon, the narrow tunnel would crush her. Her lamp swung in her hand, swirling shadows, dancing against clammy walls. She imagined that she saw small nightshades in the shadows, and Agnus Dei shivered. Would she find Mother, Gloriae, and Kyrie here, or would she find their bodies?

The tunnel twisted and narrowed. At times they had to walk slouched over, or even crawl. After an hour, Agnus Dei was sure they must be close to the southern mountainside. Where was the cave? She should see it by now. Her lamp guttered, and the shadows darkened.

"We're running out of oil," she said. "Father, do you have any oil in your lamp?"

He shook his head, and Agnus Dei cursed. She quickened her step, her boots clacking. Within moments, her lamp gave a final flicker and died.

Darkness enveloped them.

"We continue," Father said. His voice was a low growl. "Walk carefully. Crossbows raised."

Agnus Dei nodded and kept walking. She kept one hand on the clammy wall. She gripped her crossbow with the other. The south cave couldn't be far now. The sound of water dripping echoed, and wind moaned.

A screech shook the tunnels.

Agnus Dei screamed and shot her crossbow. She heard Father do the same.

The screech rose, so high pitched, Agnus Dei's hackles rose. The tunnel trembled. Two eyes opened ahead, burning like stars. Their light illuminated a swirling, inky head and white teeth.

"A nightshade!" Agnus Dei cried. "Run, Father!"

They spun around to flee, but another nightshade shrieked there too. Its eyes blazed, and it flowed toward them like smoke. Its maw opened, and it screamed so loudly, Agnus Dei had to cover her ears.

She moved her head from side to side. *Surrounded!* She could see more nightshades behind those closest to her. They filled the tunnels.

"Light, we need light," she said, but they had no oil, no torches, and the tunnel was too narrow to become dragons and blow fire.

Father slipped his hand into hers. "Agnus Dei," he said, "I'm sorry. I love you."

She felt the nightshades begin to tug her soul. Wisps of it tore free from her, like feathers plucked from a chicken. She closed her eyes, tears stinging.

"Goodbye, Dada. I love you too."

The nightshades shrieked, and Agnus Dei saw the darkness beyond them. She saw the endless worlds, the dimensions that spun her head, the space, eternal, the caverns. She prayed with trembling lips. *Goodbye, Mother, Father, sister. Goodbye, Kyrie.*

She fell to her knees, and her eyes rolled back.

Then a voice spoke.

"Enough."

The nightshades howled. Agnus Dei's soul slammed back into her body. She opened her eyes, trembling. She squeezed Father's hand. She could see now, she realized. Firelight blazed.

"Who spoke?" she demanded and rose to her feet.

Her heart thrashed.

Agnus Dei snarled and drew her sword.

"You."

Carrying a torch, Dies Irae stood before them in the tunnel. Agnus Dei charged at him, screaming, sword raised.

Dies Irae waved his hand, and nightshades swarmed. They slammed into Agnus Dei, knocking her down. She fell, cursing. She leaped up and charged again, sword swinging. Dies Irae waved his hand again, and again nightshades knocked Agnus Dei to the ground.

"We can keep doing this all day, sweetness," Dies Irae said, voice soft. He spoke from within his helmet, the steel monstrosity that looked like a griffin's head. "You would tire of it sooner than I would, I promise you."

Agnus Dei pushed herself up, sword in hand, snarling. Father stood beside her, eyes dark, silent. Agnus Dei made to charge again, but Dies Irae clucked his tongue, wagged his finger at her, and she paused.

"I'm going to kill you," she said, snarling.

He laughed and lifted his visor. Agnus Dei couldn't help but gasp. Dies Irae had changed. His face had once been tanned gold. It was now white streaked with black lines, as if oil coursed through his wrinkles. His left eye was gone. An empty socket gaped there, blazing. Starlight and darkness filled the wound, as if nightshade maggots nested there. His good eye blazed, milky white and swivelling. He looked, Agnus Dei thought, like a man possessed by demons. Which, she decided, he was.

"I think not, my daughter," Dies Irae said.

"Silence," Father said and took a step forward, raising his sword.

Dies Irae laughed. "But I am her father, Benedictus. When I raped Lacrimosa, that little whore of yours, I created two smaller whores--Gloriae and Agnus Dei."

While he spoke, Agnus Dei loaded her crossbow. She fired.

Dies Irae had only to stare in her direction. Sparks and black smoke flowed from his empty eye socket, and the quarrel shattered. Steel shards flew, hit the walls, and fell to the floor.

"My my, daughter," Dies Irae said. "You are almost as feisty as your sister, are you not? I spared Gloriae's life. Yes. I let her flee into exile. Do you know why I let her live, Agnus Dei? I let her live because she killed many Vir Requis in my service. She killed children, did you know? Maybe some had been your friends." He raised his left arm, the prosthetic arm made of steel, ending with a mace head like a fist. "But you were never in my service, second daughter. I will kill you... and that pathetic brother of mine who claims to be your true father."

Dies Irae ran forward, mace swinging.

Agnus Dei dropped down and slid forward. The floor was wet, and she flew past the charging Dies Irae. She swung her sword. The blade clanged against Dies Irae's armor, doing him no harm. Jewels flew from it, and its gilt peeled, but the steel beneath stood.

Dies Irae spun, swinging his mace. Agnus Dei ducked, and the mace whooshed over her head.

Father slammed his sword, hitting Dies Irae's helmet. The helmet dented. Dies Irae's head tilted, and Agnus Dei dared to hope that his neck was broken... but he only laughed and punched Father with his good fist, a fist covered in a steel gauntlet. The blow hit Father's chest, knocking him back.

Agnus Dei screamed. She swung her sword and hit Dies Irae's neck. The sword rebounded, sending pain up her arms. It didn't even dent Dies Irae's armor.

The mace swung again. Agnus Dei leaped back, and the tip of the mace grazed her arm. She grunted. The mace had not hit her bone, but it would leave an ugly bruise. The pain burned. She thrust her sword, aiming for Dies Irae's face, but he had managed to lower his visor. The blade hit the metal and bounced back.

The mace swung. Agnus Dei raised her sword and parried with its pommel. The mace hit with incredible force. The blow knocked back her arm, and the sword flew from her hand. It clanked behind her.

Dies Irae swung the mace again.

Father barrelled into Dies Irae, shoving him forward. Agnus Dei scurried back and retrieved her sword. She swung at Dies Irae and hit his breastplate. More jewels flew from the armor, scattering across the floor. The steel, however, remained strong.

Father swung his sword, but Dies Irae parried, almost lazily. He swung his mace toward Father's head.

Agnus Dei lunged and grabbed Dies Irae's legs. She tugged and he fell.

Father slammed his sword against Dies Irae's helmet. Agnus Dei slammed against his back. Their blows could not dent the armor, but they were dazing him, hurting him. Agnus Dei drove her sword down hard behind Dies Irae's knee, where the armor was weak. Blood spurted, and Dies Irae screamed.

"Nightshades!" he cried. "Kill them."

The nightshades, who until then had merely watched the fight, screeched. They rushed at Father and Agnus Dei, swirled around them, and howled.

"No!" Agnus Dei screamed. Once more they were tugging her soul, and her sword fell from her hand.

Red light filled the tunnel.

Heat blazed.

Fire burned.

"Leave this place!" came a dragon's roar. The fire died, and Agnus Dei saw a dragon's head in the darkness ahead, where the tunnel was wide.

"Mother!" she cried.

Lacrimosa, lying in the tunnel in dragon form, blew fire again. Agnus Dei and Father ducked and covered their heads. The firelight blackened the ceiling, and the nightshades screamed. The creatures began to flee.

Mother shifted into human form and ran toward them.

"Up, run!" she cried. "The firelight won't frighten them for long. Out of the tunnel!"

Agnus Dei looked for Dies Irae, but he was gone. She grabbed Mother.

"You're running to the south cave, Mother! Irae's got men covering that side of the mountain."

The nightshades were recovering, collecting their wisps of smoke and howling.

"It's our only way out!" Mother shouted and began to run. "Come on!"

They raced through the tunnels, nightshades howling around them, tugging at them, and snapping their teeth. Soon sunlight washed the tunnels, and they burst into the old cave, the same cave Agnus Dei had once spent a year in. Archers stood there, firing arrows.

Agnus Dei howled, shifted, and blew fire. Arrows flew around her, and once pierced her wing. She screamed, and her fire roared, and the archers fell burning.

She flew into the sunlight. The nightshades shrieked in the caves and cowered. Below her, Agnus Dei saw dozens of swordsmen and archers. She swooped at them, took another arrow to the wing, and blew fire. Her talons tore into swordsmen. Her flames burned the archers. Blood splashed the snow. Thousands of soldiers were leaving the camp below and racing up the mountain. Hundreds of crossbowmen ran with them.

"Let's get out of here," Father said, shifting into a dragon. He roared and blew fire at ten soldiers who charged at him. Mother shifted too, and the three flew. Arrows zoomed around them. One scratched Agnus Dei's side, and another cut Father's leg.

"Fly!" he roared.

They flew west, arrows zooming around them. More arrows flew, but soon the dragons were out of range.

"I thought you said we're not allowed to shift!" Agnus Dei cried over the roaring wind. Her wounds ached and blood seeped down her wing.

"Case by case basis," he called back. The forests streamed below them, and clouds gathered above.

"Why, by the stars, would you two enter that mountain?" Mother demanded. She glared at her husband and daughter. An arrow had grazed her flank, drawing blood. "Irae has thousands of men there. He was waiting for us. And you two go marching right in, like sheep into a butcher shop."

Father glanced at his wife, indeed seeming almost sheepish. "We were seeking Kyrie and Gloriae."

"We all agreed we'd meet there," Agnus Dei added, flames dancing between her teeth. "Remember, Mother?"

Mother rolled her eyes. Smoke left her nostrils. "Kyrie and Gloriae are not knuckleheads like you two. Of course they wouldn't march into a cave full of nightshades, with Dies Irae's army camped outside. They'll have returned to Requiem. I wager that if we fly there now, we'll find them."

Agnus Dei blew fire in rage. The flames lit the clouds. "If Father and I are such knuckleheads, then so are you, Mother. You also entered the cave."

Mother gave her a stare so withering, that Agnus Dei growled and bared her fangs.

"I entered the cave to save you, Agnus Dei," Mother said. "I had just arrived, saw Irae dash into the cave, and heard you scream."

Agnus Dei growled. "I don't need you to save me. I'm a grown woman now."

Mother glared. "You're a grown woman like I'm a griffin."

"You're one ugly griffin then."

Father roared. "Silence! The griffins are free now, Agnus Dei, and you will show them respect. You are a princess of Requiem."

"I am a warrior of Requiem," she said. "I'm no spoiled princess."

"You are my daughter, and I am the king, therefore you are a princess. And now kindly shut your maw. We fly to find Kyrie and Gloriae."

He roared fire, and his wings churned the clouds. He rose higher into the air, until they burst over the clouds, and flew under a shimmering sun. Mountain peaks rose below them, gold and indigo. Benedictus gave a roar that seemed to shake the skies.

"We fly to Requiem."

DIES IRAE

He pushed himself to his feet.

He stared at the blood seeping down his leg.

Jaws clenched, he walked out of the cave, stood upon the mountainside, and saw the weredragons disappear into the distance.

Bodies lay around him, blood painting the snow. Some of the men were burned, their skin peeling, their flesh red and black. Thousands of living soldiers stood there too. They froze when they saw Dies Irae, stood at attention, and slammed their fists against their chests.

He surveyed the scene for a long time, silent. Then Dies Irae left the cave, and walked through the snow to the body of a wounded soldier. The man was missing a leg. The wound looked like a dragon bite. Clutching the stump, the man stared up at Dies Irae.

"My lord," he whispered.

"Give me your sword," Dies Irae said.

The man raised his sword with a bloody, trembling hand. Dies Irae took the weapon, then drove the blade into the man's chest.

He raised his eyes and stared around him. The men still stood at attention, stiff, pale.

Dies Irae approached another wounded soldier. This man lay curled up in red snow, weeping and whispering for his mother. He clutched his spilling entrails, as if he could force them back into his belly. *Dragon claws*, Dies Irae knew.

"A weredragon attacked you," Dies Irae said.

The soldier wept and nodded.

"And you failed to kill it," Dies Irae said.

The soldier looked up with teary eyes, and Dies Irae drove his sword into the man's chest, pushing him into the snow.

The mountain was silent now. The weeping stopped. The only sound was the wind and swirling snow. Dies Irae looked over his men, the dozens of wounded, the dozens of dead, and the thousands that still stood.

"Has anyone else failed to kill a weredragon today?" he asked.

They stared, silent.

"All who killed a weredragon, raise your hands."

The men stood stiffly, pale, a few trembling.

Dies Irae called forward his captains, the commanders of the ten companies he'd brought to Fidelium. The captains stepped toward him, clad in plate armor, and slammed gauntleted fists against their chests.

"Hail Irae!" they said.

Dies Irae barely acknowledged them. He moved his eyes over the rows of soldiers in the snow. "My men disappointed me today. Decimate them."

The captains breathed in sharply.

"Decimation, my lord?" whispered one, a burly man with a battle axe. "That punishment has not been handed out since the Gray Age."

Dies Irae slowly turned his head, his armor creaking, and examined the man. "You are displeased with my command?"

The captain shook his head and saluted again, fist on breastplate. "Decimation, my lord. As in the days of old."

As Dies Irae watched, the captains arranged their companies into formation. The men stood in rows, ten men deep, fists against their chests. The captains raised their eyes to Dies Irae.

He frowned, thought a moment, and said, "The seventh row."

The soldiers in the seventh rows shifted uneasily. Sweat appeared on their brows. The captains pulled the first men from each seventh row, placed them in the snow, and swung their axes.

Blood splashed, and heads rolled.

The captains pulled the next men from formation.

Dies Irae stood, silent and still, watching as it continued. Some men of the seventh rows tried to flee. The captains shot them with crossbows. It took two hours of blood, grunts, but no screams. Not one man screamed. Dies Irae had taught them well.

When it was over, three-hundred heads were collected into a pile. Three-hundred bodies were stacked by them.

"Leave them here for the snowbeasts," Dies Irae said. "They will provide fresh meat for a while." He began walking down the mountainside, heading to the camp below. "We go to the ruins of Requiem, and we march hard. The weredragons will be heading there. I can feel it."

Soon his army snaked across the land, silent and bloody, leaving the bodies behind. Dies Irae rode at their lead on his courser. They bore the nightshades in shadowed wagons; the beasts screeched and fluttered inside them, rattling the wagon walls. When they were a half a league down the road, Dies Irae looked over his shoulder, back to the mountains.

Snowbeasts were feasting.

Dies Irae smiled thinly.

KYRIE ELEISON

As they collected firewood, Kyrie couldn't stop glancing at Gloriae. She would notice his glances, raise her eyes, and give him a stare so deep, so meaningful, that he had to look away. He knew what her eyes were saying. *Today. Again.*

He muttered and leaned down to collect twigs and branches. There wasn't much kindling here in the ruins of Requiem. Most of the trees had burned to ash. What branches they found were old, blackened, and would probably only burn for seconds.

"What we need are logs, an axe, and some rabbits to roast," Kyrie said. He tried to imagine the heat of a roaring fire, and the smell of dripping meat. It wasn't because he missed those things--though he did--so much as it beat thinking about Gloriae. And he was thinking a lot about her. About her naked body in the sun, her lips against him, her--

"Kyrie, you've dropped your sticks," she said. She was standing only a step away. He hadn't even noticed her approach, and he started, muttered under his breath, and leaned down to collect the wood.

"I think we have enough firewood now," he said, not bothering to mask the gruffness in his voice. "At least, all the firewood we'll find in this place. The whole kingdom is a wasteland."

She placed a hand on his shoulder. "Kyrie--" she began.

He walked away, ignoring her. He pointed at three fallen columns, a smashed statue of a dragon, and bits of a wall. Ash, bones, and mud littered the place. If there had been a floor, the dirt now covered it.

"This is the place," Kyrie said. "The hall of Requiem's kings. At least, I think it is. To be honest, all of Requiem looks more or less the same to me now."

She walked up behind him and placed her hands on his shoulders. When he turned to face her, she cupped his cheek and kissed him. "It's time," she said. "Now."

Roughly, he removed her hand and held her wrist. "Gloriae, no."

Her eyes flashed with sudden anger, and her jaw tightened. But then she calmed, leaned close, and kissed his lips again. "You know we must."

"But--"

She pressed a finger to his lips. "No buts. Down, Kyrie. Here by the columns."

She began to remove her clothes, staring into Kyrie's eyes all the while. First she doffed her priestess robes. Then she removed her breastplate and dropped it to her side. It clanged against old tiles. Still staring at Kyrie, she unlaced her shirt, her lips parting. She had begun unlacing her pants, too, when footfalls sounded behind.

Agnus Dei stepped toward them.

Kyrie's heart galloped.

"Agnus Dei!" he said. He gasped and his cheeks burned. He wanted to rush to her, but something in her eyes held him back.

Agnus Dei stood still, mouth open. She held a sword in one hand, and a crossbow in the other. She held the crossbow aimed at them, and it was a moment before she lowered it.

"What's going on here?" she asked, eyes narrowing.

Gloriae turned to face her sister. Her hair was down. Her shirt was unlaced to reveal most of her breasts. She removed her hands from the lacing on her pants, which she had begun to undo, and took a step toward Agnus Dei.

"Sister!" Gloriae said. She reached out to embrace Agnus Dei, who still stood frozen.

Kyrie too stepped toward her, arms outreached. "We're so glad you're alive, Agnus Dei. Thank goodness you're here."

She turned to look at him, but said nothing. Her eyes remained narrowed.

More footfalls sounded, and Lacrimosa and Benedictus stepped around a smashed wall toward them. Lacrimosa called out, and ran to them, and embraced Kyrie and Gloriae. Tears filled her eyes. Benedictus too joined the embrace, and for a moment everyone was talking at once, and sharing their stories, and mumbling their relief.

All but Agnus Dei, that was. She stood apart from them, staring from Kyrie to Gloriae and back again. Her black curls cascaded down her back, and ash covered her bodice and leggings. Scratches and bruises ran along her arms. She looked so beautiful to Kyrie; even more than he'd remembered. He walked toward her.

"Agnus Dei," he said. He wanted to take her hands, or embrace her, or kiss her, but she still held her sword and crossbow before her.

She nodded and gave him a small, mirthless smile. "Kyrie."

Kyrie cursed himself. He cursed Gloriae. This was not the reunion he'd imagined. In a thousand dreams, he'd imagined him and Agnus Dei running to each other, embracing, kissing. She'd call him pup and muss his hair, and then he'd kiss her again, and they'd be as they'd always been. Now Agnus Dei seemed icier than Gloriae.

"I... I've missed you," he said to her. "I love you."

She nodded curtly, then turned to her parents, and began talking to them about firewood and sharpening stones and unpacking their food.

Kyrie stared at her, aching. *She knows,* he thought, his cheeks growing hot. She knew he had slept with Gloriae. She knew everything; she had seen it in his eyes. Guilt filled him, suffocating. He could have stopped Gloriae. Even drunk on spirits, he could have stopped her, pushed her off him, stormed downstairs. And yet... he had stared at Gloriae's naked body in the sun. He had desired it. He had let her kiss him, let her undress him, let her lie with him.

"It's my fault," he whispered to himself. "I'm sorry, Agnus Dei."

Nobody heard him, and Kyrie felt anguish tearing inside him like griffin claws.

They stacked what kindling they had. Benedictus had carried firewood in his backpack all the way from Osanna, and soon a campfire crackled. They warmed themselves by the flames, ate old bread and turnips, and talked of their journeys.

Kyrie opened his backpack and pulled out the books *Mythic Creatures of the Gray Age* and *Artifacts of Wizardry and Power.*

"We borrowed these from Confutatis Library," he said. "Our friend Dies Irae edited them a bit."

He showed the others how the original parchments had been tweaked, some words scraped away and overwritten. When Agnus Dei saw the illustration of the hero taming the nightshades, his head replaced with the likeness of Dies Irae, she snorted. Kyrie looked up at her over the fire, hoping she'd laugh and smile at him, but she wouldn't meet his eyes.

Kyrie finished by reading from *Artifacts.* "'Lir Irae prayed to his father, the Sun God, for light to tame the nightshades. The Sun God, of infinite wisdom and power, created the Beams and filled them with his light and fire, so that Lir Irae might tame the

189

nightshades in his name.'" Kyrie cleared his throat and slammed the book shut. "In short, we don't know much. The part about the Beams is the original text. The words 'Sun God' and 'Lir Irae' are new, overwriting the original text. Who actually created the Beams, and who used them? We don't know."

For the first time, Agnus Dei spoke. "We do know."

She met Kyrie's eyes over the fire, but there was no emotion in them. They were colder and sharper than her sword. She tore her eyes away and unrolled a burned, tattered scroll. She showed them the text, which was badly damaged, missing many words.

"In the days of the Night Horrors, King T_____ite journeyed to the southern realms of G_____nd sought the Loomers o_____olden pools. The Night Horrors stole the souls of Osanna, and cast them into the d___ness, and Ta_____omers, who were wise above all others in the land. He spoke with the Loomers, and prayed with them, and they crafted him th_____e returned with th_____anna, an_____m upon the Night Horrors. He tamed them, and drove them into Well of Night in the Marble City, and sealed it. He placed guards around it, armed wit_____cape."

Kyrie thought for long moments, staring at the scroll, and trying not to stare at Agnus Dei and Gloriae. He could feel both girls watching him, and his cheeks burned, and he forced his mind away.

Instead of looking at them, he looked over the fire at Benedictus and Lacrimosa. The two sat holding each other, the firelight orange against them.

"So we know who created the Beams," Kyrie said. "The Loomers of the olden pools, in some realm that starts with a G."

Benedictus nodded. "And we know that a king of Osanna used the Beams. We know his name started with 'T', and ended with 'ite'." He scratched his chin. "We should visit the tombs of Osanna's kings; they stand in a valley a few leagues from Confutatis. We might find answers there."

Kyrie rose to his feet. He could no longer stand sitting there, feeling Gloriae and Agnus Dei staring at him. He could imagine their thoughts: Gloriae thinking of lying with him and having his child, Agnus Dei suspecting and simmering. Kyrie didn't think he could stand their eyes on him one moment longer.

"Great," he said, brushing dust off his pants. "We go back to Osanna. I'm up for a journey. We'll find out who this king is, and research him, and see how he found the Beams."

Benedictus gave Kyrie a long, hard stare, eyes narrowed. "Kid, you okay? You look like a scorpion bit your backside."

"I'm hot by the fire," Kyrie said. "I'm going for a walk."

Without waiting for a reply, he turned and left the campfire. He walked past toppled bricks and earth, and felt the others looking at him. He didn't care. His eyes burned, and he wanted to be alone. Dust rose under his boots, and he clutched the hilt of his dagger. Soon he entered a copse of burned birches. Most had fallen, but some still stood, blackened. Kyrie's boots stepped around arrowheads, shattered blades, and a helmet with a skull still inside. He knew that the ash and dirt hid many more memories of the war.

Soon he came to an old wall and tower. Only about ten feet of the tower remained; the top part had fallen over, and its bricks lay among the burned trees. The wall too had crumbled, leaving a stretch only several feet long. Around the wall, Kyrie saw the skeleton of a griffin, half buried in earth. Its ribs rose like the teeth of dragons, and Kyrie stared at it. He thought of his childhood in this land, when it had still bloomed with life. He thought of Lanburg Fields, where so many had died around him, where he lay wounded in his blood. He thought of the Lady Mirum finding him, raising him in Fort Sanctus, dying at the hands of Dies Irae and Gloriae.

And he thought of Agnus Dei. When he'd met her, his life seemed good again, full of promise. In her eyes, he found a future, a meaning to his survival.

"I love you, Agnus Dei," he said softly. "I'm sorry."

Her voice spoke behind him. "I love you too, Kyrie."

He turned to see her standing by the toppled wall, her sword sheathed. Her eyes were moist, her hair dishevelled. He walked toward her, but she raised her hand, as if to hold him back.

"Agnus Dei, I--"

"Tell me it's not true," she said. "Tell me what I suspect is wrong."

Kyrie wanted to lie. It would be so easy to. He could tell her how he'd never slept with Gloriae, tell her it was only a misunderstanding. She would believe him, he knew. And yet he could not bring the words to his lips.

Agnus Dei lowered her head, and a tear streamed down her cheek. "Why, Kyrie? She's my sister."

As Kyrie searched for an answer, Gloriae too stepped from behind the wall. Her golden hair was still down, but she wore her gilded breastplate now, and rested her hand on the hilt of her sword. Her leggings were tattered, her left boot torn, and her cloak muddy.

"Because I forced him to," Gloriae said to her sister.

Agnus Dei snarled, drew her sword, and charged.

Gloriae drew her own sword and parried. The blades clanged and locked.

"You slept with him," Agnus Dei said and snarled.

Gloriae nodded, still holding her blade against the blade of her sister. "Yes."

Agnus Dei pulled her sword back, then attacked again. Gloriae parried. Sparks rose.

Kyrie ran toward them.

"Don't fight!" he said and placed himself between them. He held his hands out, one against Agnus Dei, the other against Gloriae. Both girls shoved him aside, barely acknowledging him. He tripped on a brick, fell, and banged his elbow against a rock.

"I knew you wouldn't change, Gloriae," Agnus Dei said. Tears filled her eyes. "We should have killed you long ago. I will kill you now."

The blades clanged a third time. Gloriae narrowed her eyes, and her cheeks flushed. "Agnus Dei, listen to me. Kyrie loves you. I knew it when I lay with him. And it's still true."

The blades clashed. "So why did you two... you two...." Agnus Dei grunted and sobbed. "It's disgusting."

The blades clanged, raised sparks, and Gloriae kicked. Her foot hit Agnus Dei's shin.

Agnus Dei fell into the dirt, and Gloriae stepped on her wrist, holding the sword down. Agnus Dei tried to kick and struggle, but Gloriae pressed a knee into her chest, pinning her down.

Kyrie stood up and watched them, rubbing his elbow. He wanted to intervene, but knew he shouldn't. He knew he must only watch now, and let the sisters battle it out.

"I seduced him," Gloriae said to her sister, face blank, eyes cold. "I got him drunk, and I seduced him. He had little say in the matter."

"Why?" Agnus Dei demanded, lying pinned below her sister.

"Because he loves you," Gloriae said. "That's why. Because he missed you. Because he talked about you all the time. Because I knew that, as soon as you two reunited, you'd be together forever, you'd get married, you'd have children. I needed his child before that happened."

Agnus Dei snarled. "His child?"

Gloriae nodded. "We need more Vir Requis. There are only three females left, and we need to bear children. All of us. Lacrimosa, you, and me. I saw my chance. I took it. It only happened once, Agnus Dei, and against his will. I wanted to lie with him more times, but he wouldn't let me. If you must hate somebody, hate me, not him. He loves you. He doesn't care for me; you are all he wants."

Agnus Dei's eyes softened, and she loosened the grip on her sword. It fell from her hand.

"Get off me," she said to Gloriae. "I won't hurt you."

Gloriae removed her knee from Agnus Dei's chest and stood up. Agnus Dei also stood and stared at Gloriae, her eyes red and watery.

"Are you pregnant?" she asked.

"I don't know," Gloriae said.

Agnus Dei gave her sister a long, searching stare. Her face was hard. Gloriae stared back, face blank, ash darkening her hair. Finally Agnus Dei spoke again.

"Leave us."

Gloriae nodded, sheathed her sword, and turned to leave. Soon she disappeared behind the ruins.

Agnus Dei turned to Kyrie. His heart pounded when her eyes met his. Those brown eyes seemed full of so many emotions: Kyrie saw love, hate, rage, and fear there. Agnus Dei trembled. He walked toward her and embraced her.

"I'm sorry," he said.

She squirmed, trying to free herself. "Don't touch me. I can only imagine you touching her."

He kissed a tear off her cheek. "I know. I hate myself for it. I was stupid. I was wrong. Please forgive me."

She slapped his face. Hard. White light flashed, and stars flew before his eyes.

"Don't you dare kiss me," she said.

He held his burning cheek.

"Agnus Dei--" he began, reaching out toward her.

She brought her knee into his stomach. He doubled over, and she punched him. Pain exploded. He fell to the ground, moaning, the stars swirling before him.

"Agnus Dei, stop--" he said, but felt her grab his hair. She pulled him up, and he groaned, and stood again before her. She backhanded him, knocking him back two steps.

"Kyrie," she said, "if you hurt me again, I'm going to hurt you badly. This was nothing. This was only a taste. If you ever touch another girl, I swear by the stars, I'm going to give you the beating of a lifetime. It would make this one look like a caress."

He cursed, voice hoarse. He felt blood tickle down his chin and a bruise spread under his eye.

"Bloody stars," he managed to say. "Deal, all right? Now do you forgive me?"

She grabbed his face, digging her fingers into his cheeks. Kyrie thought she would hit him again. She snarled, eyes blazing.

"I will never forgive you," she said, "but I still love you."

She kissed him on the lips. He kissed her back, and wrapped his arms around her. She embraced him, and they kissed for a long time among the ruins. Finally they broke apart.

Kyrie took her hand.

"Marry me, Agnus Dei," he said.

She snorted. "Pup, go marry a nightshade."

They walked back to camp, hand in hand.

DIES IRAE

He stood, hands on hips, staring at the wagons. They were large wagons, twenty feet tall and a hundred feet long. Bulls with clawed feet and fire in their nostrils stood tethered to them, backs whipped and maws muzzled. The bulls were impressive beasts-- Dies Irae had once sicced them on Lacrimosa--but today he cared not for the creatures who pulled the wagons. Today he cared for the creatures inside.

"My pets," he whispered and heard them shriek. "My lovelies."

Black cloth draped the wagons, and that cloth fluttered now, and bulged with strange shapes. The shrieks inside the wagons made grass and trees wilt. The nightshades were angry. They would get angrier. A smile spread across Dies Irae's lips. He stepped toward one wagon, grabbed the black curtains, and pulled them open.

Sunlight drenched the nightshades. They screamed. Steam rose from them. They spun and swirled in the wagon, slamming against its steel bars.

"You will stay in the wagon," he told them. He knew they could break the bars if they pleased, or flow between them. His power over them--the power of Osanna's throne--kept them trapped. "You will suffer the light."

They snapped teeth, howling, and began to eat one another. A few began to eat themselves, wispy teeth of mist tearing into their inky bodies. They had blood like steam.

"Had enough?" he asked them.

They screeched, begging for mercy. Dies Irae watched them for several long moments, savoring their pain. Then he closed the curtains. The nightshades squirmed and hissed inside the wagon, hating him but serving him.

"You will learn, my pets, to tolerate sunlight," Dies Irae said. "You will learn to hunt the weredragons by day as by night. You will learn that I am your master, the giver of pain and mercy. You will fly into the sun should I ask it of you."

Dies Irae moved to the next wagon. He drew its curtains and watched, smiling thinly, as these nightshades screeched and hissed too.

"You will soak up the sunlight," he said, "until it is like moonlight upon you."

Dies Irae nodded, waiting long moments before closing the curtains. Sunlight burned them like fire against men, Dies Irae knew. But it would not kill them. It would not stop them. There was only one light, he knew, that could harm these creatures. Only one light that could truly tame them.

And that light Dies Irae kept buried and forever extinguished.

As he watched the third wagon of nightshades rattle, he thought of his daughter.

"Thank you, Gloriae," he whispered, gazing into the west, to Requiem. She flew with the weredragons now. She had betrayed him, stabbed his heart, gone to evil. But she had given him the nightshades. She had done that. "Thank you for my lovelies."

If he ever met Gloriae again, he decided that he would not kill her. He would lock her in the wagons with the nightshades, and allow them to bite her, to rip her soul to shreds, to play with her.

"Then you too, Gloriae, will beg me for mercy. But I will give you none."

He left the wagon and walked between rows of soldiers who stood at attention, fists on their chests. One man, he saw, had a nervous tic. His left eye kept winking. Dies Irae approached him.

"Is that involuntary?" he asked.

"Yes, Comma--" the man began.

Dies Irae swung his left arm, his iron arm, and shattered the man's head. He fell. The other soldiers stood still, not daring to breathe.

"I don't care," Dies Irae said to the body.

He stepped into his tent and shut the curtains behind him. Golden vases, jewelled statues of eagles, and other fineries filled his tent. The girl was there too, sitting on a divan, eyes pleading.

"Please, my lord," she began, tears filling her eyes. "Please, is my brother--"

"Your brother is dead. You'll be dead soon too."

She wept, covering her face with her hands. He grabbed her wrist and pulled her hands free.

"I want to see your face," he said. He leaned down and stared at her. She looked back, trembling. He had found her in the nearby ruins of a village, cowering with her brother in a barn.

"Yes, you look just like her... just like my Gloriae."

She shivered. "My lord, I don't know Gloriae, I--"

He backhanded her. She fell to the floor, bleeding.

"You will suffer, Gloriae, for betraying me," Dies Irae said. "You disobeyed me. You freed the nightshades. You fly with the weredragons."

The girl trembled on the floor. "Please, my lord, I don't know who Gloriae is. My name is Alendra, I... I...." She wept. "I'm only a peasant girl, my lord."

"You are a betrayer, Gloriae," he told her, and when she tried to rise, he beat her down. "You will suffer now."

The nightshades screamed inside him. He could feel their maggots squirm in his wound, the gaping hole of his left eye, the eye Benedictus had taken from him. The light of the maggot eyes burned, painting the girl a blood red. She whimpered and cowered, and Dies Irae laughed. The smoke of nightshades danced around his fingertips as he grabbed her, shook her, hurt her.

He soon stood above her dead body. Blackness like ink coiled in the air around him, and he laughed.

LACRIMOSA

From the distance, Lacrimosa could hear the youths fighting. She could not make out the words--only raised voices, clanking steel, and shouts. She stood up to rush over, to find the young ones and break them up.   Benedictus also stood up and put a hand on her shoulder.

"Let them settle their conflicts," he said, voice soft. The firelight painted his face orange and gold.

Lacrimosa shook her head in frustration. "They're fighting, Ben."

He nodded. "Let them fight. They're young, angry, and strong. All three of them are. They need to clash and lock horns; that's their way. They'll blow off steam, even if they bash one another around a bit."

Lacrimosa sighed. "Maybe you're right. Were you and I ever so young and angry?"

They sat down again by the fire. Lacrimosa leaned against her husband, and Benedictus placed his arm around her. They watched the firelight crackle among the ruins, lighting the smashed statues and burned trees.

"We were that young once, yes," he said. "But you were never angry. You were strong too, and you're strong now. But yours is the strength of water. Kyrie and Agnus Dei are fire. Gloriae is ice."

"And what are you, Ben?" she asked him.

He let out a long, deep sigh and stared into the flames in silence. Finally he said, "I am nothing now but old memories and pain."

She played with his hair, black streaked with gray. "Something weighs heavy on you," she said.

He nodded but said nothing. Lacrimosa wished she could ease his pain; she saw it every day in his eyes. She saw the burning of Requiem there, as she saw it around her. She saw Lanburg Fields, and the mountains of bodies, and all those who'd died under his banners. And she saw new pain there today; he had seen something during the past moon, but Lacrimosa knew he needed time to reflect upon it. Maybe he would never speak of it. She kissed his cheek.

"You are strong, my lord, and brave and noble. You are my husband, my king. You are a hero to the young ones; even to Gloriae."

She ran her fingers across his cheek, his skin rough and stubbly. He pulled her closer to him.

"They would fight even as toddlers, the twins," he said. "Do you remember?"

She smiled. "I do. They would fight over dolls, over candies...." She laughed softly. "Do they fight over Kyrie now?"

"That boy was trouble from day one. Do you know, I spoke to him in Lanburg Fields. I blessed him before the battle." Benedictus sighed. "I thought they had all died, Kyrie too. I thought Gloriae was gone from us forever. I thought Agnus Dei would die under the mountain. We've cheated death for so long, Lacrimosa. How much longer can we flee?"

She took his hands in hers. His hands were so large and rough; hers looked tiny and white atop them.

"We're done fleeing," she said. "The griffins are our allies; they'll fight with us when the time comes. And we'll find the Beams. We'll seal the nightshades and defeat Dies Irae."

"And what then?" he asked. "Even with Irae dead, another will replace him. One of his lieutenants will inherit the throne, and be as cruel, as heartless, as ceaseless as Irae was in hunting us."

A voice came from across the fire.

"No," spoke Gloriae. "I will sit upon the Ivory Throne then."

Lacrimosa saw her daughter step from behind burned trees. The girl's golden hair cascaded across her shoulders, strewn with ash. Her leggings were torn, her boots muddy, her armor's glint dulled. And yet she walked nobly, and her eyes stared with green ice.

"Daughter," Lacrimosa said. "We cannot ask this of you. You belong with us now, here in Requiem."

Gloriae stood by the fire, hand on the hilt of her sword. "I am Vir Requis, yes. My loyalty is now to my true father, King Benedictus. We will rebuild this land. I promise it. And I will not watch an heir to Dies Irae destroy it again. The people of Osanna know me. They have known me for years as Dies Irae's daughter, as second-in-command of their empire. If we kill Dies Irae, they will accept me as their ruler. As empress of Osanna, I will forge peace with Requiem, and help her grow."

Lacrimosa felt a twist in her heart, and she winced. For so many years, Gloriae had lived away from her, a ruler of Osanna in marble palaces. Had she finally reclaimed her daughter only to lose her again? She stood up, walked to Gloriae, and hugged her. At first Gloriae only stood stiffly. Finally, hesitantly, she placed her arms around her mother.

A shriek rose.

Lacrimosa and Gloriae broke apart and drew their blades. Benedictus leaped up, raising his crossbow.

The shriek sounded again.

A nightshade.

"But it's not night yet," Lacrimosa whispered, looking from side to side.

Kyrie and Agnus Dei came running toward them, weapons drawn. Their eyes were wide with fear.

"Behind us!" Agnus Dei cried. "Ten nightshades in the daylight. They saw us." She jumped over a fallen column, shifted into a red dragon, and flew. Kyrie became a blue dragon and took flight beside her.

Lacrimosa touched Gloriae's cheek. "Shift now; you can do it. I'll help you fly."

Soon the five Vir Requis flew as dragons, the ruins far beneath them. When Lacrimosa looked over her shoulder, she saw ten nightshades rise from the ruins like pillars of smoke. The beasts screamed and chased them.

"I thought nightshades only came out at night!" Lacrimosa shouted in the roaring wind.

Gloriae, now a golden dragon, narrowed her eyes and snarled. "Dies Irae changed them--bred them with other beasts, or tortured them to overcome their fear of sunlight."

When Lacrimosa looked again, the nightshades were closer. They swirled, dispersed, collected themselves again, and moved like ink in water. Their eyes glinted and mocked her. Their howls rose, and Lacrimosa realized that she could hear voices in those howls.

"Lacrimosa...," they screeched. "Lacrimosa, return to me...."

She realized it was Dies Irae speaking through them, his voice broken into a million hisses rising together. She shivered.

"Let's see if they still like dragonfire," she said, turned her head, and blew flames at them.

They howled. The other Vir Requis also turned to blow fire, and the flames covered the nightshades.

The nightshades screamed so loudly, what ruins remained standing below collapsed. They emerged from the inferno, teeth drawn, as if the fire only enraged them. The Vir Requis kept flying.

"Into those storm clouds!" Benedictus said, pointing. The clouds were leagues away, a tornado spinning beneath them. Lacrimosa didn't know if they'd reach them in time, but she nodded. They flew, the nightshades screaming behind. Lacrimosa felt them tug at her soul, and she squinted, howled, and blew fire at them.

Kyrie was lagging. His wings stilled, and his eyes rolled back. A nightshade flew behind him, reaching out tendrils of smoke to Kyrie's tail.

Lacrimosa raced toward Kyrie, grabbed him, and shot fire at the nightshade. It screeched, blinded, and Lacrimosa caught Kyrie. She slapped him hard with her wing. He gasped as if jostled from sleep, narrowed his eyes, and flew again.

A nightshade wrapped itself around Benedictus's leg. He roared fire at it, and flapped his wings, but could not free himself. Gloriae raced toward him, and blew fire at the nightshade.

"I am your mistress, Gloriae of Osanna!" she screamed. "You will leave this place."

The nightshades laughed mockingly. The Vir Requis shot more flames, and Benedictus managed to free himself. They kept flying. Lacrimosa tried to blow more fire behind her, to blind to nightshades, but only sparks left her mouth.

"My fire is low!" she shouted. The others seemed in the same predicament. When they blew, only small flames left their mouths. They would need rest and food to rebuild the fires inside them.

"We're almost at the clouds," Benedictus shouted over the wind and screeching nightshades. "We'll lose them in the storm."

With the nightshades shrieking and tugging at them, the Vir Requis shot into the storm.

Rain and wind lashed Lacrimosa. She screamed, but her voice was lost. Lightning flashed. She could barely keep her eyes open. She flapped her wings, but could not move forward. Wind caught her, she spun, righted herself, and strained to keep flying.

"Ben!" she shouted.

She could see him just ahead, and then winds caught him, and he flew backwards and spun. Lightning flashed again. The rain felt like a million daggers. The sound was deafening. Nightshades flew around her, screeching, spinning, tossed around like rags. Lacrimosa saw a flash of golden scales ahead.

"Gloriae!" she called, but heard no answer.

She flapped her wings, snarled, and tried to reach her daughter.

That was when she saw the tornado.

It spun before her, horrible in its sound and fury. It looked to Lacrimosa like a great nightshade, or like the terror in her heart, the pain that ran between her and her countless kin beyond the stars. It spun toward her, and Lacrimosa shut her eyes. She flew in the roar, wings useless, and Lacrimosa saw before her silver harps, and flowers on marble tiles, and sunlight between birches. She floated as on clouds, and a smile found her lips.

"Daughters," she said with a smile, reaching out her arms, and the toddlers ran into her embrace. They laughed, sunlight upon them, clad in silk, flowers in their hair. The marble columns rose around them, and hills of trees bloomed.

Lightning rent the world

Thunder boomed.

She opened her eyes, and saw rain, and saw nightshades screeching and fleeing. Lacrimosa flapped her wings, eyes stinging, the wind and rain and memories crashing against her.

"Lacrimosa!" cried a distance voice, barely audible. A black shape flew toward her, burly, reaching out.

"Ben!" she shouted.

Their claws touched, and then the storm blew them apart. Nightshades swirled around them, dispersing into wisps. The tornado sucked up some of the creatures. Others it tossed aside. Lacrimosa managed to grab Benedictus, and she clung to him. The storm spun them and finally cast them out into a world of soft rain, grumbling thunder, and rainbows.

Lacrimosa looked around her. She saw the tornado a league away, moving westward and away from her. Nightshades spun within it. One nightshade broke free and flew toward her. Lacrimosa and Benedictus blew fire at it, the last flames they could muster. Alone, the nightshade dared not face the firelight. It screeched and fled.

"Where are the young ones?" Lacrimosa shouted. The wind was still roaring.

Benedictus pointed. "I see Kyrie and Agnus Dei."

The blue and red dragon came flying from above. They had flown above the storm, and soon hovered by Benedictus and Agnus Dei.

"Where's Gloriae?" Lacrimosa asked, looking around frantically.

"Gloriae!" Agnus Dei called, also searching.

Lacrimosa flew back toward the storm, seeking golden scales. The others flew around her, also seeking. Few nightshades remained. What nightshades attacked them, they beat back with firelight. The tornado was retreating rapidly, leaving a land of puddles and shattered trees. Was it taking Gloriae with it?

"Gloriae!" Lacrimosa shouted. "Can you hear me?"

She flew, scanning the ruins below, and her eyes caught a glint of gold. She flew closer and gasped. A golden dragon lay upon a burned tree below, legs limp, head tilted back.

"Gloriae!" Lacrimosa called and dived. The other dragons dived with her. Lacrimosa reached Gloriae first. She hovered above her daughter, fear claiming her. Was Gloriae, only recently returned to her, taken from her again?

No. Gloriae was alive. Her left wing moved, and her eyes fluttered.

"Mother," the girl whispered.

Lacrimosa touched her daughter's cheek. "I'm here, Gloriae, I'm here, you're fine now."

Benedictus helped lift Gloriae from the burned tree, and they placed her on the ground.

Gloriae blinked, and her lips opened and closed several times before she could speak. "I fell. I'm... I'm not good at flying."

When Lacrimosa examined her daughter for wounds, she found bruises and scrapes, and an ugly gash along her thigh, but no broken bones. Soon Gloriae was able to stand, gingerly test her limbs, and walk.

Benedictus scanned the skies. "The nightshades are gone for now. But they'll be back soon. Shift into human form, everyone. We'll be harder to spot. Those bastards still hate firelight, but they now tolerate the sun."

They turned human again, and Lacrimosa saw that bruises covered Gloriae, and blood seeped from her thigh. She tried to tend to the wound, but Gloriae held her back, eyes icy.

"I'm fine," the girl said. "I've suffered worse."

Lacrimosa shivered. She knew when Gloriae had suffered worse wounds; it had been when she still served Dies Irae, and Kyrie had gored her with his horn. She shoved the thought aside.

When she turned to the others, she saw that Kyrie too was battered. A bruise was spreading beneath his eye. His lip was fat and cracked. He clutched his side, as if he'd been hurt there too.

"Kyrie, did you also fall?" she asked in concern.

Kyrie glanced at Agnus Dei, who shot him a venomous stare.

"Uh, yeah," Kyrie said, looking away from Agnus Dei. "I also fell."

"Fell onto Agnus Dei's fist, maybe," Benedictus muttered to himself.

Agnus Dei glared at him and clenched those fists. "Did you say something, Father?"

"Yeah," he said, voice gruff. "I said let's go. We walk from here. We go to Osanna, and we seek the tombs of her kings."

They walked through the puddles, mud, and ruins, tattered and bruised, heading into the east.

BENEDICTUS

They travelled off road. The forests of Osanna lay wilted. The trees were white and shrivelled up, like the limbs of snowbeasts. Most had fallen over, spreading white ash across the land.

"There, in the distance," Benedictus said. "Two of them."

The others muttered and lay down, pulled cloaks over them, and lay still. Leafy branches, mud, and thorns covered their cloaks, sewn and fastened with string and pins. Soon the Vir Requis appeared as nothing but mounds of leaf and earth.

The nightshades screeched above. Benedictus lay under his cloak, still, barely daring to breathe. Finally the shrieks disappeared into the distance, and he stood up. The others also stood, looked at one another uneasily, and resumed walking.

"There are more every day," Kyrie said.

Benedictus nodded. "And they're larger, too. Irae is changing them. I don't know how, but he is. He's making them stronger, faster, tougher. Next time they attack, firelight won't daunt them."

Kyrie shuddered. "How is he doing that?"

"I don't know. But I'm hoping he doesn't know about the Beams. They're our last hope."

They continued to walk, not speaking, their boots rustling the dirt and snapping branches. It was their twentieth day of walking since leaving Requiem's ruins.

Twenty days of hiding under cloaks, of seeing the ruin of the world, Benedictus thought. They had seen barely any life. Few animals remained. People were even fewer. Sometimes they saw armored soldiers travelling the roads, even several knights on horseback.

Mostly they saw nothing but toppled forts, bodies, and devastation.

Benedictus looked at Lacrimosa. She walked by his side, leaves in her pale hair. Her lavender eyes seemed so large, bottomless pools of sadness. He took her hand.

"I'm sorry," he said to her.

She looked at him. "For what?"

The young ones walked behind, speaking in hushed voices; they could not hear.

"I'm sorry that you must walk like this, Lacrimosa. Wearing leaves and dirt. Eating old rations and whatever skinny beasts we can hunt. You should be wearing silk, and dining on fine foods, and living in a palace."

She laughed softly. "Is that who you think I am? A pampered queen? Ben. I'm your wife. I'm your love, and you are mine. I would walk by you even through the tunnels of the Abyss."

He lowered his head. "You are strong, and brave, and I love you. But I've failed." He looked behind him at his daughters. "I've failed them."

Lacrimosa narrowed her eyes. "You are keeping them alive. You are leading them."

Benedictus looked ahead, to the leagues of rolling ruin, the wilted trees, the toppled walls, the animals that lay rotting on the earth. "I could have killed Dies Irae at Lanburg Fields. I pitied him. I let him live. I could have killed him under the mountain, but I was not strong enough. I'm weak, Lacrimosa. I don't know what strength I still have."

She squeezed his hand. "I know, Ben. We'll do it together. We'll find the Beams. We'll make the world safe for the young ones. I'm with you, now and always."

Benedictus turned to look at the youths.

Agnus Dei walked with a crossbow on one hip, a sword on the other. Her brown eyes were narrowed, forever scanning the world for a fight. Benedictus knew that among the youths, she was the most like him. She had his dark eyes, the black curls of his hair, the fire in her belly. Dies Irae thought she was his, that he had fathered the twins when raping Lacrimosa. When Benedictus looked into Agnus Dei's brown, strong eyes, he knew that was false. He knew she was of his blood.

Next Benedictus looked at Gloriae, and he sighed. Gloriae was twin to Agnus Dei, but she looked more like Lacrimosa. She was light like her mother, of fair hair, of pale skin. But there was none of Lacrimosa's frailty to her. This one was strong like her sister, but her strength was of ice rather than fire, a strength Dies Irae had forged into her. *She's still a stranger to me,* Benedictus thought. He wanted to earn her love, but she rarely spoke to him, and when she looked upon him, there was no feeling in her eyes, only that ice.

Benedictus then looked at Kyrie, and sighed again. Kyrie walked with muddy clothes, and his shock of yellow hair was unkempt. He held a dagger drawn in each hand. Kyrie Eleison. The son of his fallen lieutenant. The boy Benedictus had sent to die upon Lanburg Fields. But Kyrie was no longer a boy. He was seventeen now, a grown man, a warrior under his banners like Requiem's warriors of old.

"Can I make the world safe for them, Lacrimosa?" he asked.

"I don't know. But you lead them. You inspire them. That is the best you can do for them now. Look, Ben. Beyond those trees. The tombs of Osanna's kings."

Benedictus looked, and saw a valley between the dead trees. The grass was dead, splotchy with patches of snow. The sky was tan and gray. Tombs rose in the valley, the size of temples, hewn of rough bricks, beaten down and smoothed through centuries of rain and snow.

"The Valley of Kings' Glory," Benedictus said. He stopped walking and stared. Years ago, he had visited this place and seen green grass, flowers, and rustling trees. The land was ruined now, but the tombs remained, as they had for millennia. The youths caught up with him, stood at his sides, and stared into the valley. Wind played with their hair.

"A king whose name begins with T," Benedictus said. "His title will end with 'ite'. Our search begins. Let's stay together. Weapons drawn. If the nightshades arrive, hi--"

"Hide in your cloaks, pretend to be mounds of dirt, we know the drill," Agnus Dei said. "You say that once an hour, Father."

They walked into the valley, crossbows and blades in hand. The wind moaned. Snow began to fall, the flakes clinging to their hair and clothes. They approached the closest tomb, a monolith of rough bricks. Large as a castle, it was shaped like a griffin. The griffin's beak had fallen years ago, and now lay at its talons. Those stone talons rose taller than a house, dead grass rustling between them. A stone door stood at the griffin's breast. Letters were engraved into it, filled with gold.

The letters were in Old High Speech, and Benedictus read them out loud. "Here lies King Tenathax the Blessed, Defeater of Gol, Son of Tarax the Red. May the Earth God protect his soul."

Below the golden letters, in smaller words, appeared the story of Tenathax's life, a tale of battles won and temples built.

"Not our guy," Kyrie said. "His name starts the right way, but ends wrong." He scanned the smaller letters. "And it says nothing here about any Beams or Loomers. Just talk of him defeating that Gol place."

Benedictus nodded. "Let's keep looking."

They left the towering griffin of stone, and walked along the valley, until they reached a tomb shaped like a warrior. The stone warrior stood as tall as a palace. Its base alone was thirty feet tall.

They found a stone door there too, also engraved with golden letters. Again, Benedictus read aloud.

"Here lies King Tarax the Young, Defeater of Fidelium, son of Talin the White. May the Earth God bless his soul."

Here too did smaller words appear below the main epitaph, telling the story of Tarax defeating the kings of Fidelium, and destroying their temples and palaces, and annexing their realm to Osanna.

Kyrie rolled his eyes. "Every King of Osanna was named Tarax the Something, or Talin the Whatever, son of Taras the Who Cares."

Gloriae spoke softly, cheeks pink in the cold. "All but Dies Irae."

Benedictus pointed at the letters. "Look at our friend King Tarax again. See who his father was? Talin the White. Could that be the king we're looking for?"

Agnus Dei, snow in her hair, unrolled the scroll from Requiem's tunnels. She showed them the passage again.

"In the days of the Night Horrors, King T_____ite journeyed to the southern realms of G____nd sought the Loomers o_____olden pools."

Agnus Dei rolled up the scroll again. She nodded. "Talin the White, yes. Father of King Tarax. Let's find his tomb."

They explored the valley for several hours, moving from tomb to tomb. The oldest tombs were shaped as pyramids, their rocks beaten down, their letters almost effaced. Finally they found a tomb labelled "Talin the White". It was one of the simpler tombs. It stood only three stories tall, surrounded by columns engraved with dragons.

Kyrie and Agnus Dei jumped up and down. "Finally."

Benedictus examined the letters engraved into this tomb. "King Talin III, known as the White."

Smaller letters were engraved beneath his name. They all leaned in, and this time, Gloriae read them out loud.

"Born in the year 476. Rose to the throne in 482. Died in the year 489. His reign was peaceful and prosperous."

Gloriae leaned back and raised her eyebrow. "The king who tamed the Nightshades, the hero from the book, was a child? He died in childhood after a peaceful reign? That doesn't make sense."

Kyrie moaned. "Stars. We've been searching this graveyard for hours. I'm tired. Will we find no king to help us?"

Benedictus grunted. "I'm tired too, kid. Let's take a break. We'll eat what food we have."

They camped below Talin III's tomb and unpacked their supplies. They didn't have much. Lacrimosa had found some mushrooms a while back. Agnus Dei had managed to shoot two rabbits. They had pilfered turnips and some ale from a roadside tavern. They shared the food and drink, which left them still hungry and thirsty, and considered.

"We came here for nothing," Kyrie said.

Benedictus shook his head. "No, kid. We just have to go older. We've been exploring the newer tombs."

Kyrie snickered so loudly, a bit of turnip flew from his mouth. He gestured at Talin III's resting place. "New tombs? Benedictus, this is from the year 489. That was...." He counted on his fingers. "2,756 years ago."

Benedictus nodded. "2,766, actually. But our friend here is the third Talin the White. I say we find his father and grandfather."

They stood up, bellies still rumbling with hunger and throats still parched, and kept moving down the valley. Soon they reached tombs so old, they could have been mistaken for hills of scattered rocks. These tombs were mostly buried in the earth, only their roofs showing. Dead grass rustled around them.

Benedictus knelt by a stone roof which rose from earth, grass, and snow. He dug around it, tossing back dirt and snow, until he excavated the top of a doorway.

"Here, look," he said.

Faded letters appeared on the stone door. Unlike the other tombs, no gold covered these letters, and they were roughly hewn.

"King Talin the White," Benedictus read. "Wielder of Beams."

Agnus Dei leaned against the structure. "Wielder of Beans?" she asked. "Because if he has any beans around here, I'm still hungry."

Benedictus glared at her. "Agnus Dei, show more respect among the tombs of the dead. We finally found our man, and you can only make a joke? Let's dig."

They dug in the earth, until they revealed more of the doorway. However, no more letters appeared there, as had on the other tombs. The door was bare.

"Great," Agnus Dei said. "All the other kings had bloody epics written on their doorways. We finally find a match, and his door just has his name on it. Just perfect."

Benedictus nodded. "In the Gray Age, when Talin the White ruled, the tombs were simpler. It is only in later years that the kings of Osanna built great, towering tombs in the shapes of beasts and warriors, and gilded letters on their doorways. Let's step inside. We'll find more answers within."

Agnus Dei raised an eyebrow. "Are you sure, Father? Do you remember what happened last time we entered a mausoleum? You almost got a skeleton as a son-in-law."

Benedictus grunted. "Sometimes I think I'd prefer the skeleton to Kyrie."

A screech sounded above. The Vir Requis spun around to see ten nightshades in the distance.

"Into the tomb!" Benedictus hissed. "Before they see us."

He dug frantically, revealing the rest of the door. The nightshades shrieked, moving closer. The youths snarled.

"Don't shift!" Benedictus whispered through strained jaws. "They haven't seen us yet."

He leaned against the doorway and pushed. It didn't budge. Kyrie added his weight, they grunted and strained, and finally the door creaked. It took the twins to help too, and the door inched its way open.

"In, quickly!"

They scurried into the tomb. It was dank, cold, and dark. The nightshades screamed outside, louder now. Soon Benedictus saw their shadows in the sky outside.

"Did they see us?" Lacrimosa whispered, clinging to his arm.

Benedictus shook his head. "I don't think so. Their eyes must be weak in the day. We're safe."

Breathing out shakily, he surveyed the tomb. The chamber held jewelled swords, golden vases, a suit of armor, and stone chests full of gems. Golden coins covered the floor.

Agnus Dei whistled. "Nice little place Talin's got here. But where's the king himself?"

Lacrimosa pointed at a second doorway in the back of the chamber. "In there."

Benedictus stepped toward the doorway and pushed it.

Something screamed.

The doorway crashed open, and a creature leaped at him.

Benedictus fell back and raised his sword. The blade hit rusty rings of steel, bolts, and spinning wheels. It shattered, and a shard scratched his arm.

"Father!" Agnus Dei cried. Benedictus heard her crossbow fire. He saw its quarrel slam into the creature, but it ricocheted off its metallic face. The creature's hands were spinning blades, reaching for Benedictus.

He rolled aside, and one of the spinning blades cut his shoulder. He grunted and kicked, and his leg hit the creature's ribs, which seemed made of bronze. The bronze was old, green and tarnished, and it shattered. The creature leaned back and screeched, a sound like metal gears.

The other Vir Requis were stabbing it, but blades seemed not to hurt it.

"Move back!" Benedictus roared. The others stepped back, and for the first time, Benedictus saw the creature clearly. It looked like a skeleton made of metal. Its body was all gears, wheels, rusty bones. Its eyes burned with firelight. It swung its arm, and a blade flew from its hand. Lacrimosa ducked, and the blade nearly cut her.

Benedictus kicked again, hitting the creature's bronze skull. The skull shattered, raining rust. The creature tried to attack again, but Benedictus kicked its remaining ribs. They shattered, revealing a pumping heart of leather. Benedictus stabbed the heart with his dagger. The leather burst and spilled hot, red blood.

The creature twitched, then leaned over, dead. Benedictus noticed that chains bound it to the doorway.

"What the abyss was that?" Kyrie said, panting.

"A machine," Benedictus said. "Built of elder knowledge now passed from the world."

Kyrie shuddered. "And a good thing, that is."

Benedictus grunted and examined his wound. It was ugly, and full of rust, but he'd worry about it later. He kicked the metal creature aside. It shattered into pieces that littered the floor. Beyond the doorway, a staircase led down into blackness.

"I'll go take a look," Benedictus said. "If it's safe, I'll call you down."

"Ben, I'll go with you," Lacrimosa said.

He shook his head. "No. In case there are more of these machines. Stay here, all of you."

Not waiting for an answer, he stepped downstairs into the darkness. The stairway was thin, and Benedictus placed his hand against the wall.

The stairway led to small chamber. There wasn't much light, and Benedictus lit his lamp with what oil remained. He saw several more mechanical skeletons, but they lay broken on the floor, rusting. Between them lay a sarcophagus shaped like a king with a long beard. The stone king held a stone shield and sword.

"King Talin is down here," he called up the stairway. "Come take a look."

The other Vir Requis stepped down. They crowded around the sarcophagus. Benedictus brushed dust and cobwebs off, and found letters engraved onto the stone shield.

Agnus Dei, leaning over the shield beside him, gasped.

"It's the text from the scroll!" she said. "Only all the letters are here now."

She unrolled the scroll from the tunnels below Requiem. She compared them side by side and nodded. They all leaned over the shield, and Agnus Dei read the words aloud.

"In the days of the Night Horrors, King Talin the White journeyed to the southern realms of Gol, and sought the Loomers of the golden pools. The Night Horrors stole the souls of Osanna, and cast them into the darkness, and Talin the White sought the counsel of the Loomers, who were wise above all others in the land. He spoke with the Loomers, and prayed with them, and they crafted him the Beams. Talin the White returned with the Beams to Osanna, and shone them upon the Night

Horrors. He tamed them, and drove them into Well of Night in Confutatis, and sealed it. He placed guards around it, armed with Beams, so the Night Horrors can nevermore escape."

For a moment, they all stood in silence, considering the words. Benedictus stared into the stone eyes of the king, trying to imagine him fighting the nightshades, those same nightshades that now screeched outside the tomb. Finally Benedictus noticed that the others were all looking at him, waiting for him to speak. He scratched his chin.

"The Beams are from Gol," he said. "I've studied many maps, but seen no realm called Gol. The first tomb we saw, the one shaped as a griffin. It spoke of Gol; King Tenathax defeated it. Gol might no longer exist."

Kyrie tapped his cheek. "Gol... I wonder if it's related to Gilnor. We had a few maps of Osanna back at Fort Sanctus. I used to read them for fun; there wasn't much else to read. Gilnor lies to the southwest. It's nothing but swamps."

Lacrimosa nodded. Dust, rust, and cobwebs filled her hair. "I remember a song of Gilnor. Bards would sing of it in the halls of Requiem. I haven't heard the song in years, but... I remember. The lyrics spoke of the swamps of Gilnor. They said that once, thousands of years ago, a mythical kingdom stood there, a land of silver towers and bridges. The song spoke of creatures of darkness destroying the silver towers, and--"

Kyrie jumped and slapped the stone shield. "Creatures of darkness!" he repeated. "Night Horrors. Nightshades. These are all different names for those things that hunt us. They must have destroyed that kingdom of silver towers, which stood where Gilnor's swamps are. I bet you Gol was that ancient kingdom."

Benedictus grumbled. "Stop your jumping up and down, kid. Some old song of some silver towers doesn't mean anything."

Kyrie jumped again, as if in spite. "It means everything. Gilnor must mean Gol. You know the land of Tiranor?"

Benedictus nodded. "It lies far south, near the deserts."

"Well," Kyrie said, "the word 'Tira' used to mean 'fortress' in Old High Speech. Thousands of years ago, High Speech was a little different. I know the word 'Tira' from those old maps I told you about. It was written on the maps beside drawings of fortresses. Tiranor, in the south, had many forts in it; they formed a border along the desert. 'Nor' must mean 'land of' in Old High Speech. Tiranor means 'land of forts'. If I'm right, and I'm always right, 'Gilnor' means 'land of Gil'."

Agnus Dei spoke up. "But we're talking about Gol, pup, not Gil."

Kyrie was speaking so quickly now, his tongue could barely keep up. "Yes, but we're still talking about Old High Speech. That's what people used thousands of years ago, right? Old High Speech, when written down, had no vowels. Only High Speech today has vowels. The elders just wrote down consonants; they assumed you'd know how to read them. So the elders would just write 'GL', and figured you'd know how to say it properly. I'd wager people found the old books, maybe a thousand years later, and forgot how to pronounce the place names. They saw 'GL', and just read it 'Gil' instead of 'Gol'. The new name caught on. When people started writing vowels, they wrote it the wrong way. Gol must have become Gil, and Gil became Gilnor. Land of Gol." He took a deep breath. "It all fits."

Benedictus put a hand on Kyrie's shoulder. "Very clever, kid. But Gol was destroyed. Tenathax destroyed it, remember? It said so on his griffin tomb. Gol's a swampland now, and part of Osanna."

Kyrie looked giddy, rolling on the balls of his feet. "You know what? I say that's griffin dung. I bet you Tenathax was a bloody liar. See the text on Talin's shield. The nightshades attacked Gol. You've met our dear friends the nightshades. You know what they're capable of. I bet you the nightshades destroyed Gol, just like they destroyed Osanna. Years later, Tenathax merely had to walk into the ruins, annex them, and claim that he conquered the place in some glorious battle."

"You're assuming a lot, kid."

"I'm reading between the lines. You think Dies Irae is the only king to have glorified himself? They all did it, each and every one of the bastards. But these Loomers... I'm not sure who they are. Survivors of the nightshade attack on Gol, I'd guess. These Loomers found some way to survive in the ruins of Gol--the Beams. Talin must have stolen the Beams from them."

Agnus Dei punched Kyrie's shoulder. "Pup, you're making up half of this."

He shook his head. "Again, I'm reading between the lines. It says here the Loomers gave Talin the Beams. Really? *Really?* I think not. The Loomers lived in nightshade country. They'd never give up the one weapon they had. When the nightshades turned from Gol to Osanna, Talin must have heard of these Loomers surviving, and sought them out, and stole their Beams. And that's how he sealed the nightshades, and there was peace for thousands of years, until our friend Gloriae freed them."

Gloriae glared at him, but said nothing.

Benedictus grunted. "Kyrie, I don't know how you get all that. There are many pieces missing from this puzzle, and I'm not sure you have the right picture."

Kyrie grinned over the sarcophagus. "Well, there's only one way to find out." He began walking up the stairway, paused, and spoke over his shoulder. "Come on! We go to Gilnor. We seek the Loomers."

AGNUS DEI

As they entered the swamps of Gilnor, Agnus Dei couldn't stop glancing at Kyrie and Gloriae.

The mud was knee deep, and Agnus Dei sloshed through it. Kyrie was walking several yards away, mud covering him. He held a dagger in one hand, which he used to cut vines and branches in his way. Gloriae walked beside him, her hair caked with mud from a recent fall, the jewels and gold of her breastplate brown with the stuff. Once more she slipped, and Kyrie caught her. She lingered a moment too long in his arms, Agnus Dei thought, before righting herself and walking again.

Agnus Dei stifled a growl. She told herself that she should love her twin. After all these years, they were reunited; Agnus Dei knew she should feel rejoiceful. But whenever she looked at Gloriae, she wanted to punch her perfect, pretty face.

Lichen brushed Agnus Dei's cheek, and she slapped it aside, and now a growl did escape her lips. She tried not to, but kept imagining Kyrie touching Gloriae, their bodies naked together.

Don't think about it, she told herself. *You promised Kyrie that you still love him.*

Gloriae slipped again, and made a joke to Kyrie, who laughed. Agnus Dei bit her lip. Yes, she might still love the pup. But could she ever love Gloriae now?

Mother came to walk by Agnus Dei. She placed a hand on her shoulder, and when Agnus Dei looked at her, Mother smiled sadly.

"I think if you stare at her any harder, she'll burst into flames," Mother said.

Agnus Dei lowered her head. Kyrie and Gloriae were talking now, too busy with each other to notice the others.

"I know, Mother," Agnus Dei said, still watching the pair. "But I don't trust her. Even now."

Mother placed an arm around her. "She saved your life. When the nightshades grabbed you, it was Gloriae who saved you."

Agnus Dei sighed. The swamp water was deeper now, going up to their waists. "I know. It's just that...."

Mother nodded. "Gloriae and Kyrie."

Agnus Dei looked up at her mother, and saw warmth in the woman's eyes and smile. "Oh, Mother. He's just a pup, I know it, but... he was my pup."

Mother laughed. "I know, sweetness. He still is. The boy is madly in love with you."

"Are you sure he's not in love with Gloriae? Or she with him?"

Mother squeezed Agnus Dei's shoulder and kissed her cheek. "I'm sure. A mother knows these things. Agnus Dei, I don't know what happened between you three, but... try to forgive your sister. Please. We all must forgive one another now. We are all that's left of our race. If we can't live together, we won't survive."

Agnus Dei hugged her mother. "Okay. I'll try. It's hard, but I'll try."

Now that she wasn't staring at Kyrie and Gloriae, she looked closer at Gilnor's swamps. Where were these Loomers? She saw nothing but logs, lichen, trees, water, and more than anything--mud. Herons and frogs seemed to live everywhere. Mice scurried between the trees. Agnus Dei began collecting the frogs, lifting them from logs and lilies, and placing them in her pouch.

"Frog legs for dinner," she mumbled as she lifted a particularly fat one.

Movement ahead caught her eyes, and Agnus Dei stared, hoping to catch a heron for dinner too.

She gasped.

It was not a heron that moved ahead, but a huge eye protruding from the mud. The eye was the size of a mug, topped with scaly skin.

"Uh, guys?" Agnus Dei said. "There's an--"

The creature burst from the mud, roaring.

Agnus Dei shifted at once. She growled at the swamp beast. It looked like an alligator, but was the size of a dragon, fifty feet long and thin. It rushed at her, its teeth like swords.

Agnus Dei spun and lashed her tail. She hit the creature, knocking it into a tree.

The other Vir Requis shifted too. The five dragons surrounded the swamp creature, who howled and snapped its teeth. It lunged at Gloriae.

Gloriae, now a golden dragon, snarled and swiped her claws. Her claws dug into the creature, spilling blood. It screeched and bit Gloriae's shoulder, and she cried in pain.

Father snarled and leaped onto the creature's back. He bit its neck and spat out a chunk of flesh. The creature crashed into the mud, kicked its legs, then lay still.

"Are you all right?" Father asked Gloriae, blood in his mouth.

She nodded and clutched her shoulder. "It only nicked me."

They stood panting for a moment, staring at the dead creature.

"It's some kind of alligator," Agnus Dei said. "But I've never seen one so large."

Gloriae nodded. "And the thing almost r--"

Shrieks shook the swamp, interrupting Gloriae. A dozen other swamp creatures burst from the mud, howled, and charged at the Vir Requis.

Two charged toward Agnus Dei. She blew fire at one, and it screeched and fell back against a tree. The second clawed at her. Agnus Dei dodged the claws and swiped her tail. She drove her tail's spikes into its side, then pulled back, dragging the creature. She slammed it against a tree.

The burned gator charged, smoking. Agnus Dei snarled, and they crashed into each other. The creature snapped its teeth. Agnus Dei held it back with her front legs, and flapped her wings against it. It howled so loudly, Agnus Dei thought it would deafen her. Its drool splashed her. She kicked its belly, and it crashed back. She blew flames at it, and it screeched.

Teeth sank into her shoulder.

Agnus Dei screamed and reached back, digging her claws into the head of another gator. It opened its mouth to roar, and she spun around, and drove her horns into its neck. That stopped its roaring.

She kicked its body down, and looked around wildly. The other Vir Requis had killed all but two gators. The pair growled, whimpered, and sank into the mud. They began swimming away.

Agnus Dei tried to leap at them, but Father held her shoulder.

"Let them flee," he said. "And stay in dragon form. We're hidden here under the trees and moss. If those things return, I'd rather we met them as dragons."

As blood spread through the swamp waters, the five dragons began wading forward. Agnus Dei had no idea where they were going. Father walked at their lead, but she suspected he just moved aimlessly. "Gol" was all the text on the shield had said. As far as Agnus Dei could tell, the swamps of Gilnor spread for dozens of leagues.

"Maybe those gators were the Loomers," Kyrie said, walking beside her. Lichen draped over his scales.

"Don't be stupid, pup," Agnus Dei scolded him, though secretly, she was relieved to see that he now walked beside her, and not by her sister. "Did those look like Loomers to you?"

Hanging moss went into his mouth, and he spat it out. "So you know what Loomers look like now?"

"Well, I reckon that they're... old men."

Kyrie nodded. "Very old, since they crafted the Beams thousands of years ago."

Agnus Dei twisted her claws. "And they probably... have looms."

Kyrie whistled appreciatively. "Agnus Dei, by the stars, you've got it. Old men with looms. Why didn't I think of that?"

She growled and glared at him. "All right, pup, don't get smart. So I don't know what Loomers look like. But I'm pretty damn sure they're not oversized alligators."

He lashed his tail, splashing her with mud. Agnus Dei screamed like one of the gators, lashed her own tail, and splashed him back. He ducked, and the mud hit Gloriae, who gave Agnus Dei an icy stare. Soon Kyrie was slinging more mud, a twinkle in his eye and a smirk on his lips, and Agnus Dei fought back with equal fervor.

"Vir Requis!" Father thundered. "Stop that."

Agnus Dei rolled her eyes and tossed more mud at Kyrie. "Oh, Father, I'm just teaching the pup a lesson."

Kyrie froze and stared over her shoulder. "Uh... Agnus Dei? You might want to listen to your old man."

Agnus Dei frowned; Kyrie was gaping. She turned around slowly, and her mouth fell open.

Agnus Dei had once sneaked away from Mother and visited a town fair, disguised in a cloak and hood. She had seen a stall selling balls of twine. The creatures ahead looked like great balls of twine, the size of barrels, glowing bright blue. Every thread in their forms seemed filled with moonlight. They hovered over the swamp, pulsing, their light reflecting in the water.

"The Loomers," Agnus Dei whispered.

There were seven. Two appeared to be children; they wobbled as they floated, no larger than apples. The Loomers seemed to turn toward Agnus Dei and regard her, though she couldn't be sure; they had no eyes. They nodded, tilting in the air.

They began to vibrate, and a hum grew within them, until the sound formed words.

"We are Loomers. We are elders' light. We are weavers."

Agnus Dei sloshed toward them in the mud. She felt so coarse, dirty, and clumsy compared to these creatures of light.

"Do you know about the Beams?" she asked, panting.

The Loomers nodded again.

"We are Loomers. We are weavers. Our elders wove the Beams of Light. Our elders blinded the Night Horrors."

Agnus Dei couldn't help but laugh, and she fell back into the mud. "We found them! We found the Loomers. Now we can defeat the nightshades."

Tears filled her eyes. Finally, it seemed, their pain was over. Finally they could reclaim the world--for Requiem, for Osanna, for her and her loved ones.

Father approached the Loomers. He bowed his head. "Loomers of the Golden Pools," he said. "I am Benedictus, King of Requiem."

The Loomers flared. Their light turned white and angry, and they crackled and hissed.

"King?" they said, voices like lightning splitting a tree. "King Talin stole our Beams. Our elders were great weavers. Our elders crafted the Beams. Our elders blinded the Night Horrors. King Talin stole from our elders, stole the light of Gol.

We have no love for kings. Have you come to steal from us, King Benedictus?"

Father kept his head bowed. "I seek not to steal from you, wise Loomers. I seek only your aid and wisdom. The Night Horrors have emerged again, and have overrun our lands."

The Loomers flared brighter. They spun so quickly, they appeared as pulsing stars.

"The Night Horrors!" they cried, voices like storm and steam. "The Night Horrors fly again. This is blackness, weavers. This is deep blackness."

Agnus Dei rose to her feet. She sloshed through the mud. "Can you weave us new Beams?" she asked the Loomers. "We need new ones."

Father nodded. "Noble Loomers, we seek knowledge of the Beams."

The Loomers were still spinning, their light flashing across the swamp. "We cannot weave new Beams."

Agnus Dei gasped. "Why not?"

Father touched her shoulder. "Agnus Dei, please, hush." He turned back to the Loomers. "Loomers, please share your knowledge of the Beams. The Night Horrors have covered the northern realms, and we fear they will soon cover the world with their darkness. What more can you tell us? Why can no new Beams be woven?"

The Loomers stopped spinning, and dipped two feet, so that they almost touched the mud. They seemed defeated. Their light dimmed, and Agnus Dei could see the intricate network of their glowing strands.

"We are elders' light," they said, glowing faintly. "The elders lived many seasons ago. The elders wove the Beams. We are elders' light. We have not the wisdom of the old age. We cannot weave new Beams."

Agnus Dei shut her eyes. "So the knowledge of the Beams is lost. Only your ancestors knew how to make them."

The Loomers flared, their light blinding her. "Not all knowledge is lost, youngling. We have knowledge of the old Beams, the Beams of the elder Loomers. The knowledge of weaving them is lost. The Beams still shine."

Gloriae inhaled sharply. Agnus Dei looked at her, and saw that Gloriae's eyes were narrowed, her jaw clenched.

"Loomers," Father said to the beings of light, "where can we find the elders' Beams?"

The Loomers' light dimmed further, until they barely glowed at all. "We do not know. Talin stole them. Talin stole from Elder Loomers."

Gloriae stepped toward them, and spoke for the first time. Her eyes were narrowed to slits. "Loomers, what do the Beams look like?"

The Loomers seemed to regard her, shining their light upon her golden scales. "The elders built golden skulls, and placed the Great Light within them, so that the Beams will shine from the eye sockets, and look upon the world, and tame the Night Horrors."

Gloriae turned to the other Vir Requis. Her eyes seemed haunted, and her wings hung limp at her sides. For a moment she only stared, silent, and Agnus Dei thought she might faint.

Finally Gloriae spoke.

"I know where the Beams are." She winced and covered her eyes with her claws. "Of course. Of course they are there."

Agnus Dei stepped toward her sister and clutched her shoulder. "What? You knew all along?" She shook Gloriae. "Why didn't you tell us? Where are they?"

Gloriae allowed herself to be shaken. She looked at Agnus Dei with wide, pained eyes. "I saw them, but didn't know what they were. The nightshades were sealed in the Well of Night, an abyss in the dungeons of Confutatis. A doorway guards the chamber. There are golden skulls embedded into the doorway, eyes glowing in their sockets. I... I remember looking at them, but... I didn't realize they were the Beams until now."

Agnus Dei laughed and screamed. She turned toward Kyrie and her parents. "Of course! Where else would King Talin put the Beams? Once he sealed the nightshades, he put the Beams near them, so people could use them if the nightshades escaped." She began sloshing through the mud, heading north. "Come on! We go to Confutatis."

BENEDICTUS

They lay on their bellies in human forms. Burned tree branches creaked above them, and their cloaks of leaves, twigs, and mud covered them. Ahead, beyond fallow fields, Benedictus saw the Marble City.

"Confutatis," he whispered.

He stared with narrow eyes. He knew the others were staring too. Here Dies Irae ruled. From here did his nightshades and the shadow of his arm stretch across the land. Benedictus saw thousands of those nightshades over the city, even now in daylight. They screeched, nested on walls, and coiled in the air.

"How do we sneak into the city?" Lacrimosa whispered. Twigs and thorns and dirt covered her cloak. From above, she'd look like a mound of brush and mud. She peeked from her hood at Benedictus, fear in her eyes.

Benedictus watched nightshades swarm over the fields outside Confutatis, as if seeking surviving peasants. The creatures roared and returned to the city, where they landed upon a wall. Men too covered those walls, Benedictus saw. They were too small to see clearly, but their armor glinted in the sun. He estimated there would be hundreds of troops there, maybe thousands, armed with bows and crossbows.

"We can't sneak in," Benedictus said. "We've been watching for hours. Nobody's entered or exited the gates. The city is locked down. Dies Irae is waiting for us."

Agnus Dei growled beside him. "Nightshades? Thousands of soldiers? Dies Irae? Come on. We can take 'em. We'll shift into dragons and burn the bastards."

Gloriae too snarled. "Agreed. Let's attack. Head-on. No more sneaking around. We fly, we burn, we destroy. We kill Dies Irae, grab the Beams, and seal the nightshades."

Hidden under his camouflaged cloak, Kyrie pumped his fist. "Troll dung, yeah! I'm in. We fly at them by surprise. They won't know what hit 'em."

Benedictus scowled at the youths. "No. And that's final. If we fly into Confutatis, we die. There are five of us. There are thousands of nightshades; they'll tear us apart. That is, if they can reach us before those archers' arrows. I see a hundred archers from here, maybe more."

Agnus Dei clenched her fists. "I can take those archers. I'll burn them alive. I'm tired of slinking around. I could use a straight fight."

"Me too," Gloriae said.

"Me too," Kyrie said.

"Me too," Lacrimosa said.

They all turned to face Lacrimosa in shock.

"Mother, are you feeling all right?" Agnus Dei said. "*You* want to fight? You're always on about finding the peaceful solution, of using our brains instead of our brawn, of hiding instead of getting killed. You want to fight now too?"

Benedictus looked at his wife as if she were mad. She stared back at him, jaw tight, chin raised.

"My love," he said to her. "Are you sure? Tell me what you're thinking."

Lacrimosa stared at him, eyes solemn. "Yes. We fight. We charge them head-on. The time for hiding is over. We need those Beams, and an attack on the city is the only way we'll get them. But we won't fly alone." She pulled from her cloak the golden candlestick. Its emeralds glinted. "We fly with the griffins."

Kyrie and Agnus Dei's eyes shone. Gloriae, however, looked worried.

"Mother," she said. "I... I use to ride a griffin. Wouldn't they hate me now?"

Lacrimosa touched Gloriae's shoulder. "We all enslaved the griffins. Requiem and Osanna. They're free to make their choices now. They will fly with us. They will fly to thank me for healing their prince. They will fly to defeat the nightshades and Dies Irae; they hold no love for them. We will summon them. We will fly alongside them, not as their masters, but as their allies. We will charge the city, take the Beams, and defeat the nightshades."

"And face Dies Irae," Benedictus said in a low voice. That was what it all came down to, he thought. Once more, he'd have to face his brother. Dies Irae. The man who'd raped Lacrimosa. The man who'd killed their parents. The man who'd hunted the Vir Requis to near extinction.

Once more, I will meet you in battle, brother, Benedictus thought.

He remembered meeting Dies Irae upon Lanburg Fields, biting off his arm, sparing his life. He remembered duelling Dies Irae in the same place, ten years later, this time taking the man's eye.

This time, only one of us walks away, Benedictus thought. *You or I will die in this battle. We cannot both live.*

The Vir Requis retreated behind the cover of wilted trees, and Lacrimosa placed the candlestick on the ground. She inserted a candle and lit it. It flickered, nearly perished in the wind, and raised blue smoke.

"Did it work?" Agnus Dei whispered.

Nobody answered. The candle kept burning. They watched silently, until the candle began to gutter, its last drops of wax dripping. Benedictus lowered his head. He wasn't sure what he'd expected. A flash of light? The roar of griffins?

The flame gave a last flicker, then died.

The wick hissed, and the blue smoke rose. It curled, dispersed, then regrouped into the shape of a tiny griffin. The griffin of blue smoke opened its beak, flapped its wings, and flew away.

"It works," Benedictus whispered. "Aid has been summoned."

He stood up, collected his belongings, and led the others deeper into the wilted woods. He walked until they found a rocky slope that led to a stream. They climbed down, and washed their clothes, and bathed. Dead trees reached over them, their branches like knobby fingers. Three cloven shields, several copper coins, and the bladeless hilt of a sword lay on the stream's bank. A battle had been fought here.

"We wait here," Benedictus said. "Stay under cover of the trees. Stay with your camouflaged cloaks over you. Do not speak loudly, do not light fires, and do not shift."

They nodded, and for once the youths didn't argue.

"Good," Benedictus said. "Kyrie, I have a task for you. I saw an abandoned, smashed farmhouse a distance back. Go see if they have any food. No hunting. I dare not risk a fire. Get us bread, fruit, vegetables, dry meats."

Kyrie nodded, drew his sword, and headed off between the trees.

Benedictus turned to the twins. "Gloriae and Agnus Dei, I have a task for you too." He pointed between the trees. "See that toppled fort?"

Gloriae nodded. "It still stood last year. The nightshades toppled it. It looks abandoned now."

Benedictus nodded. "See if you can find new quarrels for our crossbows. If soldiers chance upon our camp, I'd rather we kill them with quarrel than roaring fire."

The twins drew their blades, nodded, and soon disappeared between the trees.

Once the youths were beyond earshot, Lacrimosa laughed softly, and touched Benedictus's arm. The sunlight danced in her eyes and smile.

"You're good at finding us quiet time."

He couldn't help but smile. "I do what I can." He embraced and kissed his wife. "Lacrimosa, you're as beautiful as the day I met you. I don't tell you that enough."

She touched his cheek. "I remember that day. I was fifteen. It was my debut. We danced in the hall of your father--I, the daughter of nobility, and you, my prince. All knew that we would marry."

He held her, and they swayed as if dancing again in those marble halls.

"I was too old for you," he said. "And I'm too old for you now. You're still young and beautiful, Lacrimosa. And I'm aging. And I'm tired. You've deserved a better life."

She kissed his lips. "You've given me the life I wanted. A life by your side. A mother to your children. I could ask for no more. We will rebuild that hall, Ben. We will dance there again, as we did twenty years ago."

He cupped her chin in his hand, and kissed her again. She looked into his eyes, and her beauty pierced him. Her skin was fair, smooth, white as snow. Her eyes were lavender pools. He streamed her hair between his fingers. Those fingers were so coarse, calloused, and her hair was like silk, a blond so pale it was almost white. They kissed again, her arms around him.

"I would make love to you," he said, "a final time."

She ran her fingers down his cheek. "We will make love many more times, my lord."

He held her. "I don't know if we return from this flight. But let us live for this moment. Let us fly for this memory."

They lay on their cloaks by the water, and Benedictus undressed his wife slowly, marvelling at her pale skin, her slim body that was bruised and scarred from all her battles. He kissed her, and held her, and lay with her by the water.

"I love you forever," he whispered to her. "I will be with you forever, if not in this life, then in the halls of our forefathers beyond the stars."

When the youths returned, supplies in their hands, Benedictus and Lacrimosa were sitting by the water, holding each other.

"Here--quarrels," Gloriae said, and spilled them onto the dirt.

"A string of sausages, apples, and two cabbages that aren't too moldy," Kyrie said, and placed the food on a boulder.

"You're getting it dirty, pup," Agnus Dei said and shoved him. He glared at her, and dumped dirt down her shirt, and she growled and leaped at him. Soon Gloriae joined the fray, laughing as she tried to separate the two.

Benedictus watched the youths, and he smiled. It was so rare to hear Gloriae laugh.

"Her laughter is beautiful," he said to Lacrimosa. "Our daughters are beautiful."

He held his wife close. She leaned her head against his shoulder, and they sat watching the young ones, waiting for the griffins.

DIES IRAE

He hovered over his throne, wreathed in nightshades. They
flowed around him, through him, inside him. He could see
through their eyes, the multitudes of them that covered the land.
He saw the weredragons cowering outside the city, covered in leaf
and filth. He saw them peeking, whispering, fearing him.

"Let us fly to him, master." The nightshades hissed, flowing
into his ears.

Dies Irae shook his head. He patted the nightshade that
flowed by his right arm. "No, my pets, my lovelies. Let them fly
here. Let them crash upon my walls and towers."

The nightshades screeched, and he patted them, soothed
them, cooed to them.

"Let us fly to them, master," they begged. "Let us suck
their bodies dry."

Dies Irae shook his head. "They are like rats, my pets.
They run. They flee. They hide. If you chase them, they will
scurry into holes. Wait, my lovelies. They will come to me. They
will try to kill me; they've been trying for years. When they fly to
our city, we will be ready."

A knock came at the doors of his hall, and Dies Irae raised
his eyes.

"Ah," he said, "your dinner has arrived." He raised his
voice. "Enter my hall!"

The doors creaked open, and soldiers stepped in, clad in
mail and bearing axes. They dragged peasants on chains. Dies
Irae saw old women, young mothers holding babies, and a few
scrawny men. When they saw the nightshades, the peasants' eyes

widened, and a few whimpered. The nightshades screamed, writhed, and licked their lips with tongues of smoke.

"The nightshades have destroyed your farms," Dies Irae said to the peasants.

One of them, a young woman holding a boy's hand, nodded. "Yes, my lord. They toppled our barn and their screams wilted our crops. We have nothing now, my lord. We're starving."

Dies Irae nodded sympathetically. "If you have no more farms, you are useless to me. You cannot grow my crops. You cannot pay my taxes."

Another peasant, a tall man with black stubble, stepped forward. "Please, my lord, we'll do any work. We'll serve you however we can."

Dies Irae smiled. "Exactly! You will serve me the way I demand. You will feed my nightshades. They shall feast upon your useless souls."

They cried. They screamed. They tried to flee. They fell, the nightshades upon them. The creatures of inky darkness swirled over their bodies, tossed them against the walls, bit into their flesh. The peasants thrashed, weeping. The nightshades sucked out their souls, and spat out their empty bodies onto the floor. Dies Irae sat on his throne, watching, a smile on his lips.

The nightshades crawled back to him, bloated, and coiled at his feet. Dies Irae patted them.

"Full, my lovelies? Good. Good. And soon you will enjoy your main course. Soon you will feed upon weredragons."

KYRIE

He walked with Agnus Dei between the bricks of a fallen fort. They walked alone, seeking supplies; the others had remained at camp.

It was, Kyrie realized, the first time he'd been alone with Agnus Dei since their fight in Requiem. He looked at her and his heart skipped a beat. She was scanning the ruins, eyes narrowed, lips scrunched. Her mane of curls bounced.

She's beautiful, Kyrie thought. *More beautiful than anything I've ever seen.*

She noticed him staring, frowned, and punched his shoulder. "What, pup?"

He put an arm around her waist, pulled her close, and kissed her cheek.

"Not now, pup!" she said, wriggling in his grasp. "We're on an important mission to find supplies."

"I know," he said, refusing to release her. "We really shouldn't."

He kissed her ear, then her cheek, then her lips. She struggled a moment longer, then placed her hands in his hair, and kissed him deeply. He held the small of her back, and whispered, "Do you know what else we're not allowed to do?"

She was breathing heavily, cheeks flushed. "What?"

"Shift into dragons."

She raised an eyebrow. "You can't be thinking...."

"Think it's possible?"

She gasped, but her eyes lit up. "You are one disturbed pup."

He nodded. "It would be horribly wrong, wouldn't it? In so many ways."

She clutched a fistful of his hair and stared at him, eyes fiery. Then she placed both hands against his chest, pushed him back, and shifted. She stood before him as a red dragon.

Kyrie shifted too. Blue dragon stared at red as they circled each other. She blew wisps of fire. Her scales clinked. Kyrie roared fire, and grabbed her, and she growled. Her scales were hot against him, and her claws dug into the earth. He clutched her shoulders, and pushed her down, and blew smoke. Bursts of flame fled her lips. Her wings flapped. His wings wrapped around her. Her tail pounded the dirt, and their necks pressed together. Smoke and fire enveloped them.

He pushed against her, again and again, and she moaned. Their scales rubbed together, chinking. Her wings flapped, but he held her down. Their smoke rose. Their tails lashed, knocking down trees. She tossed her head back, and a jet of flame left her maw. He dug his claws into her shoulders, and roared fire too. The ruins of the fort shook, and bricks rolled loose. Flames covered his world.

When he came to, they were lying on the ground, cuddling together as humans. Their clothes were singed and their faces ashy. Kyrie kissed her head.

"That was new," he said.

She nodded. "I like being a dragon."

He brushed a lock of hair off her face. "I love you, Agnus Dei. I'm so glad you forgave me. I'll always love you, and only you."

She punched his shoulder. "Oh, quiet, pup. I know you're madly in love with me. I always knew." She kissed his cheek. "Now let's get back to camp. Let's get this war over with, so we can do this again and again."

BENEDICTUS

Benedictus was teaching Kyrie to duel with swords when shrieks sounded above.

He and Kyrie, both panting, raised their eyes to the sky. They saw only the dead, snowy branches of trees. The sun was setting, burning red above the naked canopy.

"Those were griffin shrieks," Kyrie said, clutching his sword.

Lacrimosa and the twins were sitting by the stream, drawing maps of Confutatis in the dirt. They stood up and joined the men.

"They're here," Lacrimosa whispered, watching the skies.

Benedictus narrowed his eyes in the sunlight and saw them. He clutched the hilt of his sword. A thousand at least flew there, maybe two thousand. They darkened the eastern sky like a cloud.

Screeches sounded to the north.

"And those are nightshades," Benedictus said. "They've seen the griffins too."

He looked at the others, one by one. Lacrimosa stood with tightened lips, eyes staring back at him. Kyrie held his sword, eyes dark. Agnus Dei bared her teeth, and Gloriae stood expressionlessly, her hand on the hilt of her sword. Benedictus wanted to tell them that he loved them--all of them, even Kyrie. But today he would not be their father and husband. Today he would be their leader.

"Shift!" he said. "We fly. The battle begins."

The twins shifted first, becoming the red and golden dragons. Kyrie shifted only a second later, turning into a blue dragon. Lacrimosa gave Benedictus a last, deep look, then shifted into a silver dragon.

Benedictus nodded and shifted too, becoming the black dragon, and flew. He crashed between the branches and emerged into the sky. The others followed.

He saw the griffins clearly now. They flew from the east, shrieking, the thud of their wings like thunder. The sunset painted them red. When Benedictus looked north, he saw a thousand nightshades flying to meet them.

"We fight among griffins today!" Benedictus called over his shoulder.

The dragons flew toward the griffins, and Benedictus saw Volucris there, the King of Leonis, who had served as Dies Irae's mount. They met in the air, and stared into each other's eyes. The other dragons also took position among the griffins.

They turned to face the nightshades.

The creatures flew not a league away, moving fast. Their hissing rustled the dead grass and trees below. Their arms of inky smoke reached out, talons like shards of lightning.

Benedictus spoke to Volucris, not tearing his eyes away from the nightshades.

"These beasts work for Dies Irae. In the dungeons of his palace, he guards a weapon to defeat them. We must find that weapon."

Volucris nodded, screeched, and clawed the air. His eyes said to Benedictus, "We will find it."

Benedictus snarled. Only moons ago, he had fought Volucris above this city. Now they would fight here side by side.

The nightshades howled and lighting flashed between them. They were five hundred yards away now, eyes blazing.

"Dada, I love you," Agnus Dei said at his side. "I fight by you."

Kyrie nodded, roared, and blew fire. "Requiem flies again!" he called. "Hear the Black Fang's roar. King Benedictus has returned."

Benedictus roared too, and blew flames into the skies, and then the nightshades were upon them.

Benedictus swiped his claws, ripping through two nightshades. Another wrapped around him, and Benedictus felt it tugging, sucking his soul. He shook himself wildly, freed himself, and blew fire into its eyes. It screeched and fell back.

"To the city!" Benedictus shouted to the others. "We fly to Flammis Palace. We need those Beams."

Several griffins fell soulless to the ground. The others were ripping into nightshades with claws and talons. A few nightshades screamed in pain, and fell back, but did not die. Their inky bodies reformed, and they attacked again.

"To the city!"

They flew, the nightshades coiling around them, tugging at them, biting and clawing. The dragons blew fire, burning a path through their darkness. The nightshades were thicker than storm clouds, their eyes like stars, their claws and teeth everywhere. Darkness covered the sky.

From the corner of his eye, Benedictus saw three nightshades wrap around Lacrimosa. He flew at them, clawed their smoky bodies, and grabbed his wife. He pulled her free, and blew flame at the nightshades. They screeched, fell back, and Benedictus shook Lacrimosa. Her eyes opened. Her soul refilled her. She breathed fire.

"Come, Lacrimosa, to the city."

Kyrie and the twins were shooting fire in all directions. They were young and strong, their flames bright. The nightshades closed their eyes and screeched, blinded. The griffins did less damage, biting and clawing and tearing into nightshade smoke, but they were great in number, and clove a path forward. Many griffins kept falling, wrapped in nightshades, empty shells.

"Over the walls, into the city!"

They were approaching the city walls. Benedictus blew more fire--he was running low, but still had some in him--and cleared a passage between the mobbing nightshades. Soon the walls of Confutatis were beneath him.

But they flew too low. The nightshades would not let them fly higher; they covered the sky above. On the walls, the archers drew their bows.

"Kill the archers!" Benedictus shouted, but was too late. Hundreds of arrows flew. Benedictus swerved aside, but an arrow pierced his leg. Another cut through his wing, and he howled.

There's no ilbane on these arrows, he realized, but somehow that only chilled him. *Does ilbane ruin our taste for feesting nightshades?*

Those nightshades grinned; the arrows passed through them, doing them no harm. They attacked him, wrapping around him. Benedictus beat them off, flapping his wings to break their bodies. He felt them tug his soul, but he gritted his teeth, refusing to release it.

More arrows flew. Griffins screeched; a few fell dead. An arrow hit Kyrie's tail, and he roared.

"Stop those archers!" Benedictus cried. He blew flame at the walls. The archers caught fire. The other dragons blew fire too, clearing the wall of them. Griffins swarmed the city battlements, biting and clawing. The surviving archers drew swords and hacked at them.

Benedictus quickly surveyed the battle. Half the griffins had died. Cuts covered the Vir Requis. Lacrimosa flew with a wobble, and Kyrie's tail bled. The nightshades were unharmed; not one had died.

"To the palace!" Benedictus cried. "Hurry, we're being slaughtered. We need those Beams."

He hadn't much fire left. He blew weak flames, scattering the nightshades, and shot over the walls. The ruins of Confutatis spread below--toppled buildings, nightshades flowing through the streets, and soldiers at every corner. Crossbows fired, and quarrels hit Benedictus, knocking off scales. Griffins screeched and fell, thudding dead against streets and rooftops. Their blood splashed.

Benedictus saw the palace ahead, rising from a pile of rubble. Nightshades swarmed around it, forming a cocoon. One of its towers had collapsed. The rest of the palace seemed held with the inky smoke of nightshades. Their lightning crackled across the towers and walls, and their eyes streamed like comets.

Benedictus blew fire and swooped toward the palace. Arrows flew around him. They hit his chest, leg, and wing. Roaring, he ignored the pain, barrelling between nightshades, wreathed in fire, howling and biting.

Shouting, Kyrie flew at his side. His flames blazed, and his claws and fangs ripped through nightshades. Arrows clanged against him, shattering against his scales, nicking him, and he blew more fire. He swooped, scooped up archers as they reloaded, and tossed them against the parapets. The twins and Lacrimosa still flew above, wrapped in nightshades, biting and burning them.

Nightshades swarmed at the palace gates. Soldiers stood behind them, armed with pikes.

"Kyrie, the gates!" Benedictus called. "Fire!"

Kyrie nodded and blew flames at the nightshades and soldiers below. Benedictus added his own flames. The fire roared, and the soldiers below screamed. They fired crossbows and tossed javelins. Benedictus and Kyrie flew aside, dodging the missiles. Nightshades came flying at them.

Three nightshades wrapped around Benedictus. Three more grabbed Kyrie.

Darkness.

Stars swivelling.

Benedictus saw endless spaces, chambers like worlds, his soul ballooning, fleeing, flowing like night skies. Eyes burned there, and tar, and moons that fell beneath him.

Shrieks around him. Feathers. Beaks.

Griffin talons ripped smoke, and Benedictus saw his body there, an old black dragon, missing scales, scarred, bleeding. Nightshades wrapped around him, and griffins were clawing, trying to reach him, and talons grabbed his legs, and--

His body sucked his soul back in. He gasped. His eyes opened, and he saw the battle around him, the fire below, the nightshades that roared.

"Kyrie!" he called. The boy was fighting at his side. Lacrimosa and the twins swooped at him, clad in flame.

"We enter the gates!" he called to them.

He swooped, tearing into the soldiers below with his claws. They screamed, slammed at him with swords, and died between his teeth. He spat their bodies out, and drove his shoulder into the gates. They shattered, and Benedictus rolled into the palace.

He stood up to see a hundred charging soldiers. He blew fire, scattering them, and ran down the hall. He swiped his tail, knocking over several men, and bit another soldier in half.

Kyrie burst into the palace behind him, roaring fire. Blood flowed down his side, and his claws swiped, knocking over soldiers.

"Where are the others?" Benedictus asked, biting and clawing at swordsmen.

"Right behind you," came Gloriae's voice. She tumbled through the gates, a golden dragon. Agnus Dei and Lacrimosa followed.

Soon all the soldiers in the hall lay dead. Benedictus grunted; a sword had sliced his back leg. It hurt badly, and he limped. Ignoring the pain, he surveyed the others. Cuts covered them, but they were alive, panting, and awaiting his orders.

"Gloriae, do you know the way to the Well of Night and the Beams?"

She nodded. "The tunnels are narrow. We'll have to go in human form."

She shifted back into human. Blood and ash covered her, and her eyes were cold. She drew her sword, pulled down the visor of her helmet, and stepped toward a doorway. Agnus Dei and Kyrie shifted too, drew their swords, and joined her.

Benedictus looked at Lacrimosa. "Are you all right? We go underground. Are you ready?"

She looked at him, still in dragon form. Cuts covered her, and pain filled her eyes, but she nodded. "I'm ready. Let's go find those Beams. And then find Dies Irae."

Benedictus was about to shift when a voice spoke behind him.

"You have found me."

He turned slowly.

Wreathed in nightshades, his empty eye socket blazing, stood Dies Irae.

GLORIAE

She saw Dies Irae enter the hall, and their eyes locked.

"Father," she whispered, sword in hand.

But no. He was not her father anymore. She did not know if Dies Irae had fathered her when raping Lacrimosa, but she knew that he'd banished her. Hurt her. Lied to her. She snarled and raised her blade. She would kill him.

Dies Irae gave her a thin smile. She saw nightshade maggots in his empty eye socket, squirming, their tiny eyes blazing.

Then Benedictus blew fire at Dies Irae, encasing him with flame.

"Gloriae, get the Beams!" Benedictus shouted. "Take Agnus Dei and Kyrie. I'll hold him off. Go!"

Dies Irae laughed, the flames crackling around him. He raised his arms, collected the fire into a ball, and tossed it at Benedictus and Lacrimosa. The two dragons leaped back, howled, and charged.

Gloriae wanted to join the fight. She forced herself to turn away.

"Come, Kyrie! Come, Agnus Dei. We get the Beams. That's the only thing that can stop Irae now."

As she raced into a narrow hall, she thought, *I only pray that Benedictus and Lacrimosa can hold him off long enough.*

She raced down the hallway. Agnus Dei and Kyrie ran at her sides, swords drawn. Five soldiers charged at them, brandishing blades. Gloriae ran at them, screaming, Per Ignem in her right hand, a dagger in her left. She sidestepped, swung her sword, and cut one man open. A second soldier attacked at her left; she parried with her dagger, then stabbed her sword, impaling him. Agnus Dei and Kyrie swung their blades, and soon the five soldiers lay dead. The three Vir Requis leaped over their bodies and kept running down the hallway.

"In here," Gloriae said, opening a door. A stairwell led into darkness, lined with torches. She ran down the steps, Kyrie and Agnus Dei behind her. A soldier ran up from below. Gloriae tossed her dagger and hit him in the throat. Not slowing down, she ran past him, pulled her dagger free, and kept racing downstairs.

The stairwell led into dank, dark tunnels. They twisted underground like the burrows of ants. Gloriae's sword and dagger flew, cutting down all in her path. Their blood washed the floor. The Vir Requis ran down narrower, steeper stairwells, delving into the world's belly.

Finally Gloriae reached a wide tunnel, its walls cut from solid rock. The Beams lay ahead, she knew. Last time she'd been here, a hundred men had guarded the place. Gloriae tightened her lips. She would shift. She would burn them. *And once I have the Beams, I will kill Dies Irae.*

She burst into the chamber. She saw the towering, iron doorways that protected the Well of Night. Three golden skulls were embedded into the doors, their sockets glowing. *The Beams.* The chamber was empty.

Gloriae skidded to a halt. Agnus Dei and Kyrie ran to her sides and stopped, panting. They held their bloodied blades high.

"A hundred soldiers once filled this chamber," Gloriae said, staring around with narrowed eyes. "The Well of Night, where we must seal the nightshades, lies behind those doors."

Agnus Dei struggled to catch her breath and said, "Those skulls. Are they the Beams?"

Gloriae nodded.

Agnus Dei made to run at them, but Gloriae held her back. "Wait. Something is wrong."

Kyrie nodded. "Everything is wrong. Benedictus and Lacrimosa need us! I'm getting the Beams."

He shoved past Gloriae and made a beeline to the doors.

Shadows scuttled on the ceiling.

"Kyrie, wait!" Gloriae shouted.

She looked up at the ceiling and froze. Her heart thrashed, and tears sprang into her eyes. No, it couldn't be. Couldn't! She clenched her teeth and her sword, and struggled not to faint.

Kyrie saw the creatures too. He froze and stared at the ceiling, the blood leaving his face. Agnus Dei looked up and let out a shrill cry.

"What the abyss are those?" Agnus Dei whispered.

"They are us," Gloriae whispered. "Molded at the hand of Dies Irae."

The three creatures scurried down the walls like spiders, and stood facing the Vir Requis. They were sewn together from old, rotting flesh. Limbs of bodies had been attached with strings and bolts. The limbs, heads, and torsos were mismatched; they came from different bodies. Blood and maggots covered the creatures, and their teeth were rotten. Their eyes blazed.

Two were female. One had long, matted, yellow hair that swarmed with worms. The other had dank, stinking black curls. A third creature was male, a youth of yellow hair, rotting flesh, and one leg that came from a goat.

The females looked like decaying versions of Gloriae and Agnus Dei. The male looked like Kyrie.

"Welcome, living sister," said the rotting Gloriae. She opened cracked, bleeding lips to reveal sharp teeth. Maggots rustled inside her mouth. "Welcome, Gloriae."

Gloriae screamed, nauseous.

"Shift!" she screamed. "Kill them!"

She tried to become a dragon, but the magic failed her. She strained, but remained human. She looked at Kyrie and Agnus Dei; they too were struggling to shift, but could not.

The creatures laughed. "Your curse will not work here, no, darlings. You are in our realm now. We are mimics. We love you. You will join us."

Gloriae screamed and charged toward the creatures. Kyrie and Agnus Dei screamed too, and attacked their rotting doppelgangers.

Gloriae's sword drove into her mimic's chest. Its blood spurted, black, foul. The creature laughed, maggots spilling from its mouth. It dug its claws into Gloriae's shoulders, and Gloriae screamed. Poison covered those claws; they sizzled and steamed.

She pulled Per Ignem back and swung it. The blade sank into the creature's neck, and worms fled the wound, squirming up the blade onto Gloriae's hand.

She screamed, shook the worms off, and kicked. Her mimic caught her foot and twisted, and Gloriae fell.

Her mimic fell upon her and bit Gloriae's shoulder. She screamed. The creature's stench nearly made her faint. She kicked and struggled, and managed to punch her mimic's face. Her fist drove into the soft, rotting head, spilling blood and cockroaches. The creature laughed, and its claws clutched Gloriae's chest.

"You will be one of us soon," it hissed. "We will take you apart, and stuff you, and put you together again. Then we'll be together. Then I'll be with you always, Gloriae." Its bloated, white tongue left its mouth and licked Gloriae's cheek.

Gloriae kicked its belly. It grunted, and she grabbed its head and twisted. The neck, already cut from her sword, tore. The head came off, and Gloriae tossed it aside. She pushed the creature's body off her, rose to her feet, and stared down at it.

The body writhed, claws scratching. The head laughed in the corner, spurting blood. Gloriae drove Per Ignem into the torso, again and again, but it would not die.

She ran to the wall and grabbed a torch. The torso came crawling toward her, and she tossed the torch onto it.

It caught flame. The head, several yards away, also caught fire. It screamed horribly. The bugs inside it screeched too, burning. Smoke rose, and the stench nearly made Gloriae pass out.

She looked and saw that Kyrie and Agnus Dei still fought their own mimics.

"Burn them!" she cried. She grabbed another torch and tossed it at the rotting Kyrie mimic. It caught fire, screamed, and fell. She tossed a third torch at the final mimic, the maggoty Agnus Dei, and it too burned. The mimics twisted on the floor.

"It burns!" they hissed. "Why do they burn us? Why do our mothers hate us? Oh, they burn their children. How it hurts! You will burn with us soon. You murdered your children." Smoke and fire rose from them. "You will burn with us in the abyss."

Gloriae helped Agnus Dei to her feet. She had fallen, tears on her cheeks. Kyrie walked toward them, fingers trembling, eyes haunted. The three watched the mimics burn, until they were nothing but piles of ash.

Gloriae stared, eyes dry. Then she tightened her jaw and pointed at the Beams. The golden skulls seemed to stare at her, lights flickering inside their eye sockets.

"Help me pry those from the walls," she said. "We go kill nightshades."

BENEDICTUS

Dies Irae's arm swung. Nightshade smoke flowed from it, slamming into Benedictus. His scales cracked. He flew, hit a column, and fell to the floor. Marble tiles cracked beneath him.

Dies Irae stepped toward him, the nightshades swirling around him.

"My my, brother, you seem to have fallen," Dies Irae said. Veins flowed across his face, blue and pulsing. The nightshade maggots squealed in his eye socket.

Lacrimosa flew at him, screaming, her talons glinting. Dies Irae waved his arm, and the blow knocked her against the ceiling. Bricks showered down. Lacrimosa fell, hit the floor, and whimpered. Blood covered her scales. Dies Irae laughed.

"Damn you, Irae," Benedictus growled. The sight of his wounded wife blazed in his eyes, drowning his pain. He pushed himself up, his wounds aching. His eyes burned, and blood dripped into them. He could barely see, but blew fire. Dies Irae waved his arm, and the flames flew around him. Tapestries caught fire. They crackled, and black smoke filled the hall.

"Damn me, brother?" Dies Irae asked. "I am already damned. My daughter Gloriae damned me, infested me with these creatures. But I am powerful now, brother. More powerful than you ever knew me."

Dies Irae swung his left arm, the mace arm. The steel hit Benedictus's chest and knocked him down. Pain exploded. He saw only white light, then stars over blackness. He flicked his tail, and felt it slam into Dies Irae, doing him no harm.

Outside, Benedictus heard the griffins and nightshades. The griffins were shrieking in pain. The nightshades laughed. Benedictus blinked, and he could see again. He saw a window. Outside the griffins were falling from the sky.

"Yes, Benedictus," Dies Irae said. "They are dying for you. Once more, you've led thousands to die under your banners."

No, Benedictus thought. He could not allow another Lanburg Fields. He could not let Dies Irae win again.

"You murdered our father," he said, mouth bloody, and struggled to his feet. "You murdered millions. I hold you to justice now."

Dies Irae laughed again and swung his mace. Light and pain burst. Benedictus fell onto his back, cracking more tiles. He smelled his blood.

"Ben!" came Lacrimosa's cry, a world away, hazy, echoing. A streak of silver flew. Lacrimosa, a dragon of moonlight, leaped at Dies Irae. He slammed his mace into her, nightshades swirling around it. The blow tossed Lacrimosa across the hall. She hit a column, cracked it, and fell. She moaned, her eyes closed, and she hit the floor. Blood flowed from her head.

"Lacrimosa!" Benedictus cried. Tears filled his eyes. Was she dead? The blood dripping from her head horrified him, yanked his heart, pulsed through his veins. He tried to run to her. Dies Irae, still laughing, lashed his arms. Nightshades flew from them, knocking into Benedictus, tossing him against the floor.

Benedictus lay, bloodied, aching, tears in his eyes.

"Lacrimosa...," he whispered and struggled to his knees.

Dies Irae stood above him. "Lacrimosa," he said. "That is her name. That is the name I called as I raped her. She was only fifteen, did you know? I hurt her then, Benedictus. I hurt her badly. She bled and wept, and--"

Screaming hoarsely, Benedictus charged forward. Dies Irae swung his mace into Benedictus's head.

Light.

Pain.

Benedictus hit the floor.

The pain shattered his magic, returning him to human form. He lay bloodied and moaning.

"So sad, Benedictus," came Dies Irae's voice. "You've fought for so long... only to die now. Your daughters have died too. They seek the Beams. Yes, Benedictus. I know of your plans. I have known for many days, and have been waiting for you. I have placed a horror to guard the Beams, a horror I crafted especially for your children."

Benedictus struggled to rise. Dies Irae placed a boot upon his neck, pinning him down, that boot made of Vir Requis scales.

"They won't die so easily," Benedictus managed to say.

Dies Irae pushed his foot down, constricting Benedictus. He could no longer speak, could barely breathe. "Oh, they are dead already, dear Benedictus the Black. Rest assured, too, that they suffered greatly before dying. My special pets made sure of that. Your wife too is dead."

Benedictus could just make out Lacrimosa's form. She was human again--which meant she was dead, or badly wounded. She lay in blood, unmoving. Benedictus wanted to call her, to tell her of his love one last time, but Dies Irae's boot suffocated him.

Benedictus drew a dagger from his belt. Dies Irae's boot left his neck and stepped on his wrist. The dagger fell.

Benedictus took ragged breaths.

"Why, brother?" he managed to say. "Why? Gloriae, whom you loved, is Vir Requis. You too are Vir Requis, you--"

"I am no such creature!" Dies Irae screeched. His voice was inhuman, impossibly high-pitched and loud. Stained glass windows shattered across the hall. Dies Irae's face burned with green light, and the nightshades swirled around him, lifting him two feet in the air. "You are cursed. You are wretched. You are weredragon. I am pure, a being of light."

Benedictus struggled to his knees. Dies Irae kicked him down.

"No, Benedictus. You stay on the floor. You are a serpent. Serpents crawl in the dust." He raised his steel arm. "Do you see this deformity? You bit off my real arm. Do you remember, brother? Do you remember Lanburg Fields?" He cackled. "When you bit off my arm, did you ever imagine I would grow another one? A steel one that would kill you? Yes. You will die now, creature."

Benedictus looked into his brother's eye--one eye now an empty socket rustling with nightshades, the other bright blue and milky.

"Our father loved you, Di," he said.

Dies Irae froze. Di. His childhood nickname. The name their parents used to call him. The name Benedictus himself would use when the two were children.

Dies Irae stared down, face frozen. "What did you call me?" he whispered.

Benedictus lay at his feet, blood seeping, pain throbbing. "He... he could not give you the Oak Throne, brother. I know he hurt you. He did not know. He did not realize your pain. He loved you, Di. Our father loved you more than life. More than Requiem. He--"

Dies Irae trembled. His chest rose and fell like a hare's heart, thrashing. His voice was nothing but a whisper. A frightened whisper. The voice of a child. "What did you call me?"

Benedictus pushed himself to his knees. "We used to play in the temple, do you remember? The priests had left a chandelier there, out between the trees. We took the crystals from it, and pretended they were jewels, that we were rich. Us, the princes of

Requiem, playing with fake jewels, when we could have a thousand real ones! Yet these were somehow more valuable; childhood's joy lit them." Now his own voice trembled, and tears filled his eyes. "Do you remember? Do you remember the trees, and the crystals? You are my brother, Di. I loved you. I don't know you now. But you can come back. You can remember. You can--"

Dies Irae kicked him. Benedictus doubled over, coughing.

"Silence!" Dies Irae screamed, "I do not remember. That boy is dead. Gone!" His voice was like a swarm of wasps. "There is power now, and light and darkness across the world. That is who I am. I am a god, Benedictus. I am a god of wrath. You are a worm. You die. You die groveling at my feet."

Black tears flowed down Dies Irae's cheeks. His veins pulsed, darkness swarming within them. Teeth bared, his good eye wild, Dies Irae raised his mace over Benedictus's head.

KYRIE ELEISON

Embedded into the doors, the three golden skulls stared with glowing orbits. When Kyrie reached toward one, its glow brightened, and its jaw moved. Its glow was the glow of Loomers, blue and white and warm.

Kyrie wasn't sure how he'd pry the skull from the door. It was embedded deep into the iron. When he touched the skull, however, it clanked and fell into his hands. Its glow brightened, nearly blinding him, and a hum came from its jaw, a sound like spinning Loomers.

Kyrie turned to the twins, the Beam in his hands. The light bathed the girls; they appeared angelic, ghostly, beings of starlight.

"It's warm," he said. "There are two more. One for each."

Gloriae sheathed her sword and took a second skull. It hummed in her hands. Its glow suffused her face and billowed her hair.

Agnus Dei took the third and last skull. Her hair too flew, she tightened her lips, and her eyes narrowed.

"How do we use them?" she asked.

Kyrie hefted the skull in his hands. "In *Mythic Creatures of the Gray Age*, the drawing shows a man holding them up. Rays of light shoot out and tame a nightshade."

He turned the skull in his hands, so that it faced a wall. He held it high, hoping rays of light would burst from the eye sockets and sear a hole through the stone. The skull still glowed, but there was no great, searing beam of light.

"Do we need to utter a spell?" Gloriae asked. "*Ancient Artifacts* said nothing about that."

Agnus Dei marched toward the tunnel they'd come from. "Father and Mother are in trouble. We'll figure it out on the fly. Come on."

Holding the skulls, the three ran up the tunnels and staircases. They sloshed through blood and leaped over the bodies of soldiers. It was a long climb, but eventually they emerged back overground. They entered a wide hall, its tapestries tattered, its walls bloody. Bodies, broken shields, and shattered blades covered the floor. Outside the windows, nightshades screeched, lighting flashed, and thunder rolled. Griffin bodies covered the ground.

"Benedictus and Lacrimosa are behind those doors," Kyrie said. *Stars, I hope they're still alive.* He began running toward the heavy oak doors.

A hiss rose, and a nightshade slithered from a shadowy corner. It screeched and rushed at them.

Heart thrashing, Kyrie raised his Beam.

Light exploded. The sound cracked the walls. Beams of light shot from skull's eye sockets, drenching the hall. The world was nothing but white light, searing, blinding him. Kyrie nearly dropped the skull; his hands burned. He screamed, but heard nothing; the humming light overpowered all sound.

He could see the nightshade, wisps of bright gray in the light. It screeched. Its eyes burst into white fire. It struggled as if trying to flee, but seemed caught in the beams. It howled like a dying boar, hoarse, horrible. Walls shattered. It flipped onto its back, writhing, screaming.

Kyrie jerked the golden skull sideways. The beams from the orbits veered, tossing the nightshade against the wall. The bricks shattered. The nightshade wept. Kyrie had not imagined they could weep. He waved the skull again, and the beams tossed the nightshade into the corner. It lay there shivering, shrivelled up like a slug sprinkled with salt.

Agnus Dei too pointed her golden skull. More light blazed, spinning, screaming. Walls shattered. The nightshade's eyes melted. It howled. It begged them.

"Please," it cried, its voice like ripping flesh. "Please, mercy, please."

Gloriae raised the third golden skull. Beams shot from its orbits, and the nightshade burst into white flame. Smoke rose from it, it wept and shivered, and then collapsed into ash.

The Beams dimmed.

Color returned to the world.

The sound died.

The skulls vibrated gently, and once more, their eye sockets glowed a delicate, moonlight glow.

"Well," Kyrie said, "that sure beats dragonfire."

For a moment silence blanketed the world.

Then a thousand nightshades screeched outside, crashed into the hall, and swarmed around them.

Kyrie lifted the Beam, and it burst into light again. A nightshade swooped. Kyrie pointed the beams of light at it, and it screeched and flew back. More nightshades flew to his right. He spun the beams around, and they sliced through the nightshades. They screamed and curled into the corner like halved worms.

The twins were also spinning their Beams. The light seared the world, and nightshades screamed. Once caught in the light, they could not escape. They sizzled, trapped, weeping and begging for mercy in beastly grunts. Kyrie swung his Beam like swinging a club, tossing the nightshades aside.

"Don't bother killing them now!" he shouted over the roaring Beams and dying nightshades. "Knock them aside. We must reach Benedictus and Lacrimosa. They're behind those doors. They need us."

He began plowing forward, step by step, knocking nightshades aside. They screamed and fizzed and shrivelled up around him.

"Agnus Dei, beside me!" he shouted. "Gloriae, watch my back."

He could barely hear himself, but the twins seemed to hear him. Agnus Dei stood to his left, Gloriae to his right; both swung their Beams forward and backwards. They formed a sun, casting light to all sides. His golden skull trembled so violently, Kyrie clung with all his strength. For every step, he battled a dozen nightshades. Their screams and smoke filled the hall.

It seemed ages, but finally Kyrie reached the doors.

"Stars, please," he prayed as he kicked the doors open. "Let Benedictus and Lacrimosa still live."

The Beams drenched the hall beyond the doors. Agnus Dei and Gloriae behind him, he stepped through.

Kyrie's belly went cold.

The room was a mess. The columns were smashed, a wall was knocked down, the tiles on the floor were cracked. Blood covered the floor.

"Where are they?" Agnus Dei shouted. The Beams still rattled and hummed. The nightshades crowded at the doorway behind, but Gloriae held them back with her Beam.

Kyrie stared. There was a stain of blood below a cracked column. Lacrimosa's bluebell pendant lay there, its chain torn. Kyrie lifted it.

"Lacrimosa was hurt here," he whispered.

He moved down the hall. By another stain of blood, he found black scales and a fallen dagger. Kyrie could hardly breathe. The horror pulsed through him, spinning his head.

"Benedictus was hurt here. This is his dagger."

He looked up at the sisters. Both stood with Beams in hands, holding back the nightshades. Both stared at him with wide eyes.

"Are they dead?" Agnus Dei whispered. Her voice trembled, and tears filled her eyes.

Kyrie looked at bloodied footprints. They led from the hall out the doors, into the city.

"Those are Irae's prints," Kyrie said. "They're too large to be Lacrimosa's, and Benedictus has flat boots; these are heeled." A nightshade swooped through the window, and Kyrie tossed it aside, searing it with his Beam. He spoke with a quivering voice. "Dies Irae hurt them. He took them from here."

"Where?" Agnus Dei demanded. "Where did he take them? Are they dead?" She trembled. Nightshades screeched and fell around her.

Gloriae tightened her jaw and began marching toward the palace doors. Nightshades fell and sizzled around her. She looked over her shoulder.

"Follow me," she said. "I know Dies Irae. I know where he took them."

She left the palace and ran down the shattered streets between dead men and griffins. Nightshades covered the skies, howling under the Beams.

Kyrie and Agnus Dei ran behind her, waving their Beams at the walls of attacking nightshades, clearing a way between them.

"Where?" Kyrie demanded, boots sloshing through griffin blood.

Gloriae looked at him, her eyes blank. Her face was pale.

"To his amphitheatre," she said. "He's putting them on trial."

LACRIMOSA

"Court is in session," screeched the voice.

But no, she thought. This was no *voice.* It was whistling steam, and steel scratching against steel, and demon screams--an inhuman cacophony that formed words. She convulsed at the sound. Lacrimosa tried to open her eyes, but darkness tugged her. Where was she?

"All hail Judge Irae!" spoke the voice, impossibly high pitched, a voice that could shatter glass. A thousand screeches answered the words, a sound like a thousand slaughtered boars.

Lacrimosa felt something clammy wrap around her. She felt herself lifted overground, and she moaned. Her head pounded. Her eyelids fluttered, and she finally managed to open her eyes.

She gasped.

Above her floated a figure from nightmares. It was Dies Irae, but more monstrous than she'd ever seen him. Nightshades wreathed him, holding him ten feet above her. He wore a judge's black robes and a wig of white, squirming snakes. He held a circle of jagged metal, Osanna's wheel of justice, its spikes cutting his hand. Storm clouds thundered above him.

"The trial of weredragons begins!" he cried, that sound like steam and metal leaving his mouth. The veins of his face pulsed, as if insects tunnelled through them. Pus and blood dripped from his empty eye socket. Nightshades screamed around him, holding him in the air, coiling around his legs, wrapping around his shoulders. He banged his left arm, the steel mace, against his breastplate. The sound rang out even over the screeches.

"Ben," Lacrimosa whispered.

She saw him across from Dies Irae. Nightshades wrapped around him, holding him upright. Blood dripped from his mouth and leg, and his left eye was swelling, but he lived. He saw her. He tried to speak, but nightshade tendrils covered his mouth. Lacrimosa tried to reach out to him, then realized that nightshades wreathed her too. They pinned her arms to her sides, and held her an inch above the ground.

Dies Irae laughed above them, his wig of snakes hissing. "Here, in this arena, before this crowd, we shall judge the weredragons for their crimes against mankind."

Lacrimosa looked around her, and saw that they stood in the amphitheatre, the same place where Dies Irae had once unleashed beasts upon her. All around, upon the rows of seats, nightshades slithered and grunted and watched the trial. Lightning crackled between them.

"Benedictus," Lacrimosa said again, pleading, and tried to reach out to him. She couldn't free her arms from the nightshades that encased her. One nightshade licked her cheek with an icy, smoky tongue. She shivered.

Dies Irae slammed his mace against his breastplate again. "Silence in the court! Today we judge Benedictus and Lacrimosa, the Lord and Lady of Lizards." His voice was howling winds, raising his words' last syllables into screeches. Clouds thundered and crackled above him. The snakes on his head hissed.

"Dies Irae!" Lacrimosa called, finding her voice. "Cease this mockery of justice. You only mock yourself."

"Silence her!" he screeched, an electrical sound rising into a crackle.

The nightshades covered her mouth, and she shouted into them, but no sound escaped. Dies Irae cackled. He unrolled a scroll and read from it.

"Your crimes, Lizards! I shall read you your crimes. You are charged, verily, of burning alive the children of this city, and eating them, and roasting them, and biting into their innards to suck upon them." He laughed hysterically. Nightshade maggots filled his mouth. "How do you plead, Lizards?"

Benedictus managed to free his head from the nightshades cocooning him. "Dies Irae, you are no judge. Stop this show."

Dies Irae slammed his mace again. "Silence in my court! Silence, I say. Bring forth the children." His voice was a tornado, buzzing with electricity. His 'r's rolled like a rod dragged against cage bars. "Bring forth the victims."

The nightshades across the amphitheatre--there were thousands--squealed. Three swooped from the high tiers to the dusty arena. They carried burned, bloodied bodies in their smoky arms. They tossed the bodies at Dies Irae's feet.

Lacrimosa looked away too late. The image seared her. Three children, burned and twisted, black and red. Who had done this? Had Dies Irae murdered these children as mock evidence for his mock trial?

He was fully mad now, Lacrimosa realized. He knew not fantasy from reality. The nightshades had festered in his brain and broken it. Did he truly believe she and Benedictus had burned these children?

"I find you guilty!" Dies Irae cried. The nightshades lifted him higher. Lightning crackled around him, and the snakes on his head screamed.

"Dies Ira--" Benedictus began, but the howls of nightshades and the booming thunder overpowered his words.

Dies Irae floated upon the nightshades ten feet back, and approached a structure hidden beneath a black curtain. *What horror lies there?* Lacrimosa thought. What more could Dies Irae reveal to still shock her?

Dies Irae ripped off the curtain, and Lacrimosa wept.

It looked like a gallows heavy with bodies. But these bodies were not hanged. They were gutted, bled, and hung on meat hooks. Some bodies were but children. A makeshift butcher shop for humans.

"Behold!" Dies Irae cried. "The weredragons have prepared these bodies to feast upon them. They stole our women, our youths, our children. They butchered them. They planned to eat them. They dined upon them in their halls of scales and flame."

Lacrimosa lowered her head, shut her eyes, and wept. How could such horror exist? How could such evil fill a man? How could a human, for Dies Irae had been human once, sink into such insanity? She shivered. All she had ever wanted, ever fought for, was the song of harps, a life of peace, of leaves and earth and sunlight and stars. How had she come to here, this trial, this stench of blood and fire?

"Ben," she whispered. She would die here, she knew. Close to him, but unable to hug him, to kiss him one last time. The nightshades tightened around her, and she opened her eyes, and looked to Benedictus.

Their eyes met.

"I love you," she whispered to him. He mouthed the same words back to her.

Nightshades flowed into her mouth, but she kept her eyes on her husband. *I wanted to grow old with you. To watch our children get married, have children of their own. That's all I ever wanted. But we end here in pain and horror.*

"I find you," Dies Irae said, "guilty. Guilty! Guilty as charged!"

He banged his mace against his breastplate, and the nightshades howled as if cheering. Winds flowed among them, and the clouds roiled.

Dies Irae kept reading from his scroll. He read of the earthquakes they caused, of the temples they toppled, of the illnesses they spread. He shouted about how they destroyed the world, and stole the souls of millions. As he read, he laughed and screamed.

"Guilty! Guilty to everything!"

Finally he tossed the scroll aside, and pulled a sword from his robes. It was a black sword, raising smoke, a jagged sword that sucked in all light.

"Behold the sword of the executioner," he said, and held it aloft, presenting it to the crowd of nightshades. "Behold the bright blade of justice."

Benedictus was struggling against the nightshades. His face was red. He was trying to shift; Lacrimosa saw scales appear and vanish across him. The nightshades were crushing him.

She saw her husband, and she heard the birches rustle. She could see them again, wisps of golden leaves, and harpists between them, and columns of marble. She saw Benedictus in green and gold, and she walked with him arm in arm, as dragons glided above through blue skies. Tears streamed down her cheeks, and she clung to that memory, those ghosts of a land destroyed and burned. She would die with those memories, that love of her home, that love of Requiem.

"Goodbye, Benedictus," she whispered. "Goodbye, Requiem. May our wings forever find your sky."

Wreathed in nightshades, Dies Irae floated above Benedictus.

"Now, in this arena...," Dies Irae said, speaking slowly, theatrically, savoring every word. "Now, we carry out the punishment. Death. Death. Death!"

Silence fell.

The thousands of nightshades leaned forward, licked their lips, and stared.

The clouds ceased to grumble.

Dies Irae smiled a small, thin smile.

"Death," he whispered.

He raised his sword above Benedictus.

Lacrimosa closed her eyes. She would not watch this. She would remember Benedictus among the birches, smiling and strong, her king. That was how he would remain forever in her memories.

Light fell on her eyelids, and she smiled as she wept, for it seemed to her that the light of Requiem's stars glowed upon her.

A buzz hummed, angelic in her ears, like the sound of dragon wings.

"I'll be with you in our starlit halls, Ben," she whispered. "I'll watch over you, Agnus Dei and Gloriae. I'll watch you from the stars, and be with you always."

"Mother!" they cried. "Mother!"

She smiled. The memories of their voices seemed so real.

"Mother, you're alive!"

Lacrimosa opened her eyes... and she saw them.

She shouted and wept.

"Agnus Dei! Gloriae! Kyrie!"

At first, Lacrimosa thought that she floated through the starlit halls, the spirit Requiem beyond the Draco constellation. White light washed the world, bleaching all color, banishing all shadow. But no. This was still the amphitheatre, now drenched in light. Three dragons were flying toward the amphitheatre. Gloriae. Agnus Dei. Kyrie. They held the Beams in their claws. Lacrimosa knew they were the Beams; great light burst from them, spinning and singing. The world hummed and glowed.

The Beams' light hit the edge of the amphitheatre. The nightshades there, upon the top tiers, screeched and writhed. They turned sickly gray and thin in the light, and their screams shook the amphitheatre. Cracks ran along the stones.

"It's over, Dies Irae," Benedictus shouted over the shrieking nightshades and humming Beams, his voice almost lost. "We have the Beams. It's over."

A nightshade still wreathed him, but it was hissing and squirming. The nightshade holding Lacrimosa spun around her, grunting. The Beams did not shine on them directly, but the light still burned them.

"Mother!" Agnus Dei cried above. She, Gloriae, and Kyrie had almost reached the amphitheatre now. The Beams' rays were moving down the rows of seats, like light through a temple window travelling across a floor.

"When the light reaches you, you're dead, Irae!" Lacrimosa screamed. "You've filled yourself with nightshades, and now you're going to burn."

Dies Irae was staring at the dragons. The nightshades around him squirmed and grunted and screeched. The snakes of his wig blistered, then burst. His good eye blazed, and his skin seemed stretched nearly to ripping. The beams had moved down the tiers of seats, leaving seared, dead nightshades. They were now travelling across the arena floor, stirring the dust. The beams were a hundred feet away, then fifty, then ten, then five....

Dies Irae screamed. An inhuman scream. The defeated cry of a demon.

He turned to stare at Lacrimosa, his good eye burning, his empty eye socket gaping.

"We will meet again, Lacrimosa," he said.

Then he turned and stabbed Benedictus through the chest.

"Ben!" Lacrimosa screamed.

"Father!" came a cry above.

"Ben! Ben!"

The nightshades wrapped around Benedictus burned and fled. The nightshades around Lacrimosa smoked and flew from her. She fell to her knees, weeping.

"Ben!"

She saw Dies Irae open a trapdoor in the arena floor, that door tigers, bulls, and other beasts would once emerge from. He disappeared into the tunnels. Lacrimosa rose to her feet, ran to her husband, and knelt by him. She held him.

"My love." Tears streamed down her cheeks.

He lay in her arms, the sword buried to the hilt in his chest. He looked upon her with glassy eyes, and a soft smile touched his lips.

"L-- Lacrimosa," he whispered, blood in his mouth.

The beams washed them. Nightshades screamed and flew around them. Lacrimosa clutched her husband, touched his cheeks, wept into his hair.

"Please. Don't leave me."

He held her hand. "Watch over the young ones," he whispered. "I love you, Lacrimosa, daughter of Requiem."

Sobs shook her body. She embraced him. "I love you forever, my lord."

When his head fell back, and his eyes stopped blinking, Lacrimosa raised her head and howled, a dragon's howl, a cry she thought could rend the heavens. She did not know how much time passed. Nightshades screamed. Beams blazed. There was a great battle. Lacrimosa was aware of nothing but her husband. She cradled his body in her arms.

It seemed that ages passed, the turns of seasons and the reigns of kings, as she held her husband, until the nightshades fled the world and only soft light washed her.

Still holding her king, Lacrimosa looked up. In the soft light she saw her daughters approach, walking in human forms, their steps slow. Kyrie walked behind them, bathed in dying light.

The Beams dimmed.

Darkness covered the world.

Agnus Dei saw her father, and she let out a cry like a wounded animal. She ran forward and knelt by his body, weeping. She held his hand, saw that he was dead, and cried to the sky.

Gloriae stared, face pale, silent. Her mouth was open, her eyes confused, shocked, her hands open.

Kyrie fell to his knees by his king, and shook him, and cried his name. Tears streamed down his cheeks.

"Dada!" Agnus Dei cried through her sobs. Lacrimosa held her, desperate, digging her fingers into her shoulders. Kyrie embraced them. Gloriae knelt by them, looking around, dazed. They wept as one, trembling, their tears joining, falling upon the body of Benedictus.

"My king," Lacrimosa whispered to him. "My husband. My love."

"Dada," Agnus Dei whispered, running her hands over his face.

Lacrimosa kept waiting for Benedictus to open his eyes, to cough, to wake up, to hold her. She kept checking his breath, again and again, finding it gone, his life fled from her forever.

Eyes blurred, she saw Volucris lead the surviving griffins into the arena. *So few remain.* Blood covered them. The beasts saw her holding Benedictus, tossed their heads back, and cried in mourning. Their shrieks thudded against her ears, and Lacrimosa sobbed and held her husband.

Arrows flew. They clattered against the ground around them. Lacrimosa looked up, and through her tears, she saw soldiers streaming into the arena. They fired arrows and drew swords.

Agnus Dei and Kyrie howled, shifted, and blew fire. Gloriae and Lacrimosa soon joined them. Flames filled the arena that night, and blood washed it, and dozens of soldiers died by fang and claw. But many more soldiers streamed in, a city full of them, and Lacrimosa knew they could not win this fight.

She lifted Benedictus's body in her claws. He seemed so small, so light. She flew with him, the arrows whistling around her, until she was out of their range. Her daughters and Kyrie flew at her sides, tears flowing down their cheeks.

The Vir Requis fled the city, and flew over burned fields, over toppled farmhouses, over wilted forests, over the ruins of the world. No more nightshades flew here. Their darkness was gone, but the darkness of Lacrimosa's world seemed greater than ever, and she did not think any light could banish it. The light of her life had been doused.

The dragons flew into dawn, into night, into dawn again. Their wings scattered clouds, their roars pierced the sky, and the tears of Requiem fell as rain upon a ruined world.

The world, Lacrimosa knew, could no longer be mended. Not for her. Not for her children. Never more for Requiem and her life.

King Benedictus had fallen.

AGNUS DEI

They buried her father in the ruins of Requiem.

She stood above the grave, wrapped in her cloak. Snow fell. It filled her hair, turned her black cloak white, and covered the shattered statues, columns, and memories. The snowflakes glided, swirled in the breeze, and stung her cheeks. The world glittered under a soft sun.

"Requiem is beautiful again, Dada," she whispered.

Her tears fell, and she knelt in the snow, and placed a lock of her hair upon his grave. A ribbon held the strand, bright red, a single piece of color in a white world. Her tears made holes in the snow.

She straightened and stared at the grave. They did not bury him among kings; those mausoleums were gone now. Agnus Dei buried her father in a graveyard of soldiers, so he would rest forever in the company of bravery, and sacrifice, and other men of sword and fang.

"You were a hero to your men," she whispered, and a sob shook her. "A leader. A great king. You were a father to them too. You were a father to us all. Goodbye, Dada."

It seemed unreal, but a dream. How could he be gone? How could she carry on without him? How could she find strength within her to continue this war? Father had always known what to do, where to go, how to fight. How could she live without his wisdom, his strength, and his love? Anguish clutched her, so that she could not breathe.

With trembling fingers, Agnus Dei clutched the hilt of her sword. "I swear to you, Dada. I will rebuild Requiem. I will rebuild our home. I will continue to walk in your path, and not stray from it to the left or right. I love you, Dada. Forever."

She backed away from the grave, tears on her cheeks, snow on her lips. Her mother embraced her, and Agnus Dei buried her face against her shoulder. They wept together, trembling.

Gloriae stood by them, staring at the grave, eyes wide, disbelieving. She had not spoken since leaving Confutatis. She kept looking from the grave, to Agnus Dei, to Lacrimosa, and back to the grave. Finally a sob fled her lips, and tears sprouted from her eyes.

"Mother," Gloriae whispered and joined the embrace.

Kyrie stood, face hard, tears on his cheeks. He stared at the grave, lips moving silently. Agnus Dei left her mother, and clutched him, and wept against him. He held her, gently at first, then desperately.

"I'm going to look after you," Kyrie whispered. His tears fell. "I don't know how to carry on without him. He was my king, my compass. I don't know how to fight this war without Benedictus. But I promise you, Agnus Dei. However I can, I will look after you, and Gloriae, and Lacrimosa. You have my word. You have me forever."

"Oh, Kyrie," she said, and clung to him, her tears on his shoulder. Her heart seemed like a ball of twine, too tight, and she trembled.

She left Kyrie's embrace, and took a step back, and shifted into a dragon. She knelt before the grave, and tossed her head back, and blew flame. The column of fire rose into the snowy sky, spinning and crackling.

The others became dragons too. They stood in a ring, tears on their cheeks. They blew four pillars of fire, a farewell of sound and heat and light... for one fire extinguished.

The story will continue in...

LIGHT OF REQUIEM

Song of Dragons, Book Three

NOVELS BY DANIEL ARENSON

Standalones:

Firefly Island (2007)
The Gods of Dream (2010)
Flaming Dove (2010)
Eye of the Wizard (2011)

Song of Dragons:

Blood of Requiem (2011)
Tears of Requiem (2011)
Light of Requiem (2011)

KEEP IN TOUCH

www.DanielArenson.com
Daniel@DanielArenson.com
Facebook.com/DanielArenson
Twitter.com/DanielArenson

Acknowledgements

I'd like to thank several people for their help with *Tears of Requiem*.

Thank you beta readers Greg Baum, Janelle DeCelis, Debra Martin, and Jonathan Thompson.

Thank you Anne Victory for editing the manuscript.

Thank you authors Michael Crane, David Dalglish, Robert Duperre, Amanda Hocking, Jason Letts, David McAfee, and Sean Sweeney.

CPSIA information can be obtained at www.ICGtesting.com
Printed in the USA
LVOW12s1334180615

442968LV00002B/147/P